LIFEFORM

An Original Novel

M. Alan Jacobs

ISBN: 1463566417
ISBN 13: 9781463566418
Library of Congress Control Number: 2011909728
CreateSpace, North Charleston, SC

Chapter One

It was 0045 hours. It wasn't time yet.

The man and woman waited where the cover was good. In the tall grass on the back side of the hill, they were well away from the floodlights but close enough to hear the shouting and the machines.Of the two of them, Doc was the one with doubts. Not so Malone. She'd said the two of them were presumed dead. No one would be expecting them. So there was no reason not to sleep while they waited. Lying in the dark next to Doc, she was following her own advice. She was inert. Her breathing was regular.

Doc knew it was easy for Malone. She had no conscience and no fear. She had no personal stake in the outcome other than her life. And from what Doc had already seen, Malone didn't seem to value her own life a whole lot more than anyone else's. That meant she didn't value it at all. Malone was all about the job.

On the other hand, everything that really mattered to Doc was now at stake. That made sleep impossible. So he kept one eye on the luminescent face of his diver's watch and tried not to shiver.

0120 hours. Not yet.

Doc shivered. The air was impossibly cold. The drizzle was even colder, falling from a freezing black cloud that now stretched across twenty square miles of tropical terrain. All were wrong for the Amazon rain forest. All were anomalies. So was the destruction surrounding him in a darkness as bleak as the back of the moon. Miles of lush forest felled and scorched by the object in its final seconds before impact. The impact crater was an anomaly too. A wedge-shaped gash in the earth where instead there should have been a circular, inverted cone. It meant the object's angle of impact had been low. In fact near level trajectory. That meant the object was of artificial design. Artificial design had alone been enough reason to send a scientific team. But there had been other reasons too. More important reasons.

Perched on the edge of the impact crater was Doc's target, the supposedly secure complex assembled to study the object. Back in D.C., the location was designated Crash Site Alpha Bell Tower and stored on a hard drive that was also supposed to be secure. Doc accepted that the scientific team and marine force who'd originally occupied the complex were probably all dead. And clearly the complex was in the wrong hands. But there was still hope that the three people who mattered to him were alive and inside. It was up to Malone to get him to them. And having it up to Malone was for Doc the same as facing another anomaly. She was unpredictable.

0200 hours. Almost time.

The shouts and the machines fell silent. The floods remained on. Their light diffused over the top of the hill. Doc waited for an additional thirty minutes. Then he turned to shake Malone. She was already awake and alert. She touched his shoulder and whispered one word.

"Now."

Doc turned his back to Malone as she stripped off her jeans and shooting jacket. He glanced over his shoulder briefly. Her naked back was toward him. She was smearing herself in mud. Her jeans were already cut as short as possible, and her shoes were gone. He watched as the last traces of red hair and pale skin vanished.

Doc kept one eye on her as he pulled off his shirt left handed. Pain shot through his broken right ribs when he slipped his arm out of his sleeve. The safety pins were still in place holding the wound over his ribs closed. Through the bandage, he couldn't tell if the skin was hot or swollen. But the wound was over twenty-four hours old. In the tropics, that was long enough for bad things. Wound infection and maybe worse. There was nothing he could do about it. He opened his Swiss knife and cut away his pants legs so he'd match Malone. The move was painful.

"Time to hurry, Doc." Malone was suddenly beside him. "I'll do it for you."

She worked quickly, helping him smear his six foot frame in mud. Around the bandage and wound, she was gentle. Her touch was deceptive given what she was used to doing with her hands. She helped him with the rest, smearing the mud into his face and hair.

She eyed her work. But they both knew he'd never be mistaken for an Indian. His build was too tall, his muscles too lean, and his face too angular. She rubbed more mud into steel-gray hair that badly needed a barber. It was no good if the light reflected from his head. She nodded back to him that he was covered.

"This will fool them only at a distance, even in the dark." Doc whispered. "And not for damn long."

"Enough to make them think we're loose Jivanos. Hopefully pull their attention toward the prison and give us a shot at our objective." Malone paused only or a second. "Our best option is to not let them see us. Remember that."

Out of the corner of his eye, Doc watched Malone grab up her shooting vest and check it for the quiver of poisoned darts. Looking satisfied she grabbed up a blowpipe. Doc kept the second blowpipe, then grabbed up the camouflage cape made of liana shrubs he'd cut and woven with vines. The shrubs were lifeless. That was perfect.

"We come down behind the generator," Malone whispered. She didn't wait for Doc to indicate he'd heard her. She moved like a cat. Doc fixed one eye on her and the other on the halos formed around the floodlights atop the perimeter fence. Their light diffused into perpetual swirling cloud that stretched miles in all directions. Their grid was arranged with the larger illumination arcs inside the fence. Outside of the fence, the arcs were of narrow depth. Between them, dark places reached the fence. Blind spots!

Doc ran side by side with Malone, bare feet pounding the earth. Halfway down the hill, he dropped to his belly beside her. The pain from his broken ribs instantly knifed into him. He took a minute to catch his breath, then caught up with her as she inched forward. He kept abreast of Malone as she descended toward the cyclone fence. Doc checked her position every five paces. He didn't want Malone at his back.

The steady whine of the oil driven generators rose in Doc's ears, mixing with sudden rain coming down hard and cold. Twenty-five yards from the cyclone fence, the earth changed. More mud and less vegetation. And all of that vegetation was dead or dying. Malone moved close to Doc. He pulled the liana bush cape over them both. She inched forward alongside him, close enough for him to feel her breathing. He felt her face close to his as they both looked at the target.

The cyclone fence was over eight feet high. The concertina wire was razor sharp. Music emanated from speakers next to the floods on each pole. The music fought with mechanical sounds from the generator motor. Macabre, Doc told himself. Whoever was in charge of the compound was just plain macabre.

Doc swept his eyes beyond the fence and across a stretch of flat, muddy ground where he made out the shadowy outlines of the bunkers. The bunkers must have been added by whoever had taken Crash Site Alpha Bell Tower from its small security force of American marines. Originally there had been only the complex and the bivouac and the fence. Doc strained and thought he saw the nearest of the modular, steel units. They'd been intended for use in space, but they'd ended up in the upper Amazon jungle, put in place to study something that *had* come from space.

He reminded himself of what lay beyond. A mile-long crater shrouded in a nearly impenetrable cloud of frozen carbon dioxide. The cloud was self-renewing. It came from something in the crater's far end, from an object not of Earth origin. In what had once been secure circles, the object was designated Alpha Bell Tower. Alpha was chosen because it meant first. But Bell Tower was chosen for what? Maybe it was chosen because it meant sentinel. Or maybe it was chosen because it meant ringing the toll. Who knew? The choice was all in the mind of someone way higher than Doc in the Pentagon. Of course that someone now knew less than Doc.

"Heads down," Malone said in a hushed voice. Doc complied.

A single sentry approached along the inside perimeter of the fence. His path took him between the generator and the fence. His weapon, an MP5 with an integral silencer and flash suppresser, was slung over his shoulder so he could rub his hands together and try to keep warm. The sentry wasn't expecting trouble. That part was good for Malone. The rest wasn't.

"He's wearing a mic," Malone whispered.

Doc narrowed his eyes and strained to make out the sentry's radio headset. He cursed. His plan called for a leg shot with the dart. Feeling the pain and having a leg collapse from under him, the sentry would think first of snake bite. The sentry's natural response would be to yell for help, and the plan counted on the generator's drowning out the sentry's voice. The plan assumed the curare would completely paralyze the sentry before he made the decision to fire his weapon. The plan was now dead on arrival.

"No good," Malone muttered. "He yells in his headset, he's heard."

The sentry moved around the generator. He clicked on a flashlight as he disappeared into the shadows. It would take the sentry fifteen minutes to complete one walk around the entire perimeter. Malone waited until the sentry's flashlight vanished around a curve in the fence. She signaled Doc to move.

Doc kept up with Malone as the two of them crawled forward to the fence, keeping themselves covered in the cape. She took both blowpipes and loaded them. Then she asked Doc for his Swiss knife. As Doc gave it to her, he peered out through the camouflage cape and saw the sentry return around a different side of the generator. The sentry was warming his face with a thermos mug.

"Don't move, Doc," Malone whispered. "Not a twitch." She unfolded the blade, outstretched her arm, and scraped the lowest wire of the cyclone fence. It whined loudly in the rain.

The sentry threw down his mug, dropped to one knee, and raised his weapon. Radio chatter reached Doc's ears. The running came within seconds, followed by shouts and a half-dozen bouncing flashlight beams. Doc buried himself under the cape and froze next to Malone. He turned the luminescent surface of his watch down in the mud.

"Not a twitch, Doc. Breathe shallow."

Flashlight beams swept the earth. A shaft of light penetrated the cape, entering between the leaves and stinging Doc's eyes. He shut them and froze, ticking off the seconds in his head. Against him Malone felt like stone.

The footsteps of several men approached in the rain, accompanied by shouts. They were on the outside of the fence. Doc's instinct was to stand up and run. He prided himself that he never followed first instincts. He tightened his fingers into the earth and waited.

The rain came down harder, soaking his skin under the leaves. He prayed it wouldn't wash away the mud, wouldn't create a surface that would give him away. A burst of radio chatter came from only a few feet away, followed by Russian voices. They laughed and faded away, taking the lights with them.

Malone waited. Doc counted the seconds in his head, ticking them off one by one. It became quiet except for the rain and the generator. After five minutes, Malone whispered a last time, "This one's the real thing."

She scraped the fence with her knife. The whine was long and loud.

A single flashlight swept the steel, followed by cursing and the click of a weapon's bolt. The light swept directly into Doc's face. He shut his eyes and held his breath, praying the light had not caught his retina reflection. The beam moved away. Doc looked up to see the sentry's profile against the fence. The sentry's flashlight beam was moving.

Malone's first dart hit the sentry in the throat. He dropped his flashlight, clawed at his neck, and tried to yell. Nothing came from his mouth but a course wheeze. He tried to spin and raise his weapon. Malone's second dart hit him in the shoulder. His arm fell limp, his hand instantly dropping his gun to the mud. He staggered but collapsed before he reached the generator.

"Dig to fricking China." Malone hurled herself at the fence, fell on her knees, and dug with both hands. Doc did the same, keeping one eye on the downed sentry. The man's chest wasn't moving.

"I made the damn darts too strong," Doc cursed.

"Shut up and dig or we're all dead." Malone found the bottom of the cyclone fence. "Thank God! It's shallow."

Doc worked fast, his mind spitting the facts at him. The curare from the darts wouldn't touch peripheral nerves or brain. Curare was too bulky a molecule to penetrate the blood brain barrier. It did its job at the junction between nerve and skeletal muscle. The brain could give all the commands it bloody well wanted, but skeletal muscle simply wouldn't respond: not arms, not legs, not voice box, and if the dose was high enough, not the diaphragm. When the diaphragm stopped, breathing stopped, and asphyxiation followed. The brain would be conscious all along, screaming for air until the lack of oxygen brought the heart to a stop.

"Dig faster," Malone hissed.

In less than five minutes, they were under the fence and into the compound. Malone bolted into the shadow of the generator. Doc ran in the opposite direction, dropping to check the sentry.

"Doc!" She tried to whisper above the rain. "Keep moving."

He ignored her. In the light from the fallen flashlight, he saw the sentry's face was blue and his eyes frozen. Doc felt for a carotid pulse. It was 160 and skipping beats as the oxygen-starved muscle of the heart threw beats independently of the pacemaker. Doc rolled the sentry on his side to keep his airway clear of the rain. He retrieved the two darts. There was nothing else to do unless he wanted to perform CPR and wait for capture.

Malone motioned violently from the shadows.

Doc joined her beside the generator. She grabbed his face with both of her muddy hands and pulled him close. "Get things clear. That's the enemy."

"I don't kill people."

"I do. And if you pull that shit again, I'll kill you. I won't have any choice."

Doc followed her quietly along the power lines that snaked between dark bunkers. He searched for noise. He wanted to hear familiar voices and know that those he'd come for were still alive. He wanted to hear all three of them alive and talking. He wanted to know where they were being held. But he heard nothing except the rain pounding on canvas tents and mud roofs. And just beneath the rain, he listened to the music crackling from the outdoor speakers. It was Wagner! It was *Tristan and Isolde,* an opera of tragic lovers. For the second time, he considered the someone he did not know, the someone who now controlled Crash Site Alpha Bell Tower. Psychotic, Doc told himself. The bastard had to be.

Ahead the bunkers ended in open ground that stretched fifty feet to the first module of the complex. Doc ran silently with Malone and froze with her beside a darkened tent. The open ground leading to the module was brilliantly lit by floods, each light wrapped in a halo created by the wet air. Huge power lines snaked in the mud and climbed a concrete pier that interfaced with the entry module. A separate, smaller cable dropped from the module and ran back into the bunkers. Malone studied it. She kept her voice low.

"The smaller cable is a phone line. It means there's a command post somewhere behind us."

Doc nodded. He studied the steel stairs that climbed the nearest concrete pier to connect to a steel landing. The landing interfaced via an air lock to the first module. One guard was in sight huddled against the pier. He looked bored.

Malone dropped him with three darts, one into his neck and two into his broad back. She sprinted the distance in spite of the mud and pulled him behind the pier. Foam was pooling from his mouth as she relieved him of his sidearm and buckled the holster around her naked waist. Doc retrieved the darts before climbing the stairs behind her.

She froze just under the landing. In the floods, it was visible from every part of the compound.

"Guard's clothes," Doc suggested.

"No time," Malone answered. She took one look back. The bunkers were in the shadows and lifeless. Beyond them, flashlight beams moved near the cyclone fence. She took a breath and padded across the landing. Doc followed.

The key punch code was 7-99, the date of Object Alpha Bell Tower's arrival from space. Doc punched in the digits. The outer airlock hatch opened with a hiss. The pressure inside was below atmospheric but still higher than the level in isolation modules. Doc and Malone flattened against the inside wall and cranked the outer hatch shut. The vents whined. Doc felt his ears pop as the pressure dropped. Malone peeked through the glass port of the inner hatch.

"Two technicians on duty. Both have sidearms." She reloaded the blowpipes and handed one to Doc. He looked at it hesitantly.

"You have to do it," she insisted. "If you don't, I use the gun." She showed him the 9mm Beretta she'd taken from the outside sentry. A round was already chambered. Malone thumbed back the hammer and released the safety.

Neither guard turned around as Malone cranked open the inner hatch. She and Doc fired at the same time, darts hitting each technician in the upper back. The curare began its work in the shoulders and backs in the split second it took the two technicians to spin in their chairs to see what had stung them. The effect was already spreading as they faced the nearly naked, muddy woman and man who'd shot them with blowguns. Malone raised her pistol and motioned for them to freeze. It didn't take long. Both crumpled out of their chairs, landing in heaps on the steel floor.

"Remember! They can still hear," Doc said as he stepped over a technician and sat at a keyboard. He winced as he lifted his right hand to the keys. It was his ribs again.

"Doesn't matter," Malone answered as she removed the technicians' guns and kicked them away. She studied the service module, finding the keypad she wanted. The keypad was striped diagonally, yellow and black. In its center a red button was protected by a glass cover. She made sure the cover was unlocked. Nearby was a field phone, the flat black receiver cradled in a Kevlar box fitted with a hand-cranked battery. Malone reasoned that the field phone connected to an outside command post.

She stood at Doc's back and looked at the computer screen. Feeling her at his back, Doc tightened. She said, "Find out what they've done."

"In front of you is what they've done." Doc made sure her eyes were on the screen and not him. He scrolled down the columns of numbers. They were grouped under headings: air vents, seals, and hatch locks. "They've locked down the isolation area and kept it under constant watch."

"You're saying the Bell Tower agent has been isolated?"

"No question. It has." Doc continued scrolling through data, this batch directly from the laboratory programs. He found the files he wanted and chose a summary. The object had brought something from space, something that killed every lifeform in its path. The search for a cause had focused on a microbial agent. The scientific footwork was extraordinary. The cause of the killing had been identified as an extraterrestrial virus. Doc shook his head.

"They think they've identified a virus."

A virus did not make sense. A virus could jump some species but not all species. And no virus could jump from animals to plants to bacteria. Yet the data in front of Doc's eyes reached exactly that conclusion. A virus had traveled to Earth inside Object Alpha Bell Tower. The virus was capable of interacting with gene sites specific to every lifeform on Earth and killing everything in its path. The so-called virus had been isolated and stored. But then things had gone wrong, according to the computer data. Doc related it to Malone.

"What I'm seeing is beyond the worst-case scenario."

"What kind of worst-case?"

"What they're calling a virus was identified in the isolation lab." Doc hesitated telling her more. But he had no choice. "The panels indicate they've cut isolation off from the rest of the complex. Hard wires, sensing devices, and air vents. All sealed from the outside."

"Meaning?"

"Meaning containment has failed." He glanced at Malone. "Whatever they isolated, it's free! That's why they locked down isolation."

Doc switched chairs and moved to the next computer screen and keyboard. The feed came from an external camera and sensors. The sensors displayed temperature and nitrogen pressure in a bunker. A camera inside the bunker relayed an image, rows of steel dewars lighted under halogen lamps. The surfaces of the dewars were beaded with condensation. They each bore a universal biohazard symbol.

"God in heaven!" Doc realized he was sweating. "They've moved specimens to a bunker. They plan to transport it."

"That explains the airstrip we saw them building."

"That would be my guess."

"What's being transported?"

Doc pointed to the screen and the dewars. "They're taking a sample of the Bell Tower agent with them. They think it's a virus. But who knows what it is? Identity aside, they plan to fly it out of here."

"What can be done about it?"

"Mop Up." He said the words as if he'd said the end of the world. He knew what Mop Up meant: cleansing in a sick sort of way. It was cleansing with over ten thousand degrees of thermonuclear heat and the force of 340 kilotons of explosives. All would be delivered in the form of a tactical nuke via fighter bomber from the carrier *Nimitz*. Doc said, "We have to get to their transmitter and signal Mop Up."

"We'll never get to the transmitter. It's too well-guarded."

"It's our only option."

"I'm sorry to hear that, Doc." she answered softly. "I really am." She raised her Beretta with one hand and pointed it between Doc's eyes. She lifted the glass cover on the yellow and black keypad with her other hand and depressed the red button.

The alarm that followed was shrill and continuous.

Chapter Two

The field phone rang immediately. Malone kept her pistol leveled at Doc and answered it, raising the flat receiver to her face. She barked into the phone, "Speak English."

She waited for someone on the other end to comply. She listened, then responded. "No. Isolation has not been breached. I punched the alarm."

She listened again and kept her pistol pointed at Doc. He held his hands where she could see he was no threat. His mind raced. Malone had not been asked to identify herself. Whoever was on the other end of the phone had heard Malone's voice, a woman's voice, and had assumed the voice belonged in the complex. Doc held his breath and prayed. He listened and got his answer.

"No," Malone said into the phone. "This is not Dr. Waterstone."

Doc felt his legs start to give. He said his thanks to God, steadied himself, and kept his expression impassive in front of Malone. Now he knew that at least one of the three people he loved was alive and that she was here. Dr. Kay Waterstone had been his counterpart for years. Unlike him she'd kept her professional life to herself, thinking that doing so would allow her daughter, April, to live a normal existence. He'd told Dr. Kay, as she liked to be called, that she'd been very wrong. In their line of work, there was no such thing as normal lives for their children. Had Dr. Kay let April into her confidence, April would be far away from this place and safe. But Dr. Kay had not taken his advice. She was not one to take advice at all. But now Doc knew Dr. Kay was still alive. That meant one down and two to go. Dr. Kay was alive and near. Now he needed to find her daughter and his son.

"Keep your palms atop your head, Doc." Malone motioned with her automatic pistol. Doc complied with his left. He couldn't lift his right. He let his lean muscles relax to save energy. He knew what he was going to do. He smiled back at Malone and saw that his smile unsettled her. That was good. She made sure the two technicians on the floor were still motionless before she spoke into the phone.

"Your two men in here can't talk. I'm doing the talking. I'm armed, and if need be, I'll vent the isolation modules to the outside. So get me someone who can make decisions and put him on this phone."

Malone backed against a wall while keeping her gun where she could easily swing her aim to either Doc or the two technicians felled by the darts. Doc looked for any signs of weakness in Malone's face. He saw none. In his mind, he began to write his own script for her. In his, she'd demand that the party on the phone bring all of the hostages inside. And once they were inside, Doc would be able to proceed with his own plan. But none of that was going to happen. Malone wasn't going to play by his rules. She had her own agenda.

"I'm still here." Malone spoke into her field phone. She listened only briefly then began dictating conditions. "That's right. I want the man in charge. He comes in alone and unarmed through the main air lock. If the wrong guy comes in or if I see a weapon, I blow his brains out and vent isolation."

The phone line went dead. Malone cranked the battery and tried to get an answer. The line stayed dead. She held her pistol in both hands and glanced at the hatches.

"They cut you off," Doc said.

"I expected it."

"They'll cut the power next."

"I think they won't." She glanced at the technicians crumpled on the floor. They were starting to move.

"Time's short, Malone." Doc kept his left hand raised. His right lagged.

"I don't need much time." She kept the 9mm Beretta pointed toward him, her hand never wavering. "If I vent isolation to the outside, what's the safest place in the neighborhood?"

"You're standing in it."

"What's the second safest place?"

"The air lock," he answered. "Temporarily."

"Don't need much time. I hold a big card." She motioned Doc toward the computers, told him to sit, and told him to keep his hands in sight.

Doc did as he was told. Gun to his head, he surveyed the files on the hard disc and opened the environmental controls. He found the icon for emergency lock-down procedures. They were easy to reverse, easy to open isolation and vent it to the outside. That didn't matter. He told himself he'd never do it. He ran his eyes across the length of the module, saw the naked wiring and unused work spaces. The active banks of computers and monitors occupied only one wall. They'd been fit in a hurry. He saw two security cameras, also added in a hurry. Both were moving on their tracks. They were pointed in his direction. He turned to Malone.

"You were working for the opposition all along, weren't you?"

She didn't answer him. She backed against the wall, keeping him in the corner of her eye. She watched the air lock as it made a hissing noise. The warning light indicated that the outer hatch was opened, then closed. Another hissing noise indicated that the air lock was repressurized. Movement flashed across the hatch window, and Malone moved so she could aim at either Doc or the hatch. She raised the Beretta in a two-handed grip to just below firing position.

The inner hatch opened. The man who entered ignored Doc and spoke in the other direction.

"Hello, Malone."

"You could at least look surprised to see me." She tightened her grip on her gun and raised it.

"I have no reason to be surprised."

Doc saw that the man who entered was tall and formidable, dressed in dirty marine fatigues with a silver leaf on the collar. Doc didn't linger on that observation. Doc's attention went to the man's face, what was left of it. Nerve-deprived, rubbery skin hung limp over crushed bones. The eyes were violet, hypnotic, insane.

"Dr. Jules Verne Tech, meet Victor Rykoff," Malone said.

Doc said nothing. He watched both adversaries.

"Friend of yours?" Rykoff asked.

"We travel in the same circles," Malone answered.

Rykoff looked at Doc for only a second. Then he let his eyes wander briefly over Malone's muddy, mostly naked body. His face was dead, expressionless. Malone ordered Rykoff to place his palms on a bulkhead and spread his legs. As he did, she patted him down. She didn't find a hidden weapon.

"You're stepping out of character, Victor. You're playing by the rules." She backed away, letting him turn and face her. She stood where she could point her pistol at him or Doc with one turn. "Lock the inside hatch."

Rykoff pulled the square hatch into its jam and cranked the hand wheel. The air-seal light winked for several seconds before illuminating.

"Who told you I was coming, Victor?" Malone asked. "Was it Briggs?"

"Briggs was cheap inside help. That's why he's dead." Rykoff said it softly, lowering his hands to his sides. His gaze was intense and unsettling. Doc made himself look away, a childhood horror rumbling in his head. Never look directly at the Medusa.

"What brings you to me, Malone?" Rykoff asked. "You get bored in the Balkans?"

"I'm never bored."

"You said you wanted to talk," Rykoff said. "So talk."

Doc listened. Something in Rykoff's voice was wrong. It took Doc a second to realize that something was missing. There was no fear, no hate, no anything.

Malone asked, "You've isolated a virus from Bell Tower, haven't you?"

"Maybe."

"You've had a lab accident too. You've locked down the isolation modules, but you've also salvaged some of the virus."

"Maybe." Rykoff's eyes were probing, sizing Malone up.

"Well maybe," Malone said sarcastically, "my people would be interested in a buy."

"I'm not much interested in a sell."

Malone showed the slightest waver in her gun hand, not much of a waver, but enough for Doc to notice. He knew it wasn't fear. It was uncertainty. She recovered and forced a smile. "The money would be right."

"I already have money." Rykoff stepped away from Doc, widening the distance Malone would have to sweep her pistol to shoot both of them. "In fact, I have considerable money. I financed this entire operation myself. My buyer was skeptical, so I did the whole thing spec."

"Who is your buyer?"

"Use your imagination."

"We'd pay you better, much better."

"It wouldn't be the same. Your side would never use the virus. My buyer would. That's real terror."

Rykoff moved toward the air lock, and Malone motioned for him to freeze. Rykoff did as she ordered, standing where his body blocked her view of the glass hatch. One of the technicians at Malone's feet started to crawl on his belly. She stepped out of his reach, keeping her gun pointed at Rykoff. "My people would settle for just a sample."

"They won't get that either." Rykoff's eyes lingered on Malone's lithe, muddy form. "Countermeasures could be developed. My buyer wouldn't like that. Neither would I."

Doc watched Malone sweat. He knew she wasn't afraid. She couldn't be afraid. She was a psychopath, just like Rykoff. Two psychopaths arguing for possession of something that could end all life on the planet. She was sweating because Rykoff was a tough match, even for her.

Rykoff's voice turned gentle, almost soothing. "Was this your primary plan, Malone? Fighting your way in here and buying your way out?"

"No. That was my backup."

"What was your primary?"

She nodded toward Doc. "He was. But that didn't work out."

Doc shifted slightly in his chair, hiding the darts he'd removed from the men Malone had dropped. The darts were still stuffed in the small of his back, the tips capped with plant pulp. They were still potentially lethal. Malone knew he had them. She hadn't taken them back.

"You're out of options, Malone," Rykoff said softly.

"I have one more. I shoot you and vent the complex."

"Not much of an option."

"I'm not crazy about it, either." She held her gun in both hands. "But I'll do it."

Doc knew Mop Up was out of the question. No way to reach the microwave transmitter and signal *Nimitz*. But he had to try. Step one was getting out of the module. Doc let his hand rest against the keyboard. The environmental window was still on screen, the commands within a click of the mouse. He made the calculations in his head: how long it would take to drop the air pressure in the module, who would pass out first, whether he could even drop the breathable air that low, and whether he could finish the job with the darts.

"You didn't come here to die, Malone," Rykoff said.

"Give me another option."

"Same one I gave you in the Balkans."

"No good. Back then all I had to do was walk out. This time is different. I can't go back empty-handed."

"Why?"

"For starters, lots of questions. I won't have good answers."

"Sure you will. You're a skilled liar."

"Not nearly skilled enough."

"What if I give you a little start?"

"Depends how little."

As Rykoff considered an answer, Doc leaned forward to rest his face on one hand and rub his eyes. With his hidden hand, he clicked the first command and selected the evacuation pump. The icon turned red on the screen. The pump made no noise as it began to evacuate the air they were breathing. That was good. Doc told himself that at the first symptom of dizziness he'd hold his breath. He'd have the advantage over everyone else in the module. Outside he'd probably never make it to the transmitter. But he had to try.

One of the technicians pulled himself to sitting position. Malone took another step backward, gun wavering a little more, but still pointed at Rykoff. "I'm running out of patience, Victor. What are you going to give me?"

"Dr. Waterstone's data."

"Not enough. I want Dr. Waterstone herself."

"Not an option."

Listening Doc felt himself go weak. Then he felt rage. He locked his muscles, welding himself to his chair and fighting the urge to stand and smash what was left of Rykoff's face. Doc forced himself to wait, one eye on the monitor screen. The pump icon was still red. But atmospheric pressure wasn't changing. The evacuation pump was too slow, but it shouldn't have been.

"Settle for the data, Malone." Rykoff kept his arms to his side. "It's comprehensive. Molecular analysis of the virus and its toxins, autopsy data on the human victims, real-time on the experimental animals. The data is..."

"Marketing, but otherwise useless." Malone forced a harsh laugh. "Just your way of letting my people know what you've got."

"The painless way to let your people know."

"I'm not your little messenger girl. You're starting to piss me off."

Rykoff shrugged. "There are other ways to make a point." He leaned forward, eyes intense. "Let's say a demonstration somewhere in a third world hole filled with the kind of people that no one really cares about. I calculate there would be enough carnage for a black and white photo on the back page of the *Times,* taken with morning coffee and a dash of obligatory sympathy for the suffering masses on the other side of the world."

"Am I supposed to care?" Malone asked sarcastically.

"I'm trying to appeal to your better side, Malone."

"I don't have a better side. You'll have to up the ante." She raised the Beretta. "This is the last time I ask."

Rykoff paced, but not too far. His body blocked any view Malone could have of the outside hatch. He continued, "For the demonstration, my home village should do nicely. It's the least I can do for the descendants of the men who did this to my face." He touched his sunken cheek. "My face doesn't feel. My fingertips do. They feel something cold and dead every time they touch my face. You know all about that, don't you, Malone?"

"You know what he wants, Doc?" Malone grinned out of the corner of her mouth.

"I think so," Doc answered.

"I know so. Same deal he offered in the Balkans. She kept her eyes fixed on Rykoff, her gun hand relaxing. "He lets me live if I lie down with him. Then I serve as his little messenger, take his data disc back to the people who write my paycheck."

Doc glanced sideways at the laptop screen. The pump flow was red, but internal atmospheric pressure wasn't budging. He realized why. There was a breech in the system. He knew where it was.

"Know what, Doc?" Malone took a deep breath. "I'm going to take his offer." She released the pistol hammer under her thumb and handed her weapon to Rykoff. He took it.

At Rykoff's back the inner hatch of the air lock flew open suddenly, slamming steel against steel. Three mercenaries leaped through the opening, their automatic weapons raised. Two laser points fixed on Malone's face and one centered on Doc's head.

Doc looked at the hatch indicator. The light read "closed" and "locked" in spite of the fact that the hatch was open. It explained why the module wouldn't depressurize. Rykoff hadn't really resealed the hatch. Nor had he entered the air lock alone. The mercenaries had been with him. They'd cut and re-circuited the light on the hatch.

"Does this mean our deal is off?" Malone forced a smile.

"No, our deal is just starting." Rykoff reached over Doc and clicked off the evacuation pump. He looked at Doc the way he would a bug. "Any comment, Dr. Tech?"

"No comment at all. I'm not a psychiatrist."

Chapter Three

The darkness in the steel room was not total. The tiny red indicator on the intercom threw off some light. So did the tracking indicator on the security camera, blinking in synchrony with the steady whir of the motor swiveling the lens between targets. The camera was probably designed to work in low to absent light. That much H.I. Tech guessed as he stretched his lean, lanky frame out in the top bunk. The whirring camera motor meant that on the other end it was somebody's job to watch them, even in the dark. That was expensive in terms of manpower, he knew. And it meant that the mercenaries thought of him as more dangerous than he did himself. That helped.

H.I. knew it was best to sleep. Doc's rules said it was. In a bad situation, sleep while you can. You may not get the chance to do so later. The same went for eating, another of Doc's rules. So true to form, H.I. had eaten the canned food he'd been served earlier, even though Dr. Kay and April hadn't touched theirs. Doc would be proud of him, following his rules. But then again Doc had gotten him into this mess.

H.I. Tech considered his options for the hundredth time and didn't like them. He was only sixteen, and he was going to probably die. He had time to think about it now, and instead of being afraid he was actually pissed. That was a surprise to him. And it was also a surprise to him that he was thinking about getting kicked out of school. That had been Doc's doing also, though not deliberately. In fact Doc was responsible for all of his problems except one. Yet here he was following Doc's rules. Go figure.

H.I. turned his head toward the ceiling, which was only inches from his face. But sleep wasn't going to happen. And he did need time to think of a way out. His original escape plan, making a deal with the big South African who'd captured him, looked dead. The South African's nickname, Bulldog, was completely fitting. Bulldog was a mercenary who'd already proven himself tenacious when given a target. He'd also proven himself greedy and aggressive, aka hungry and mean. But Bulldog was not a cowboy. He worked for paymasters, not causes. He weighed his risks and placed his life above money. No matter what H.I.'s promise of wealth, it was unlikely that Bulldog would still honor the deal he'd made with H.I. Too risky, and the South African would know so.

H.I. rolled to his side, and the motor on the camera stand whirred as the lens followed him. Maybe it was run by an infrared motion detector, and maybe no one was watching him at all. But he couldn't count on maybe.

From the bottom bunk, he heard whispers coming from Dr. Kay and April. To him the two often looked more like sisters than mother and daughter. Ok, so what if they were maybe nineteen or twenty years apart? And so what if Dr. Kay was raven haired and dark while April was blonde with gilded skin? Each had the same slender build with all those great curves. Each had the same liquid blue eyes that could burn a hole through you when they were mad or make little creases under them when they smiled. But there was also a big difference. April didn't often smile. And April was the one thing in H.I.'s life that Doc had not messed up. That thing H.I. had messed up himself, and she hated his guts for it. She'd said it more than once.

He strained to understand what they were saying. They weren't dwelling on escape. Nor were they dwelling on the Bell Tower lifeform and the end of the world. Mostly their whispers were a lot of making up. Their whispers were punctuated with muffled crying between mother and daughter. Hearing them H.I. guessed there'd been a lot water under the bridge. Or maybe it was just something that took their minds off the inevitable. Maybe they were making their remaining time count for something. Taking their minds elsewhere or making time count were actions that both seemed stupid given that they were locked in a steel room on the edge of oblivion. H.I. realized he was starting to think like Doc. That couldn't be a good thing.

Below him April and Dr. Kay suddenly laughed in the dark. H.I. guessed that laughter was something the mercenary on the other end of the open intercom and camera would find perplexing, if there was a mercenary on the other end. H.I. almost laughed himself. But then the compartment hatch slammed open.

Two flashlights shined in his face. H.I. blinked then followed the beams as they dropped to catch Dr. Kay and April holding each other. H.I. squinted to make out the forms behind the flashlights, two armed mercenaries holding a third person. The mercenaries shoved the third person into the room, slammed the hatch behind him, and locked it. Boot steps regressed along the grated floor and vanished.

In the dark, H.I. heard someone moving along the wall. The light switch clicked and H.I. shut one eye to protect himself from the sudden sting. With one eye squinted open, he made out the figure now facing the bunk. He was an Indian covered in mud and naked except for short pants. H.I. looked again, this time with both eyes wide open, and realized he was not seeing an Indian.

"Doc?" It was all H.I. could say.

April yelled for Doc a split second after him. But Dr. Kay's reaction was entirely different.

Dr. Kay swept April aside and threw herself into Doc's arms. Their kiss went on a long time, and it wasn't a cousin kiss or a friend kiss. Doc crushed Dr. Kay's slender form with one arm, his other pressed against his side. He held her like he'd never let go. But eventually he did let loose. He had tears in his eyes, something H.I. had never seen before. But the tears were nothing compared with the kiss. H.I. stared the whole time. He couldn't help himself.

"You okay, son?"

"I'm fine. How are you, Doc?" H.I. almost addressed him as "Dad", like a normal son would have addressed a normal father. But hey!

"You okay, Babe?" Doc stroked Dr. Kay's hair and face. She nodded.

"Well, I'm not okay." April grabbed at Dr. Kay's arm. "When did this bullshit between you two start?"

"It's a long story, Baby."

"It better be," April turned to Doc. "When did you two become an item?'

Doc ignored her. "Is the cam sound-capable?"

"No," Dr. Kay answered, still holding Doc. "Sound is relayed on the intercom."

Doc glanced toward the switch on the intercom box. The small red light showed the intercom was active. He checked his watch and gently untangled himself from Dr. Kay. "I need some clothes."

Dr. Kay opened a steel drawer under the bottom bunk. It was filled with workman's fatigues, all dirty and crumpled. Next to it were socks, underwear, and crumpled towels. Eye on the security camera, Doc grabbed a towel and unfolded the sink from the steel wall. He began to sponge away the mud. Dr. Kay moved to help him. As soon as she touched his side, he gritted his teeth in pain.

"What did you manage to do to yourself this time, Doc?"

"Gunshot, I think." Doc said. "Grazed the chest wall. I don't think it penetrated."

Dr. Kay went over Doc like she would a patient. As she did so, she moved fast. With trembling hands, she cleared mud from the bandage and then from the tape encircling his chest. He winced. She stopped. "You break a rib too?"

"I think so. When I fell. Hurts like it."

"What butcher dressed your wound?"

"My CIA escort, Alex Malone." Doc winced as Dr. Kay went back to work. He answered Dr. Kay's next question before she could ask it. "Malone's a whole other story."

"So where is Malone?" H.I. asked.

"Yeah! Where's the bitch?" April didn't get an answer. "She is okay, isn't she? If she's not okay, I didn't mean the part about calling her a bitch."

"Malone's made private arrangements with our host," Doc said.

"Bitch! What did I tell you?" April threw herself back on the lower bunk. "I told you she was dirty back at the airport in Washington."

H.I. considered it. Malone's being dirty and selling out now didn't make sense. She could have sold out a lot earlier with a lot fewer risks. She could have turned April over to the mercenaries in Villa Lobos. Instead she'd pulled April and H.I. out of harm's way. She could have jumped for her own life back on the *Portos Blanco.* Instead she'd helped H.I. and April jump to safety then remained with Doc on the wrecked boat. H.I. told April what he thought.

"You're naïve, Tech." April shifted her gaze to the sink.

Dr. Kay finished removing Doc's bandage and tape. His bruising was extensive. His wound was ugly, held together by safety pins. It was also infected. Red streaks were spreading to surrounding tissue. Dr. Kay's hands began trembling again. She moved to the intercom, punched in numbers, and depressed the switch."

"Medical." A technician answered on the other end.

"This is Dr. Waterstone. I need some things." She rattled off a list. She listened as the voice on the other end stated that Rykoff would have to be disturbed for permission. Dr. Kay spoke again. "Then disturb Rykoff. He'll be pissed if you don't. I need those things now."

Five minutes later, the lock clicked, and the door opened with a hiss. H.I. asked himself how he'd missed the fact that the door was air-tight. He didn't dwell on his mistake. There were two armed guards in the door frame. One delivered a large canvas pouch to Dr. Kay. Both waited with weapons in hand, while she went to work on Doc.

"Looks bad, Doc. I don't know how you're still functioning."

"Will power, divine intervention, or both."

Dr. Kay worked fast again. Made Doc swallow two levofloxacin. Then removed the safety pins, debrided the wound, and packed it with kerlix soaked in iodine. Then another bandage and clean tape around Doc's ribs. She nodded to the guards when she was done. They collected the medical materials in the pouch. The door sealed tightly behind them, and a loud locking mechanism tumbled into place.

Dr. Kay finished helping Doc sponge away as much mud as possible. Then Doc struggled into the workman's clothing from the drawer beneath Dr. Kay's bunk. H.I. could see that the moves were painful. He watched Doc slip into the one blind spot the security camera could not find.

H.I. knew where Doc's mind was going. Sizing up the room. Looking for some way to beat the locks, the monitors, and the guards. But clearly impossible, H.I realized.

On the other hand, maybe the deal with Bulldog could be brought back into play. Bulldog had access to the helicopters. And by now Bulldog could plainly see that Rykoff was on to something much bigger than an ordinary smash-and-snatch job. Bulldog had been hired to take over the site and prepare a runway to fly something out. But then he'd been ordered to kill all of the American scientists as well as the American and Brazilian security teams deployed around the crater. He'd have to know this whole thing could not be about some downed, experimental craft. By now Bulldog could plainly see that he'd been lied to by the man who'd hired him. But Bulldog would never believe the other truths, that the thing in the crater had come from space, killed all life within a mile radius, and entombed itself in a cold cloud that defied explanation. So H.I. had fed the big South African an alternative, that the object in the crater was the core of a new energy source worth billions. Bulldog had been convinced. Of that H.I. was sure.

H.I. turned his attention to Dr. Kay's laptop so he could finish producing discs that would look to Bulldog like blueprints of an energy plant. He clacked at the keyboard and tried to forget the things he'd seen on the keyboard before Doc's arrival. He tried to forget what Dr. Kay had said at the time. But it all came back to him, and he realized his sweat was cold. What she'd said seemed impossible.

"It's found me. That's why no one can leave."

"What's found you?"

She'd told him. And he'd seen the evidence on the screen of her laptop. But now it all a seemed unreal. A nightmare that maybe he'd dreamed after falling asleep in the bunk before Doc's arrival. But he had not fallen asleep. And it was no dream. He shoved the memory out of his mind. He watched the machine reboot. The screen filled with nonsense hieroglyphics.

"Anyone notice this machine won't access the system?" He waited for an answer.

No answer came. April and Dr. Kay had their eyes on Doc. So H.I. toyed with the keyboard. Nothing worked. The hieroglyphics went on for a minute, then disappeared. Dr. Kay's ID photo replaced them, joined by April's. They were identical in face, save for the twenty or so years that separated them. As if one were a mere copy of the other, they had the same blue eyes, same high cheek bones, and same round mouth. But where there was wisdom in Dr. Kay's eyes, there were street smarts in April's. On computer screen, the two faces began merging into one. They were doing it without any crunch from the hard drive.

It had a visitor. It's found me. That's why no one can leave.

H.I. stared at the screen. "The lifeform in the crater has been contained, hasn't it?"

"We're safe for the time being," Dr. Kay said.

"That's not an answer." H.I. looked again at the images on the laptop screen. Dr. Kay's and April's. They were merged into one face, in some ways even more beautiful than either of the two of them. Then H.I. realized the beauty wasn't in the physical features. It was in the expression. So peaceful. And then the two faces separated, each now distinct and even more beautiful. Data began scrolling underneath them in a language H.I. could not understand. He shut the lid.

"The Bell Tower life form is no mere virus, is it?" H.I. looked at Dr. Kay as he spoke.

"No. It's much more than that."

"Because a mere virus is just a strand of DNA or RNA wrapped in protein. By itself it can do nothing. By itself it can't even survive or reproduce."

"That's right."

"A virus lives by invading other living things, doesn't it? Invades them and turns them into a host. Finds a place where its genes can attach and take over and force the host to build its progeny."

"Only if it can find a specific host." Dr. Kay nodded.

"But what happened here is way beyond that, isn't it?" H.I. held his breath. "What you've found here can invade all earth life forms."

Doc interrupted. "What's been found here would require a universal genetic pass key. If one exists."

"It does exist. It's all in the data on this laptop," H.I. answered. He looked at Dr. Kay. She wouldn't meet his gaze. He continued, "The lifeform carried here by Bell Tower can do this, can't it? And it can because it is not merely a virus, is it?"

"No, it's not just a virus." Dr. Kay looked at Doc.

"It can think, can't it?" H.I. asked. But he knew the answer. "It built the spacecraft that carried it here, the one in the crater?"

"Yes."

"Bullshit," April said. "Bugs don't think."

"Why?"

"They don't think because they're too small. And they don't ride in spaceships."

"That's wrong. Actually Earth microbes are riding in spaceships right now. They're taking interstellar rides. We sent them."

"Bullshit."

"No, this is not bullshit. The Voyager satellite launched decades ago will eventually travel to another star, and when it arrives it will be carrying unintended passengers."

"Earth microbes," April said. "But they'll be frozen dead."

"They may not be dead at all. Live bacteria have survived rides on other satellites in Earth orbit."

"So you think the Bell Tower lifeform is an unintended passenger, a microbe that arrived here alive?"

"No. I'm only pointing out that interstellar spaceships are a function of the passenger, not the vehicle. And that Bell Tower's passenger has a power more remarkable than space travel."

"It's more remarkable because it can build genes?"

"No, it doesn't build the genes. It manipulates the ones all Earth life shares. That makes it an ultimate weapon. That's how it kills."

It kills everything in its path.

H.I. thought of the stretch of lush rain forest that Bell Tower had reduced to a frozen crater deader than the surface of the moon except for a half-sphere the size of a building and home to a lifeform small as a virus. An intelligent lifeform! An evil and destructive lifeform! He remembered his nightmares. How long ago had he had them? Had it been a few hours or a few days? In the dream the word had appeared over and over on the blackboard.

Extinction.

In the nightmare Raymond Marsden had shouted the warning, because he had understood Bell Tower. But that was just a bad dream. In real life Marsden had been ridiculed and had been led to kill himself by jumping from a hotel room window.

It wiped the dinosaur from the face of this planet. Now it's back.

"This is a crock," April said. "Bugs don't think."

"Actually, they could." H.I. tried to log off and power down. But the laptop would not follow his commands. He shut the cover and kept talking. "Human-built computers are already moving toward microscopic size. Microchips will be history. They'll be replaced by strands of DNA or molecules, arranged in layers and shuffling electrons in three dimensions instead of two. We're talking real power, the ability to think."

"Does one of these microcomputers exist?"

"No."

"So because someone thinks it can be built, you think it must already exist?"

"I'm just saying that it's possible, and I'm saying that intelligent life could exist on that level."

H.I. watched April slip back into the bunk. She hadn't noticed the image on the laptop, and H.I. wasn't going to fill her in. She didn't need to know that the viral-sized lifeform from Bell Tower had the ability to manipulate electronics or that it recognized Dr. Kay and April, a scientist and her brood. It was searching for them. That he did not want her to know.

"You still didn't answer my question," H.I. said to Dr. Kay. "Is the lifeform in isolation completely contained?"

"For now at least, it is. It's frozen in liquid nitrogen."

But not contained, H.I. thought, because it could do much more than invade other lifeforms and manipulate genes. It could access electronics. And it already had access to all of the electronics in this complex.

Doc interrupted, "It's 0345 hours."

"You want us to try and get some sleep while we can?"

"No. I want you to get out of your chair."

H.I. did it calmly. Just as calmly, Doc took the chair in his left hand, raised it over his head, and used it to smash the surveillance camera from its swivel. He did the same to the intercom box.

"We have less than a minute," Doc said, wincing from the pain in his ribs. He removed bamboo darts from his clothes. "Listen carefully, and do exactly what I tell you."

Chapter Four

Malone lifted her head and let the hot spray run down her naked skin. When she turned, Rykoff's face was floating outside of the transparent shower wall. It was battered and lifeless except for his eyes. They were violet, penetrating.

"I liked you in the mud."

"I didn't." She took her time working a lather over the mounds of her breasts, knowing he was watching every move. She counted on it.

Rykoff touched the plastic from the outside, denting the surface against her skin. The portable shower cylinder swayed on its suspension wire. It was meant only for one. Rykoff unzipped the side, spoke without emotion. "You know there was a time in Sarajevo when I wasn't sure I could trust you."

"Was there?" She turned her back to him to let him run his hands over her soapy skin. His fingers wandered like big spiders, touching her shoulders and spine before moving lower. His hands were manicured, smooth, cruel.

"Oh, yes. There was a time."

She closed her eyes and let the water hit her full in her face. She felt his hands wander slowly over her buttocks, his palms flattening and then squeezing hard enough to hurt.

"I'm surprised to hear that." She said it slowly. She turned to face him and let the water run off the pointed ends of her breasts. He reached for her. She pulled away, keeping her eyes fixed on him. She turned off the water and outstretched a slim arm.

"You are, as you Americans say, a piece of work." He handed her a towel.

"Is that so?"

"You know it's so. It's what I like about you." He stepped backward so she could climb out of the shower cylinder. He stood close as she padded onto the floor of the bunker. She felt the hard wood under the canvas covering. Beneath them she heard the water draining away.

"I'm your type, am I?" She buried her face in the towel. It was dry, not clean. It smelled like medicine.

"You're so much more than that."

She understood what he meant. It sent a chill down her spine. She kept her back to him, avoided looking at him. "Are you saying we're alike?"

"We're both survivors. We're both ambitious. I knew that in Sarajevo when you killed your own partner. What was his name?"

"Ramsey. His name was Ramsey." She wrapped the towel around her, mounding her breasts up toward him and letting the tail end fall open over her buttocks. She reminded herself she had to do this carefully. He was no fool.

"I knew it again tonight, Malone."

"Knew what?"

"That you're a realist. I saw that about you when you discarded Dr. Tech."

"That move was a no-brainer. Dr. Tech would have been in the way."

"Of your job?"

"Not the job. Just the way I have to get it done."

"Which is?"

"Making a deal with you. He'd be opposed. I wouldn't." She raised a leg, planted a foot on a chair, and dried her hair. She closed her eyes and felt Rykoff's course breathing touch her skin. Pheromones, she told herself. That's what Doc would have called it, dissecting passion as if passion were a lab animal. She didn't ask herself if Doc ever felt passion. She knew he did. She even knew the woman for whom he felt the passion, the lovely Doctor Waterstone. His files and hers had been clear about the relationship they denied.

Malone felt Rykoff's breath quicken. Pheromones! Malone told herself she wanted the air lousy with pheromones. She felt Rykoff's gaze wandering over all of her. She opened her eyes and saw what was on the table. She'd seen it before when she'd first entered the bunker. She studied the distance. "How long has it been, Victor?"

"How long has it been since what?"

"Since you've had a woman?"

He didn't answer her, just sat in a chair next to the table. Sat there and let his eyes drink in the sight of her.

"It couldn't be that long, Victor. Not for a man with your attributes."

"Are you referring to power and money?"

Malone looked beyond Rykoff. In the semi-darkness of the bunker, she saw surgical lamps and steel cabinets loaded with vials. Where there were vials, there would be sedatives and narcotics and needles and syringes. She knew Rykoff used them to alter his face, but that the effect was never better than temporary. That was important to remember.

"That's buying, Malone. I don't like buying."

"What do you like?"

"I like winning."

Malone saw dim reflections in the windows of the steel cabinets. She saw the back of Rykoff's head, capped in white hair. She saw her own naked form. It was small and slender and curved. To the casual eye, maybe even vulnerable. But vulnerable was wrong. She scanned the cabinet windows for locks. There were none. The glass reflected a low shape, maybe a cot, maybe a surgical table. She couldn't tell.

Rykoff shifted in his chair. The move was purposeful. He was out of reach of the table. He was also out of reach of what lay on the table. A Beretta M9 automatic pistol. Loaded, it held fifteen nine millimeter rounds. It was within her reach, not his.

"You didn't answer my question," Malone spoke. "How long has it been since you've had a woman?"

"Sarajevo! You!"

"You're lying! When you don't even have to."

Malone buried her face and hair in the smelly towel. She looked at the table and the Beretta pistol. She looked beyond them to the shadows on the bunker's canvas door. Two of the shadows moved ever so slightly. She knew what they were.

"I like winning too," she said just above a whisper. She flicked her chin, throwing damp, red hair out of her face.

In that same second, she reached over the table and grabbed up the gun in her hand. Out of the corner of her eye, she saw the shadows move and saw Rykoff start to stand. She swung toward Rykoff and knew immediately the weight of the gun was too light. She spun it in her hand and pointed the pistol grip toward Rykoff. The shadows on the canvas door froze. Rykoff took the pistol.

"You shouldn't leave those lying around," Malone said. "You never know when they might go off."

"This one's not loaded." Rykoff lay the gun back on the table. She kept her eyes on his as she drifted across the floor and leaned full into him. Standing on tiptoe, she slowly ran her hands over him and felt him respond. She opened his shirt and brushed her face against his chest. His muscles were hard as body armor. She touched her face to his cheek. It was cold as ice. It felt like death.

"Not just another pretty face, are you Victor?"

"Once I was." He touched her all over. He took his time. He was rough. "I had a handsome face. They took it away."

"Who took it away?"

"The Russians did. My own countrymen did this to me. They didn't want my life. They just wanted to take away the tools of my trade, my face and my voice."

"Why?" She felt her own breath quicken. It shouldn't have. Rykoff repulsed her. She cursed herself even as she felt herself respond to his touch.

He whispered between breaths. "It was because of what I did after I did the job. They thought I was going independent. They were right. I was."

"You're the independent type." She pressed her lips to his ear and murmured. "Can you feel my lips?"

"No. My face can't feel."

"There?" She held him tighter and found his belt. "Can you feel me there?"

"Yes."

"What job were you doing for the Russians?"

"I was organizing the Slavs. I had them all: Serbs, Bulgars, and Montenegrins. We were ready to drive out the Turks."

Malone winced. Drive out the Turks? He wasn't making sense. What if the bastard was psychotic? That would make things tough, damn tough.

"You don't believe me, do you, Malone?"

"We can talk about it all night long." She smiled and slipped out of his grip, her arms still reaching for him. She stepped backward until she felt her legs brush the metal rim of a cot. She lay back to make room for him. The sheets were cold and damp.

He stood at the edge and held her face like a vice in his manicured hands. "The Russians were afraid of what I'd do with the Serbs. So they…" He stopped talking as she touched him.

She forced a moan, opened one eye, and searched the bunker. The shadows were frozen against the canvas door. Two guards just outside, she figured. They'd be listening to everything and ready to storm in and blow her brains out if she made the wrong move. They were Rykoff's insurance! She looked up and saw his dead face. His eyes were open, staring down.

"Why don't you close your eyes and enjoy the ride?" she whispered.

"I can't close them. I can't use any of the muscles in my face. I can't taste with the front of my tongue. I can't smell.

They smashed both facial nerves when they broke all the bones in my face. They used a lead pipe."

"That's ancient history, Victor," she whispered. "Who's buying Bell Tower?"

"That should be obvious."

"It's not obvious. Who's buying?"

"There's a lot you don't know about me, Malone. There's a lot you wouldn't believe."

Her head was beginning to spin. Steadying herself, she whispered. "I know all I need to know." She reached for Rykoff. She guided him next to her on the sheets and cradled his head in her breasts. His skin was cold as ice. She didn't think about the cold. The world was spinning. Something was damn wrong.

She held Rykoff tight, told herself his caution would be down and that she'd make her move. She looked for the steel medicine cabinets. They were miles away, swaying like crazy. Or was it her head that was swaying? What was wrong with her? Her breathing quickened with his. It wasn't supposed to.

She looked for the Beretta. It was still on the table, swaying in and out of her vision. She forced herself to think. The weight of the Beretta had been light. Empty clip! That's why she'd handed it back. She told herself she'd use it like a club. If she could get to it! She tried reaching. Her arms wouldn't obey. They spun in space. Rykoff briefly forced them behind her head.

"Life demands risks, Malone. You know all about risks."

She tried to answer him. The words wouldn't come.

Rykoff's voice was a whisper. "My buyer was a risk. My buyer wouldn't pay up front, so I'm here on my dollar. My buyer will pay big on the backside."

"My people will pay more." Her voice was weak. She gripped the bed with both hands. The world was spinning. She stopped talking as he touched her again.

"But your people like to make all of the rules," Rykoff said.

"What do you care?" She let go of the bed, found herself holding him, pulling him to her, crushing herself against him as her eyes searched for a weapon.

"I like my own rules, Malone." He pulled away suddenly. His voice was cold, almost mechanical. "You knew that in Sarajevo."

She reached for him. Her arms swayed in the wrong direction. He stared at her, said it slowly. "You've misjudged me."

The handcuffs came out of nowhere. He cuffed her to the cot railing, tightened the cuffs until they hurt. He stood over her, his voice a million miles away. "I always win, Malone."

The last thing Malone remembered was Rykoff's sarcastic whisper.

"I always win," he said.

Then nothing.

Chapter Five

Malone became aware of a hum in the darkness, aware that she was naked and cold and on her back on the canvas. Her jaw hurt. Everything hurt. Rykoff must have hit her more than once. She couldn't remember. He'd probably questioned her, and when he hadn't gotten answers he'd hit her. She promised herself she hadn't given him answers.

She tried to move. She couldn't. Her arms were bent behind her head. Her wrists were handcuffed to a long chain wrapped around the leg of a metal cot a few feet away. She was alone on the canvas floor. She rolled toward the hum and saw Rykoff asleep in pajamas atop the cot. His eyes were closed with paper tape. His nose and mouth were covered in a clear plastic breathing mask linked to a machine by tubing. The machine was flat and white, like the base of a vacuum cleaner. A few lighted buttons were visible on the front panel.

She realized it was some special modification of a BIPAP machine, meant to keep Rykoff's damaged airway open, so he wouldn't asphyxiate during sleep. It provided the assistance during both inspiration and expiration. No ordinary therapy would do for his injuries. His machine was custom-built. It took up lots of space and made constant noise. But without it, sleep could bring death. Malone wondered how Ryoff had survived in the beginning, after the Russians had broken his face and before Rykoff had gotten his machine. Maybe he'd survived by sleeping only a little bit at a time, each try interrupted the choking and air hunger that would bring him back awake. There would have been no REM sleep or dreams. Taken together, the makings of a harsh sentence. But Rykoff deserved even worse. His broken face and a life without deep sleep or dreams seemed only a start. But even that had been reprieved by technology. Technology was unfair.

Malone tried again to remember what happened to her. Her mind was empty. Why? The medicine smell in the towel he had given her. Some kind of sedative or a hypnotic. The sick bastard had drugged her! Then he'd questioned her, and when he hadn't gotten the information he wanted, he'd done other things.

She hurt all over, hurt deep. She could move her eyes and close her lids without a problem. She could move her arms and legs. Rykoff hadn't broken any bones. She thought of him without anger. Anger wasn't needed because she was going to kill him. That had been her intent from the second she and Doc had initiated the backup plan. Doc's job was to get his loved ones out, something of no importance to her. Her job was to pretend to make a deal with Rykoff so she could get to the backup objective. She reminded herself that Doc and the others had to be expendable if she were going to neutralize Bell Tower. She knew she would succeed at her job, just as she knew Doc would fail at his.

She winced at the thought. Doc was paying the penalty for playing in the big leagues.

Malone rolled on to her belly and extended her neck so she could see her wrists. She wriggled both inside their handcuffs. The jaws on both were tight. With the fingers of her right hand, she explored the base of her left cuff. Two tiny keyholes. All she needed to get free was a bobbie pin. But finding a bobbie pin was unlikely.

She searched through the darkness. Rykoff's discarded marine fatigues were piled in the seat of a chair within reach of her legs. In one try, she had the shirt gripped in her toes. She pulled it to where she could reach the collar with her hands. She removed the oak leaf insignias first. They were no good for what she had in mind. She removed his combat engineer pin next. The pin mounted in back was long enough and thin enough to do. She bent the end of the pin twice by inserting it in the keyhole and twisting. The final shape was a tiny crank handle. She slipped it into each keyhole. The ratchets opened and released the jaw. The cuff opened, and she was free with the handcuff dangling from her right wrist.

Rykoff lay on top of the sheets, the chest of his muscular body heaving with the steady hum and pressure of the modified BIPAP machine. His hideous face was buried in tape and a breathing mask. Malone's first impulse was to finish the job the Russians had started. Look for a heavy, blunt object. Bash in his skull. Bash it until she saw brains.

She knew she wasn't going to kill him that way. Not her style. Besides, it was not necessary. In a few hours, Rykoff would be vaporized beyond ashes. So would the compound and everything for miles. Personal revenge wasn't necessary. Her calm returned. Her brain cleared.

She needed clothes. Rykoff's were too big. She searched the bunker and saw only one shadow on the canvas door. One guard was still walking sentry and watching over his master. Malone gripped the handcuffs in her right hand and made a fist. She slipped naked across the canvas floor and opened the flap.

The lone guard stood with his back to the flap door. She was glad to see he was smaller than Rykoff. He stood smoking a cigarette, his weapon slung over his shoulder. His demeanor and stance showed he was tired, and tired was careless. But she knew it happened to the best of them.

The guard turned too late as Malone waded into him. His first mistake was hesitating so he could stare at her naked body. His second mistake was leaving his chin open. She threw all of her strength into her right fist, reinforcing it with the handcuffs as she smashed into his chin. She felt his jaw crack and heard his neck snap backward. He collapsed in a heap.

Malone grabbed him by the ankles and dragged him into the darkness inside the bunker. She felt for the artery in his neck. No pulse. She must have hit him at a freak angle and broken his neck. Just as well, she told herself. She took his clothes. To make them fit, she knotted his shirt bottom at her waist and rolled up the sleeves. The pants were baggy. She tightened the belt and rolled up the legs. She discarded his boots. They were too big.

She froze and tilted an ear skyward. Something was different in the compound. What?

She put it out of her mind. She threw the dead guard's pistol belt over her shoulder and checked his 9mm Beretta. The clip was full. The safety was on. There was a round in the chamber. She holstered the pistol and noted the belt was fitted with three thirty-round clips for the MP5 submachine gun that lay at the dead man's side. Malone grabbed up the MP5 and extended the weapon stock. She pulled back the cocking handle and flipped the selector switch from safety to single shot. She froze again.

She knew what was different in the compound.

There were no tractor sounds. There was no shouting. There was no noise of any kind, except an occasional cough drifting from one of the bunkers. Why was there no noise? The answer had to be that the airstrip was complete.

Malone realized time was shorter than she'd allowed. She checked the dead man's watch. It was 0445 hours. Somehow, in spite of Rykoff, she was on schedule. She took the dead man's hat, buried her hair, and pulled the brim over her face. She moved among the bunkers.

The compound lights threw rings in the wet air and reflected a haze from the sky. The clouds were low and swirling. In her mind they looked angry. She remembered Doc's explanation, that their point of origin was the crash site. It didn't matter, Malone told herself. The crash site, and whatever had fallen from the sky, had very little time left in their existence.

She passed the first bunkers and found the bulldozer unoccupied and abandoned at the edge of the fence. It was pointed in the right direction, toward the rain forest. In a few minutes, she'd need it. She noted its location and kept her bearings. She moved noiselessly in the dark and found the communications bunker.

A cluster of microwave dishes and radio antennae angled toward the sky. No sentry was posted. The flap doors were closed and illuminated from the inside by one light. She cracked the flap with her weapon and saw one technician at the equipment, his head nodding off. Malone flipped the selector switch on her weapon to safety and slipped to the technician's back. He didn't stir. She used the MP5 like a club and felt his skull crack. Without checking him for life, she rolled his body away from the table and sat at the keyboard. Her hands were shaking but not out of fear. She felt excitement! She tapped in the information she'd memorized at Langley.

IT SYSTEM:	**BELLTOWER SPOKE**
USER ID:	**KWATER (LAST LOGGED ON 0830, 12/10/1999)**
PASSWORD:	**XXXXX**

Dr. Waterstone's password was "April." Malone shook her head. The idea of a password was that it not be discoverable with random guesswork. It was careless of the good Doctor Waterstone to have used her daughter's name, and careless was bad for security. Malone hit the return key and asked for permission to enter the system. The machine answered immediately.

PERMISSION TO ENTER SYSTEM GRANTED

She checked the watch. It was 0455 hours. She tapped in the message that would be uplinked to a satellite and downlinked to the combat information center of the *USS*

Nimitz. It would be the last message from Crash Site Alpha Bell Tower.

MESSAGE IS MOP UP. REPEAT. MESSAGE IS MOP UP.

Malone signed out of the network. She searched the software and found the command she wanted. She used her own password and activated the hidden computer virus that turned the hard drive to garbage. The communication system was down. "Mop Up" was irrevocable. Mop Up was thermonuclear destruction of Crash Site Alpha Bell Tower and everything in its vicinity!

Rykoff would be reduced to atoms. She had assumed the thought would make her smile. It didn't. She checked the watch. It was 0457 hours. How long did she have? The answer was a couple of hours, enough time to reach minimal safe distance. The bulldozer would get her there.

Malone grabbed up the MP5 and used the barrel to open the bunker flap. Outside there were no signs of activity. The bulldozer was in sight, but Doc and the others were not. She checked the dead man's watch. It was 0500. Doc was late, and late meant not coming. Malone felt a tinge of regret, shrugged it off, and made her way to the bulldozer.

Doc had known the risks, Malone reminded herself. He'd agreed to the backup plan. He'd accepted that if he were late, she'd leave him. Doc was arrogant. He didn't need advice and didn't need help and didn't trust her. He'd have to live or die by his own actions.

The bulldozer was unguarded. Malone climbed into the cab, slung her weapon over her shoulder, and started the motor. She glanced once in the direction of the Bell Tower control complex. Time up. Doc was on his own.

Malone took both gear levers in her hands and turned the heavy machine on its treads, pointing it toward the cyclone fence. She lowered the scoop and tightened her grip to move forward.

The gunfire came from her back.

In a split-second she was crouched and protected by the steel seat. She pointed her weapon through the back window. Gun flashes lit the blackness. They were coming from the direction of the control complex. Yells followed. So did more gunfire. She knew Doc was making his move late. She told herself that was his problem and not hers.

Chapter Six

Less than a half-minute after Doc smashed the surveillance camera and intercom panel, the hatch slammed open. Two guards pointed automatic weapons into the compartment. Safeties clicked off.

"Everyone is to step from room."

The guard doing the talking spoke broken English with a Russian accent. His partner looked like he'd been woken from sleep. Both looked pissed. Doc entered the corridor first. The metal grating echoed under his boots.

"Everyone is to lie on floor."

Doc hugged the grating first. H.I. followed, lying prone alongside Dr. Kay and ahead of April. The lineup was according to Doc's plan.

"Everyone is to make arms behind back."

H.I. lay with his face pointed directly into Dr. Kay's eyes. She tried to wink but couldn't. So she clenched her teeth. Behind her April was in position.

"No one is to move. No one is to talk."

Boots crunched on the grating as the first guard stepped over H.I. His smell stung H.I.'s nostrils. Mud and sweat. H.I.

looked up and realized Doc's mistake. The guard's boots came up too high.

Don't do this, Doc. The plan isn't going to work. Call it off.

The guard with the accent stood with his gun aimed at everyone's backs. H.I. reasoned that his weapon had to be set on single-shot because an auto burst would ricochet. The other guard, the sleepy one, slung his weapon and moved through the hatch into Dr. Kay's compartment. That was going by the book, like Doc had predicted! Empty the compartment and immobilize the prisoners in the corridor. One guards the prisoners, and one searches. That was good for Doc's plan. But Doc's plan was still going to be a bust.

Sudden radio static echoed through the open hatch. The sleepy guard searching the compartment had the mic on his radio open. That was bad for Doc's plan, very bad. Cursing followed the static, as the guard surveyed Doc's damage: a busted surveillance camera, a busted intercom box, and a loose ceiling vent. Maybe the guard would notice the camera was missing from its busted wall mount. Maybe he wouldn't. H.I. heard him throw his weight on the rim of the lower bunk and lift himself toward the vent. Doc also heard it and took it as a cue to make his own move.

"Not to move or I shoot boy!" The guard with the accent was suddenly behind H.I.'s back. H.I. felt the gun aimed at him and felt his own sweat fall to the wet grating underneath his face.

Doc froze with his hands bunched up inside his sleeves. Gun aimed at H.I., the guard with the accent gave Doc another command. "You show your hands."

Doc opened his hands, and a single bamboo dart rolled into sight on the grating. There were two more darts, both hidden from the guard. H.I. knew where they were. But it didn't matter where they were, because Doc's plan was going badly.

"Don't move!" the guard with the accent shouted as he kicked Doc's dart out of everyone's reach. H.I. sensed the weapon swiveling toward Doc. But a shot never came. The noise from inside Dr. Kay's compartment changed everything.

In that instant, the sleepy guard inside Dr. Kay's compartment was fully awake. He was looking inside the ceiling vent and not liking the box-like shape that he failed to recognize as the busted surveillance camera. In front of the box was Doc's luminescent watch. In the wee hours of the morning, the guard's sleepy brain interpreted what he saw as something else completely. He acted on instinct and yelled a warning.

"Bomb!"

In the corridor, the guard with the accent lowered his weapon and cursed in Russian. He hesitated a mere second before leaping over Dr. Kay and toward the compartment hatch. Dr. Kay caught him in mid-stride, grabbing at his legs and yelling hysterically. The guard tried to sweep her out his path.

"Not to scream."

She yelled louder and grabbed at the air. The guard's eyes wavered between his partner inside the compartment and her in the corridor. He grabbed her by the hair and pointed his gun again. The panic in his voice was unmistakable. He shifted his weapon toward H.I.

"To stop or I shoot boy."

"Bomb!" The guard inside the apartment yelled again.

"Bomb!" Dr. Kay yelled with him.

In the corridor, the guard with the accent took a step backward. Now his boots were within inches of April. Dr. Kay screamed as if insane. For the guard, everything was happening at once. Just as planned. And H.I. saw April make her move. But the guard's boots were still too high.

So H.I. reacted without thinking, pushing himself up from the floor and directly into the guard's line of sight. For a second the guard's eyes were angry slits in a broad face that badly needed a shave. Then they went wide with confusion. His legs buckled, and his weapon fell out of his hands. He collapsed to the grating, twitched, and became flaccid. Just above his boots were the two bamboo darts April had jammed into his legs.

Doc threw himself against the compartment hatch, slamming it shut faster than the other guard could get down from the bunk. H.I. reinforced Doc with his own 160 pounds as the guard inside pounded the hatch with the butt of his weapon. Doc closed the outside lock.

"We're totally screwed," H.I. said. "He has a radio."

"Don't be negative." Doc swept up the fallen guard's automatic weapon and ran the length of the module. He flattened at the side of the hatch to Node 1 and pointed the weapon inside.

The hatch leading to the safe lab was closed and locked. Directly opposite, the hatch interfacing the service module was wide open. Through it, the entire service module was exposed to view. Banks of data screens and video monitors were unattended. A field phone was buzzing, unanswered.

"We have to move fast." Doc bolted across forty-three feet of the service module, slung his weapon, and checked the air lock hatch. He raised his wrist and saw that he had no watch. He asked for the time.

H.I. searched the monitor bank and looked for a clock. He found Bell Tower instead. It was motionless on the monitor screen, shrouded in its own freezing vapor. Its skin twitched, and the overhead lights in the service module blinked. As the lights restored, H.I. glanced toward Doc, remembered what Doc wanted, and peeled his eyes from Bell Tower. A clock display was superimposed over a camera feed from the isolation lab. On screen, frozen fog swirled inside the lab's steel walls. H.I. skipped the time readout and looked at the digital readouts. The lab's compartment temperature and atmospheric pressure were rising.

It's contained for now in liquid nitrogen. It won't last.

"Time!" Doc yelled again.

H.I. read the display. "5:05 a.m."

For a second Doc's lean muscular shoulders sagged. Then he held his weapon in one hand and opened the air lock hatch. He waved everyone against a wall and entered the air lock alone. Inside he smashed the single bulb with the butt of his weapon.

The field phone line was still buzzing at H.I.'s back. He ignored it and moved into the air lock as Doc flattened against the outer hatch. Doc nodded to him to swing the hatch open. Outside it was pitch black. There was something wrong about that.

"What happened to the floods?" H.I. whispered.

Doc stepped through the outer hatch and crouched on the stairs. H.I. followed and let his eyes adjust. Ahead there was no activity. The shadows between the bunkers and tents were still. The drizzle was falling continually. It was noiseless and cold and coming from a cloud that seemed even lower than H.I. recalled. Through the mist and dark, the compound was silent all the way to its perimeter fence. There was no sound except the field phone buzzing at their backs.

"Let's go," Doc whispered.

H.I. felt Dr. Kay behind him and April behind her. The three of them stepped onto the steel landing at the same time. As they did the floodlights came from everywhere. The chatter of automatic weapons followed. But no bullets pinged against metal. The weapons were being fired into the air. Their chatter was brief.

"Make it easy, my china." Bulldog's voice came from a megaphone. "No place for you to go. So just drop whatever weapons you've picked up and walk down the stairs, eh."

"Keep down," Doc whispered. He clicked off the safety on his weapon.

"Don't be bloody arseholes!" Bulldog yelled. "No place for you to go."

Doc fired once. Glass and sparks shattered from one of the floodlights. It faded to a glow before dying. Doc shifted his aim toward another light. He didn't get the chance to fire. The lights were shut off, leaving absolute darkness and cold. Footsteps thudded in the mud, moving in on all sides.

Doc positioned his weapon toward the stairway. H.I. heard a click and knew Doc had flipped his selector switch to full automatic. Laser target spots came from the darkness, painting the stairs and landing from all sides. But there still was no shooting.

"It's about a five-to-seven-foot drop to the ground," Doc whispered. "When I start shooting, roll over the edge."

"Bullshit," April answered. "I'm not doing this again."

"When you hit the ground," Doc continued, "run under the complex. Stay between the piers until you reach the crater rim."

"No freaking way," H.I. said. He meant it. He was not abandoning Doc.

"You have to," Doc said. "All three of you."

H.I. would have argued, but he heard the same noise Doc seemed to hear. A heavy, treaded vehicle was clanking toward them in the darkness. He thought of a tank or half-track and knew Doc's weapon wasn't going to discourage either one.

"We're out of time, Doc. We all have to run."

But no one got the chance to move. Automatic weapons fire erupted from all directions, lighting up the treaded vehicle clanking toward the stairs. It was a bulldozer rumbling forward as bullets sparked against its steel. Crouched in the cab, the driver fired back.

In that same second, Doc opened fire from the landing. The landscape took on the appearance of an old movie, flickering in light and dark as mercenaries tried to take up position around the rampaging bulldozer. One of the mercenaries stood holding a rocket-propelled grenade, and the driver cut him down with a short burst. The gunfire stopped and the world went black again. But the darkness lasted only for a few seconds.

Then the gunfire came back with a vengeance, concentrating on the bulldozer now only fifty feet away. The driver remained crouched, as gunfire from two directions raked the cab. Using the gunfire for cover, a mercenary clutching a grenade bolted toward the treads. The driver fired over the side and dropped the running man in front of the bulldozer scoop. The grenade explosion burst white hot against the steel, tossing fragments of earth as far as the landing where H.I. lay flattened. Something fell in front of his face. It was a human finger. For a second he thought the yell that followed was his. But he was wrong. It was April's.

"Malone!"

"Stay down!" Malone yelled from the bulldozer cab. She spun the treads and nudged twenty-five tons of machine against the stairway. The scoop lowered like a shield between the stairway and the shooting. Malone flicked on a small flashlight that lit the way into the cab. Around her the glass windows were shattered from gunfire.

"I should have left you," was all she said.

Chapter Seven

Malone killed her flashlight. The image of the glass splayed into cracks around bullet holes stayed in H.I.'s eyes. Ahead of him Dr. Kay and April felt their way into the cab. Doc jammed his way in next, and H.I. followed. No one was shooting at them. H.I. said so.

"They don't want to hit the complex," Doc answered.

The lifeform is contained for now.

H.I. thought of gunfire ripping the complex, cracking open the isolation lab and spreading the Bell Tower lifeform. But no way could the guards have been told the truth. In fact they already had shot in the direction of the complex. So why weren't they shooting?

Malone shouted above the motor noise, "Kid, can you drive one of these things?"

"No. But I'm a fast study."

"Two gear levers and two clutch levers!" she hollered. " Right track and left track. Ignore the hand throttles and use the foot throttle. It works the opposite of a car. You step on it to idle down. Got it?"

"Piece of cake."

Malone crouched on the left side. Doc took the right. H.I. slammed the decelerator throttle to the floor, eased the clutch lever, and jammed the right track into gear. The diesel motor whined and almost stalled. H.I. released the foot decelerator fast. The bulldozer lurched forward on its right track. Metal ground against metal as twenty-five tons of bulldozer tore the landing away from the complex.

"Mop Up?" H.I. heard Doc ask Malone.

"Done," Malone shouted back.

Malone crouched as the first laser spot wandered into the cab. More followed. On her signal H.I. hit the decelerator and clutch, then threw the second lever into gear. He released the decelerator again. The bulldozer lumbered forward. Malone stuck her arm out of the window and lit the air with a pistol flash. H.I.'s ears rang all the way into his teeth. For a millisecond the flash lit the bunkers and the guards moving between them. They were running parallel to the bulldozer, following without shooting.

Malone yelled to Doc, "Where'd you get your weapon's instruction?"

"FBI range at Quantico."

"Switch to automatic. Fire short bursts."

Doc held his fire. "How long to Mop Up, Malone?"

"Not long enough," she answered. "Minimum safe distance is ten miles."

"It can't be reached on the ground," Doc said.

"I know that."

They both opened fire at once, shooting over the bunkers in the bulldozer's path and forcing running men to the ground. Doc reached for the hydraulic lever and adjusted the scoop. H.I. released more pressure on the decelerator throttle to let the speed and momentum increase. The bulldozer flattened the first bunker like an empty tin can.

"Can you fly a Huey?" Doc called to Malone.

"No, just fixed wing stuff," Malone replied. "But I'm the only pilot you've got."

H.I. pulled the right track out of gear, spun machine in the mud, and drove over a second bunker. He threw the right track back in gear and spun the bulldozer into a fence. The whole perimeter ripped from its foundation, falling in a wave of protesting steel. Malone fired another shot in the air to light more wrecked terrain and running guards. They were following the bulldozer.

"They'll jump us at the airstrip!" Doc bellowed.

"I'm going to give them some distraction," Malone yelled back.

She ordered H.I. to take the left track out of gear. He popped the clutch and spun the bulldozer. The cyclone fence imprisoning the Jivanos Indians materialized out of nowhere. The bulldozer hit the fence at an angle, tearing it down with one tread as steel whined against steel. The force twisted the fence sideways and snapped the threading. Steel fragments pinged against the scoop.

"Stop!" Malone shouted.

H.I. pulled the right track out of gear. Malone unscrewed the flash suppresser on her automatic weapon, pointed the barrel out of the left window, and fired into the air. The terrain again flickered like a silent movie, lighting up Jivanos Indians scrambling over the wrecked fence that had been their prison. They ran sheltering their women and children. A half-dozen guards split off to chase them. The rest flanked the bulldozer.

Malone ordered both tracks forward. As H.I. complied, she hit the hand throttles. The bulldozer surged ahead. Wind sucked though the windows and stank of rotting vegetation and cordite. The treads found the mesh surface of the airstrip, and the bulldozer picked up speed. Malone saw what lay in their path before H.I. did. Both of them saw it too late.

The parked Huey came out of the dark all at once. The roof of the bulldozer's cab hit a rotor blade, bending it upward and showering sparks. The air filled with the scream of metal slicing metal. The bulldozer's scoop gutted the Huey's fuselage like a tin can. The force spun the Huey ninety degrees on its runners and ruptured its fuel tanks. Leaking fuel spewed into a giant puddle under raining sparks. The exploding fireball thudded against the bulldozer scoop and shot burning liquid past both sides of the cab.

The explosion hurled Malone into the dark. One second she was yelling and fighting for the controls. The next she was gone. The bulldozer continued pushing the wrecked Huey like a rolling fireball. Burning fuel trailed on both sides of the cab. The heat was terrible.

Instinct took over for H.I. He jammed the decelerator peddle to the floor and hammered both clutches. The bulldozer stopped instantly. Fire climbed over the right tread and pounded the bullet-riddled windshield. Doc gave him a hard shove out of the left door behind Dr. Kay and April. H.I. bounced over the tread and landed on Malone as Malone belly-crawled across the tarmac while dragging her weapon and cursing. Nearby Dr. Kay, April, and Doc flattened. Holding her chest and coughing, Malone pointed toward drums stacked at least a hundred feet away. But no way did H.I. think they could make it. He was right.

The floodlights came from two sides of the tarmac. Doc shot one out. Automatic weapons fire angled from two sides, forcing Doc down. A voice came from the loud speaker. The voice sounded calm, almost soothing.

"No one has to die. All you have to do is stand and walk."

"Fricking Rykoff!" Malone coughed.

"How long do we have until Mop Up?" Doc hissed. He ripped the ammo magazine from his weapon. He worked fast, fiddling with something.

"We have a couple of hours, tops." Malone winced. She was in a lot of pain.

Rykoff's voice on the speaker was filled with regret. "Two rocket-propelled grenades are trained on your position. It is not my wish to use them."

"Hide these anywhere you can." Doc started dropping bullets into H.I.'s palm.

Rykoff's voice boomed a last time. "You have twenty seconds to surrender!"

Chapter Eight

More than a thousand miles east of Crash Site Alpha Bell Tower, Malone's transmission downloaded to a receiver inside the combat information center of the *USS Nimitz*. The message was loaded to a floppy without being read and then carried forward to a stateroom in the flag quarters. Its recipient uploaded the message to the flat screen of a PC. Its recipient wasn't happy. He was afraid.

"How long ago did *Nimitz* receive this?" Captain Trent Bishop wiped sleep from his eyes. He was hoping he wasn't seeing the screen right. He knew he was asking a stupid question. The message time was displayed clearly. At the doorway to Bishop's quarters, the ensign from combat information center answered anyway.

"It was received at 0445, sir."

"What time is it now?" It was another stupid question. Bishop knew it wouldn't make the damn thing go away.

"It's 0502, sir."

"Dismissed."

"Sir, I'm supposed to receive the floppy after you've erased the message."

"Sorry! It's damn early." Bishop keyed a nonsense command and wondered whether his ensign would notice the hard drive wasn't grinding. Screw it if he did. Bishop handed the ensign a second floppy already lying on his desk. The ensign never saw the switch. "It's all yours. Take it back to CIC."

"Goodnight, sir."

Bishop waited until the door to his quarters was closed to take a second look at the floppy he'd stolen. He looked at it a long time. He jammed it back into his machine, hoping he'd imagined the content. He hadn't.

LOG:	98723150
TIME:	0355 ZULU
TO:	ETRAC
EYES ONLY:	T. BISHOP, R. MORGAN
FROM:	K. WATERSTONE (I.D. and PASSWORD VERIFIED)
SUBJECT:	CRASH SITE ALPHA BELL TOWER
MESSAGE:	MOP UP. REPEAT. MOP UP.

Bishop exited the program, removed the disc, and locked it in his safe. It was a violation of his orders to keep the disc. Screw his orders! He wasn't going down the toilet by himself. And there was no doubt there would be a damn, dirty, big flush when this one was over. It would probably drown all seven privy to what was about to happen. That would be himself, Admiral Morgan, CAG, and the four ordnance men. Bishop reminded himself there were about to be eight. CAG would have to brief the pilot.

Bishop picked up his phone, made sure his line was secure, and called Admiral Morgan's quarters. The voice on the other end of the line wasn't sleepy. Never was. Bishop repeated the message. "Received at 0455. Mop Up," he said. "Sent and repeated."

"You erase the disc?"

"There's no way I erased it."

"Good." Morgan paused, then spoke quickly. "Let's get this done. Notify CAG."

Twenty-eight minutes later, CAG, Commander Air Group, sat perched atop his desk in the ready room of Strike Fighter Squadron Thirty-Six. Behind his back were dozens of photos of planes and pilots. Among them was the official squadron emblem, a snake perched over the top of a magician hat and wand. The snake protruded its tongue through fangs beneath the squadron's name, Sidewinders.

The lone pilot, Lt. Commander Shane Jacket, was dressed in a flight suit and reclined in a padded seat in the front row. Jacket, call sign "Psycho," asked one question. "Sir, why is a marine guard posted outside?"

"That will be apparent once I brief you." CAG gave Psycho his orders and watched the color leave Psycho's face.

"Sir, is this some kind of performance test?"

"This is not a performance test, Lt. Commander."

"An exercise?"

"Not an exercise."

"Why me?"

"Because you'll do it. And because you won't talk about it later."

Psycho turned and looked to the enclosed area at the back of the room. Inside was a computer terminal interfaced with the TAMP system. TAMP stood for tactical air-crew mission planning.

"You have thirty minutes on TAMPS." GAG lit a cigarette, changed his mind, and stubbed it out.

"Am I by myself in the strike?"

"You'll have an E2 running strike control."

"Will the E2 crew be aware of my ordnance?"

"No."

"Who is aware?"

"That's not your concern."

Psycho walked to the back of the ready room, sat at the TAMPS terminal, and enabled the software. He felt CAG standing at his back and smelled CAG's tobacco odor. Psycho pulled up his mission plan, saw that the target was identified only as a jungle coordinate designated Tango Alpha.

"What is the target, CAG?"

"Not your concern?"

"Bullshit. I'm dropping a tactical nuke inside a friendly country in peace time."

"You don't want to know the target, Psycho."

CAG thought of what he'd been told of the target. It was a guarded crash site dug in the rain forest by a meteor that could spread disease to all life on Earth. Mop Up meant dropping a nuke on the site to contain it. Would the operation remain a secret? No way! Would the true nature of the target ever get out? It didn't matter. No one would believe it. Not the media and not congress. They'd be too busy destroying everyone involved in the decision. The lives of those involved would be over. Except the president was scandal-proof, CAG reminded himself. The president probably didn't know what was going on, or at least he would claim that he didn't. Maybe he'd even find a way to blame it on the other party. CAG told himself that part didn't matter anyway. He reminded himself he was going to do his duty.

CAG tried another cigarette. "You don't want to know the target. You just want to do your job."

Chapter Nine

Putin was working the shift on the hangar's radio when the message came through. "Team Bus, this is Dugout. Do you copy?"

"Copy, Dugout. This is Team Bus. I read you five by five." Putin stubbed out his cigar and answered. He checked his watch. 0500 hours! He didn't recognize the voice on the radio, but knew it didn't belong to Rykoff.

"It's the bottom of the ninth, Team Bus. Repeat. It's the bottom of the ninth."

"Message understood, Dugout. Team Bus will be in the lot by 0800. Over and out."

Putin clicked off the power, stood, and zipped up his leather flight jacket. The rain was still thumping on the hangar roof. Inside the air was cold and penetrating. So much for summer at the bottom of the world, he told himself. His bones felt more chilled than they would on the other side of the world in Moscow, where it was winter. Here the air was wet, Putin remembered. It would be heavy. That was something to consider during takeoff.

Putin crossed the hangar floor. Dawn light filtered through open, steel doors. It was a wet, gray Antarctic light falling on the southern most tip of the South American continent. Putin thought he could smell the sea and even hear the gulls in the Beagle Channel. Then he dismissed his senses. It was just his imagination.

He found his copilot, Chernov, asleep with the others in the hangar office. Chernov was stretched out on top of a desk, his breath hanging in the wet, cold air. All but one of the others were asleep on the floor. The North Korean, Park, was missing. Putin told himself his suspicion was correct. Park was secret police. He had to be. Putin roused his copilot.

"Get your ass out of bed, Nikolai."

"This is no bed." Chernov cursed, "And it's damn cold." Chernov squinted in the light coming from the open hangar doors. "Doesn't it ever get dark in this climate?"

"In winter, it's dark all the time. Where's the Korean?"

"He took a walk. He said he couldn't sleep."

"Find him. We're rolling in ten minutes."

In fact it was thirty minutes before Putin started the four Allison T56-A turboprops. It was another ten before he had the C-130 Hercules positioned for takeoff. The delay was the Korean's fault.

"Where'd you find him?" Putin asked Chernov as they sat in the cockpit.

"He was watching the penguins," Chernov answered from the right seat. "There must be ten thousand of them on the rocks."

"Keep your eye on him. I don't trust him."

"You said the same thing about Rykoff."

"I don't trust anyone, Nikolai," Putin answered, "except my wife and you, my friend."

"I think you're wrong about Park."

"How so?"

"I don't think he's a wild card. I think he's scared. I think he knows the cargo."

"Unlucky him."

Putin scanned the terrain. Jagged peaks capped in snow rose seven thousand feet to the west and south. To the northeast, the rough waters of Ushuaia Bay stretched to the rougher waters of Beagle Channel. Beyond the channel the wind swept the gray hills of Isla Grande.

"I still say you're wrong about the Korean." Chernov ran his eyes over the instruments and tried to shake off sleep.

"Maybe so." Putin lifted one headphone off an ear. In the other he listened for the tower. Putin spoke to Chernov, "Maybe he's not a spook. Maybe he's a head case."

"He didn't talk like a head case. He was watching the penguins like it was his last day on Earth. He was talking about this place, the land of fire. He told me how the explorers saw the Indian torches on the beach. Now the Indians are gone."

"He's talking about survival of the fittest. Our North Korean thinks like a true comrade." Putin sneered. "He and Stalin would have been good buddies."

"He wasn't talking about Stalin. He was talking about the scientist who passed through here in the last century."

"Darwin?"

"Yeah, Darwin. He passed through here. The channel is named after his ship, *Beagle*."

"Park is a Korean head case. He's the wrong man for this job."

"No. He wasn't crazy. He was scared. He said that things were going to change. He said that the penguins might all be gone and that people might all be gone. I think he was talking about the cargo. Did Rykoff tell you what the cargo will be?"

"He didn't tell me, my friend. And I didn't ask. We just do our job and get paid, like good little capitalists. In case you haven't heard, the revolution is dead. And that, my friend, is a good thing."

In his left earphone, Putin received the tower's permission for takeoff. Putin scanned his instruments. "Let's get this big bastard airborne. Give me full flaps and give me some power."

Chernov pushed the four throttles forward. Putin felt the power build, released his brakes, and let the plane lumber forward. He remembered the wet, cold air and gently coaxed the C-130 off the runway. He gained altitude slowly and pointed the nose slightly northwest. The compass settled on 355.

"He acted like it would be the end of the world," Chernov said.

"I wouldn't worry about the end of the world, my friend. I would worry about Rykoff."

Chapter Ten

"Your time is up. Surrender or you get the grenades." Bulldog's voice was on the microphone. Floodlights swept past the fire swallowing up the Huey and the bulldozer. The heat was terrible.

H.I. kept his head down. "Where's Rykoff?"

"He's probably gone to fire the grenade himself." Malone coughed. "We're out of options."

She struggled to her feet directly in the floodlights and showed her weapon over her head before dropping it. Then she grabbed her side. Doc stood and kept Malone from buckling over. He nodded to H.I. to hide the bullets he'd passed to him. H.I. had already had hidden them by passing them to April, knowing she could hide them in a place he prayed Rykoff would never search.

"Stay cool!" Doc kept his left hand high. He did the best he could with his right, wincing from the pain in his ribs.

Bulldog's men closed in from both sides of the landing strip, weapons aimed. Behind them figures in hazmat suits used extinguishers on the flames engulfing the charred skeleton of the Huey. Wind blew the black, thick smoke toward the complex and smothered the floodlights. The smoke funneled into overhead cloud. A single figure holding a rocket-propelled grenade launcher emerged to approach Malone. As the figure came out of the shadows, H.I. got his first look at Victor Rykoff's face. It was more hideous than H.I. had imagined. It was a face meant for nightmares.

"You've made a bad choice." Rykoff towered over Malone.

"I'll live to make better."

"That's unlikely, Malone." Rykoff laughed hoarsely. "There are no more fences for you to walk."

Rykoff grabbed Doc's weapon out of Doc's hand, tested the weight in his grip, and ripped the parabolic ammo magazine from its port. Rykoff looked over the magazine carefully, his eyes seeming to display amusement. The rest of his face was as dead as a rubber mask. He conferred in private with Bulldog, then turned back.

"I expected more imagination from you, Dr. Tech."

Doc didn't answer.

Rykoff turned to Dr. Kay. "You and your daughter will come with me."

Dr. Kay saw Doc nod "ok". Hesitantly, she grasped April's hand and tried to get her to follow Rykoff. April protested. But seeing nods from both Doc and Malone, she moved in the direction Dr. Kay was pulling her. The nearest of Bulldog's men closed the gap and raised their weapons toward HI., Doc, and Malone. H.I. heard them click open bolts to make their automatic weapons ready. He wondered if he'd hear the shots that killed him. Instead he heard Rykoff shout orders.

"Take your time with the rest of them. Make it especially painful."

H.I. felt his knees start to buckle. He forced strength back into them and reminded himself that April and Dr. Kay still had a chance. Rykoff still needed Dr. Kay, so he still had to have April as leverage. That was why he was taking the two of them with him. As for Doc, Malone, and himself, H.I. thought they were all as good as dead. H.I. looked at Bulldog and tried to read the big South African's face. But Bulldog's attention was elsewhere.

Bulldog was standing clear of the other men and looking toward the remaining helicopters. H.I. hoped he was thinking about running for his life. Maybe Bulldog was even still buying into the lies H.I. had told him about the thing in the crater being the core of a new energy source worth billions. Maybe the big Neanderthal was not only thinking about running for his life, but also thinking about running away rich. Maybe there was still a chance for the deal H.I. had cut with him: the software of the energy core in exchange for a ride out. But Bulldog wasn't looking in H.I.'s direction. Not good, H.I. told himself. Not good at all.

Bulldog conferred with another man, then walked away in the direction Rykoff had taken. The other man walked toward H.I., his face illuminated by the flames from the burning copter and bulldozer. As he got closer, mutual recognition flashed. The man's left cheek bore four parallel gashes. April had inflicted them with her fingernails in the helicopter on the way to Crash Site Alpha Bell Tower. The man was a South African like Bulldog. Maybe they were friends. Maybe Bulldog had taken him into his confidence.

"All of you on the ground, face-down, now!"

H.I. did as he was told, expecting a gunshot to the back of the head. Behind his back he heard the Russians follow the South African's orders to lower their weapons. H.I. looked at Doc and nodded at him to get ready to make a move against the guards. Any move would do now that their weapons were lowered.

"Don't resist," Doc whispered back. "Just cooperate."

H.I. froze against the steel mesh of the tarmac and locked his legs together hoping his strength would come back. He heard muttering in words too soft to understand. Two of the Russians moved around him, grabbed Doc by the ankles, and dragged him a short distance away. H.I. watched as they used their combat boots to kick the hell out of Doc, working him over until Doc was coughing up blood. H.I. winced every time he heard contact made. They stripped Doc's clothes off of him and shook them out.

"Nothing but a pissing pack of cigarettes."

The South African dropped the pack just inside Doc's reach, and Doc grabbed at them. That didn't make sense. Doc didn't smoke. The South African stepped on Doc's hand.

"Guess you ain't heard the news. Smoking is bad for your health."

The South African was still standing on Doc's hand when H.I. launched himself at him. Halfway to his target, H.I. noticed the Russians were laughing but not moving. Just before he reached the South African, H.I. felt fire lance into his leg. The world turned upside down, and the surface of the tarmac smashed the back of his head. In one effortless move, the South African had disabled him with a kick. Bright lights danced in H.I.'s eyes, and the world tried to leave him. The kicks that followed took the air of his chest. He threw up more than once, soaking his fatigues in vomit and filling his nostrils with the stink. But it didn't last. The Russians ripped away his fatigues and kicked him some more. The world left him for a moment, and then he became aware of the cold steel tarmac against his face. He was pointed at Malone. The South African was standing over her.

"I've saved the best for last," the South African said. "You don't remember me do you?"

Malone didn't answer him.

"I wouldn't expect you to remember me. Rykoff's lovely drugs do that. They're also supposed to make you spill everything. But you spilled nothing. Good training, I told the boss. So I made up the difference with pain. And you talked. Everyone always does."

Malone kept her mouth shut. H.I. moved his palms to help himself to his feet. The nearest weapon was only inches away, pointed down, and held in a loose grip by one of the Russians. But the Russian was looking at Malone. All H.I. had to do was move a few inches, jam his finger into the trigger guard, and guide the barrel toward the South African.

"Stay put, kid," Malone coughed a warning.

The South African worked her over while the Russians watched. H.I. felt the pain every time the South African's boot made contact. Then they pulled away her fatigues to search them. They found nothing. They stood over her while she fought to get air back into her lungs. H.I. saw the older bruises on her pale form. They'd hurt her badly the first time.

"Search ain't done yet," the South African said. He directed two of the Russians to hold Malone. Then he moved toward her. But he never got to what he intended. He was interrupted by an approaching Russian.

"Rykoff," the approaching Russian said out loud. The rest he whispered to the South African.

"All righty then," the South African said. "Pull on your fatigues and start walking.

It took them a while to do what they'd been told. Smelling the vomit on his clothes, H.I. wretched again. This time he had nothing to bring up. He wretched until his belly hurt. Then he caught his breath and helped Doc support Malone as they staggered forward under guard. She stumbled, holding her side and coughing worse. The air was thick with acrid smoke from burning aviation fuel. The team in hazmat suits was trying to pull the bulldozer away from what was left of the Huey. There were Russians all over the airstrip.

"I'm sorry about the copter, Malone. I didn't see it."

"Not your fault, kid. I didn't see it either."

The three of them limped as they followed the tread tracks back into the compound. This time everything was lighted by floods. Not a good thing, the floods being on. They showed H.I. things he didn't want to see, not then, not in nightmares, and not ever.

The Jivanos' prison was flattened. The perimeter fence lay open on one side. Not all of the Jivanos Indians had escaped. Mercenaries with raised weapons stood over the dead ones. The dead lay twisted in impossible positions, half-naked with faces smeared in blood mixed with ceremonial paint. Some were women. Some were children. Their eyes were open and dead as glass. Already the flies were swarming.

"How you feel, kid?' The South African with the scratched face moved alongside H.I. But H.I. didn't answer him. The South African pulled him away from Malone and Doc, letting the two of them stumble forward, supporting each other. He lowered his voice as he continued to speak to H.I. "My name's VanRensburg. Bulldog is *my china.* That means "my friend." He let me in to what you told him. Be ready to move when we come get you. And don't do anything else stupid."

VanRensburg moved away.

The compound fence was collapsed and shredded. Beyond the twisted metal, floodlights fell on smashed bunkers and scattered debris. The communications bunker with its microwave dishes and clustered antennae was still intact. The door flap was open, and inside Bulldog stood with another Russian, surveying stacked radio parts and computers. Bulldog looked in H.I.'s direction for a second, then went back to his field phone.

"The transmitter is intact, but the computer is bloody useless." Bulldog glanced in Malone's direction as she limped by the bunker on the way to the compound. "She must have bloody used a bloody computer virus. I'm telling you, man. The sat com is now worthless."

In the dark H.I. thought he saw Malone smile. A Russian gave her and Doc a shove.

"You should have stuck to the plan," Doc said to Malone. "You should have left when I was late."

"I should have." She coughed. "Next time I will. Count on it. Except there won't be a next time."

The stairs and landing at the Bell Tower air lock were nothing but mangled scrap metal. A ladder was leaned across the wreckage. Doc helped Malone climb. It was painful for both of them. Beyond the air lock and inside the service module, every monitor and keyboard was occupied. H.I. knew immediately what he was seeing.

Fear!

Something bad was going on with the instruments, but that wasn't what frightened the men at the controls. They were blood-chillingly afraid of Rykoff. He was standing over them. His violet eyes were cold. He held an automatic pistol in his hand.

"Exit all the programs and reboot." Rykoff gave the order with the calm of someone who didn't tolerate mistakes. Across the back of his skull, leathery skin quivered under fine, white hair.

"It won't exit. The programs are still running," a technician answered. "They are running by themselves."

"Impossible."

"Not impossible. Computer virus..."

"Are you saying a computer virus is giving program-specific commands in two different I.T. systems?" Rykoff backed away from the monitors and cursed. "That's impossible."

H.I. caught a glimpse of the screens and felt his skin turn cold even though the temperature in isolation was rising. The lock-down procedures were being disabled. Pressure seals were disengaging.

"It's a computer virus!" The technician was sweating. "Must be!"

"From where?" Rykoff yelled.

One monitor relayed input from a crater camera. Bell Tower's skin occupied most of its screen. It was quivering like living flesh.

"Go to the main bus and kill all power to the system!" Rykoff shouted. "Go manual and initiate full emergency containment!"

Technicians barked orders into hand radios between bursts of static. Immediately the lights and ventilation systems died. The service module turned red under the emergency lights. Battery-driven fans activated. In the red light, Rykoff turned toward Malone. Everything below his eyes was rubbery, formless, and dead.

"Bus is disabled!" a technician shouted. "Servers are down. Emergency seals are closed by hand crank."

"Good." Rykoff refocused on Malone as he spoke. His eyes looked like torches. "Cut the lines to the computers. We'll splice and reboot one by one. Everything except environmental and ventilation."

"Da!"

Rykoff spoke slowly to Malone. "I want your computer virus extricated from my systems."

"It's not my computer virus," Malone said. "I just did your com bunker."

Rykoff turned to Doc. "You are trying to spread the Bell Tower agent?"

"No." Doc didn't smile. "Getting my flesh and organs turned to mush is not on my agenda."

"One of you or both of you are lying."

"Or neither," Doc muttered.

Rykoff ordered that H.I., Doc, and Malone be moved out of the service module. A lone Russian holding a hand gun directed them into Node 1. The Russian kept out of their reach and followed them through Node 1 into the habitat module. After the three of them limped into Dr. Kay's compartment, the Russian closed the hatch from the outside. The locking mechanism tumbled into place. Inside the compartment, H.I. watched Dr. Kay throw herself into Doc's arms. Doc winced.

Dr. Kay didn't let go. "Rykoff told us you were being shot."

"We're no longer expendable." Doc held her. "Rykoff has other problems."

"What kind of problems?"

Doc didn't answer. He pointed to Malone as Malone tried to painfully lower herself onto the bunk. "See what you can do for her."

Dr. Kay let go of Doc and moved to Malone. H.I. shifted his gaze to April. There were things he wanted to tell her. But before he could, the compartment hatch opened and Rykoff stood in the frame. He looked like something right out of hell.

"Tell me, Malone. How did you get a virus into the module computer?"

"I didn't." Malone coughed and bent over.

"You're lying."

"The only thing I nailed was the sat com. It's nailed for good."

"So all by itself, the computer is trying to reverse negative pressure in isolation and bleed off the positive pressure everywhere else? All by itself, the security system is giving commands to open the isolation hatches?"

"Beats the shit out of me. I'm not running this hacienda."

Rykoff turned to Dr. Kay. His voice turned soft. "Any thoughts, Doctor?"

"Bell Tower," she said. "Just like I've warned you all along."

"Make me a believer."

She laughed at him. It was a mean laugh, not at all like Dr. Kay. "Open your eyes, you psychotic son-of-a-bitch. That thing in the crater is a total unknown. Just think of everything that's happened, everything our human eyes have observed, and ask yourself for an explanation based on human experience and known phenomenon."

"All explainable," Rykoff answered in a soft voice. "Chemistry and Physics 101. Basic genetics and virology with a little sophisticated technology thrown in. Electromagnetic pulse weaponry. Nuclear reactor..."

"Wrong!" Dr. Kay cut him off. "Try a spacecraft that can fence in radiation while selectively letting radio waves pass. Try a virus-sized lifeform that can jump every species in its path."

"Nothing can..."

"Nothing on Earth, Rykoff. This isn't from Earth. It's an unknown. It invades its prey's genes and alters genes so that its prey kills itself. And in case you haven't figured it out, we are the prey. We are the enemy. And by *we*, I mean every living thing on this planet."

The normal lights blinked on as power was restored to the complex. The ventilation remained off. Rykoff seemed unaware of the sweat collecting on his forehead. His eyes remained calm, almost kind. "It really doesn't matter, Dr. Waterstone. Power is restored. The computer will stay down. The systems are in manual lock. Nothing will escape containment."

Rykoff played with an object in his hands. "We have another problem. One of you is hiding something." His eyes almost filled with regret. "Surely not you, Dr. Waterstone. You wouldn't be that foolish."

Rykoff opened his hands. The object he held was a parabolic weapon clip. "This came from one of the MP5s surrendered on the airstrip. It's a very empty clip. There were not that many shots fired from your end. No casings lying on the ground. I find that curious, don't you?"

No one answered him.

Doc glanced at H.I. But H.I. didn't look back. Rykoff studied April. Every slim muscle in her frame tightened, and Dr. Kay tried to shield her. H.I. held his breath, but not just because he didn't want Rykoff to touch her. He had another reason, a damn important one.

Rykoff focused his gaze on April. He made his voice as gentle as a parent's. "If you'll just return the bullets, the matter will be closed."

April said nothing.

"Perhaps a more complete body search would be in order," Rykoff said without emotion. "I have a full medical facility. Malone knows all about that facility. Don't you, Malone!"

"Bite me!" Malone said. "Sorry! Forgot. You don't have teeth."

Rykoff started to answer. Malone cut him off. "Tell me something, Victor. When the Russians beat in your face, did you get a thrill out of it? Just a tiny sexual thrill?"

Rykoff didn't flinch. "Take the girl. Full cavity search."

"No!" Dr. Kay screamed and tried to shield April. "She doesn't have them."

"Then tell me who does."

"She doesn't have them. I don't have them. That's all I…"

Dr. Kay stopped, as one of Rykoff's technicians appeared, tapped Rykoff on the shoulder, and addressed him in Russian. "Team Bus."

"Da," Rykoff answered. He checked his watch and spoke to the two Russians standing outside the compartment. "See the hatch stays closed."

Rykoff left, and the hatch closed. H.I. heard a welding torch ignited on the other side of the steel. Doc used his hands against the inside surface and immediately found the hot spot around the latch and lock pad.

"Why did you provoke him?" Dr. Kay exploded at Malone.

"So he'd get pissed off and start making mistakes. So far he hasn't made any," Malone said. "Beats waiting."

"Waiting for what?" H.I. asked.

No one answered him. Malone tried to sit down on the bunk. She grabbed her chest and almost collapsed. Dr. Kay moved toward her immediately.

"You short of breath? You taste blood in your throat?"

"No! I don't think I punctured a lung," Malone answered. "See if there's something you can use to wrap my rib cage." Malone unbuttoned her shirt and Dr. Kay looked at flesh pockmarked in cigarette burns. Dr. Kay's face went pale.

"Who did this to you?"

"Rykoff!" Malone answered. "After he drugged me. The drugs didn't make me talk. So he let the South African have a turn. Rykoff probably even helped him."

"I'm sorry."

"No, I'm the one who's sorry. I apparently told him that you are the only asset we have who can manage what he's harvesting from Bell Tower."

"Guess that's why we're alive," Dr. Kay said.

"Being alive may not be a good thing. For now just wrap the ribs tight and pretend you didn't see the other." Malone winced as Dr. Kay did what she'd asked.

Doc jerked his fingertips from the steel door where it was getting hot. He placed his ear against another part of the door. "They're gone," he whispered. "Where are the bullets?"

H.I. looked in April's direction. She spoke softly, "I have them."

"Let's have them," Doc said.

"Turn around," April answered.

They did as she asked. H.I. could hear April struggling out of her clothes. Bullets clinked as they dropped to the floor. H.I. heard Dr. Kay gasp. Then April put her clothes back on and told everyone they could turn around.

"All I could save was ten." She flicked blonde hair out of her face and passed a handful of 9mm bullets to Doc.

"Have to do," Doc said. He held the ten 9mm rounds in his palm, then pocketed them. He began to thump on the door. He asked Malone. "How much time have we got?"

"Not enough, Doc."

"Until what?" H.I. asked Malone.

"Mop Up."

"What's Mop Up?" April asked.

Chapter Eleven

Dawn at her back, *Nimitz* turned into the wind.

The pilot of the E-2C Hawkeye snapped a signal salute through his left window, and twin steam pistons accelerated him from zero to a hundred fifty knots. A hundred feet forward, he felt his Hawkeye leave the bow catapult while pushing three G's. Two seconds later he climbed on twin turboprops, sun reflecting from the massive, down-looking radar dish mounted above the Hawkeye's wings.

Pscyho watched from the cockpit of his F/A-18 Super Hornet, perched on the shuttle of Cat 2 and aimed toward the port bow. Wind forced its way though his raised canopy. The voices on his helmet headset were distorted in static, but Psycho listened. He understood.

"Sun Fire Control, this is Coach. We are inbound and climbing to Angels twenty."

"Roger, Coach. You are clear to Angels twenty. Over."

The Hawkeye was unescorted. Psycho understood why, even though the crew of the Hawkeye did not. They had been told they were running a deep penetration strike exercise for the new Super Hornet with its improved fuel fraction. A necessary lie. After Psycho was done, they would know the truth. Anyone in the air would see the mushroom and know the truth. The fewer people in the air, the better. So CAG had sent the Hawkeye to its orbit without the usual escort of two Tomcats. Afterward the crew of the Hawkeye would have to be debriefed. But only afterward.

Psycho stole a glance to his right and saw the ordnance crew in red jerseys climbing back into the weapons elevator forward of the catapult control station. Their faces were hidden in goggles and red helmets, but he knew their features would look nervous. Should look nervous! They'd racked a nuke under his wing. Psycho wondered if they were even part of *Nimitz's* crew. He wondered if they knew the target. Probably not. Best not.

"Mop Maid, this is Sun Fire Control. Two minutes."

"Roger, Control," Psycho answered into his radio and scanned the deck a second time. Now the green shirts had the deck between Cat 1 and Cat 2 to themselves. One of them held up the chalkboard, and Psycho read the number written to signal the weight of his plane. Psycho hand signaled an okay. There was no way the green shirts could tell that the bomb racked under his wing was a nuke instead of a conventional joint direct attack munition. Both weapons would look the same. Both would be elongate and configured with guidance fins. Both would be non-reflective gray.

Psycho closed his canopy. He thought of Hiroshima. The men who'd flown Hiroshima hadn't known the weapon they were dropping. They'd known only afterward. Psycho knew before.

He tried not to think about it. He watched the hand signals that told him the jet blast deflector behind his F/A-18 was raised and that the holdback was attached to his nose gear strut. He looked at the sun shimmering in a thousand places on the sea. He looked at the green shirts and ran his engines up to full power, throwing in his afterburners.

The green shirt fired off his last hand signal. Psycho snapped back a salute and felt the shooter release the steam from the catapult. The holdback released simultaneously. Psycho felt his eyes and face flattened with the g-forces, and two seconds later he was over the water. He settled at four hundred knots and two hundred feet, beginning a shallow climb.

"Coach, this is Mop Maid." Psycho contacted the Hawkeye.

"Roger, Mop Maid."

"I am feet wet, lima lima. Vector two hundred twenty."

"Roger, Mop Maid. Vector two hundred twenty until ingress."

"Roger." Psycho ran his eyes over the computer-driven instruments and locked his autopilot. He pulled up his cathode-ray tube satellite map display and checked his waypoints and fuel. The new FA-18 Super Hornet was fitted with internal fuel tanks, a big improvement over the old F-18. It would actually get him to the target, but he'd need an air refuel on the way back. He locked on to the identification friend-or-foe system in the Hawkeye and set its position on his map. He was gaining on the Hawkeye a hundred miles each hour. When he was over the target he'd be just at the edge of the Hawkeye's radar perimeter.

Psycho thought of the Hawkeye crew, jammed like sardines between racks of electronic consoles and operating three radar systems. They'd be watching everything. Watching everything and knowing nothing until afterward. Just like the crew at Hiroshima. One flash and eighty thousand killed so that a million more could be saved. Kill many to save many more.

"Coach, Mop Maid. I see land."

The Brazilian coast came from nowhere, taking up the whole horizon: flat, green, and endless. At four-hundred knots closure, Psycho disengaged his autopilot and climbed to avoid treetops. The jungle shot under his wings, and the FA-18 bounced in the changing air temperature. He wondered if he was seen by Indians or fisherman. They'd probably think he was a UFO. He signaled the Hawkeye.

"Coach, Mop Maid. I am feet dry."

"Roger. Stay lima lima until ingress. Vector two hundred twenty-five."

"Roger that."

Eye on his heads-up compass, Psycho barely moved the stick. Beneath him the jungle was endless carpet. He locked his autopilot and toggled up his weapons systems on his computer screens, enabling the weapons guidance pod under his left wing. Radio chatter buzzed in his helmet.

"Mop Maid, Coach. The sky is clear. We are picking up civilian radar only on your seven and eight."

Psycho acknowledged message understood. There was no other traffic in the air. The only radar signatures were commercial aviation, one in Macapá and one in Belém.

"Mop Maid, you are clear to tango alpha. You are clear to the target."

"Roger. Vector two hundred eighty-five at one hundred miles. Ingress at twenty miles." Psycho looked through the left side of his canopy, across the jungle carpet, and all of the way to the Rio Negro River. The river was as massive and black as outer space. Ahead of him low rain clouds painted the horizon and blurred the distant highlands. He checked his next waypoint, the mouth of a valley.

"Mop Maid. Civilian radar on your ten. Vector two hundred eighty-five."

"Roger." Psycho knew they meant Manaus. He bled off altitude and accessed his targeting pod and computer. His global positioning system received a signal from the overhead satellite. It verified his position to within three feet, matching it against his target. His computer calculated altitude, speed, and angle of climb needed to toss the bomb ten miles to the target.

The Rio Negro came from the left and shot under his wings. The clouds swallowed the massive dark water and green carpet. Psycho locked his eyes on his heads-up display, keeping his altitude above the trees. The transparent display was projected on clear glass above his instruments. Ahead of him was a valley. Miss it and he'd slam the earth.

"Mop Maid. Stay two hundred eighty-five. You are in the groove."

"Roger."

Psycho leveled at three hundred feet and followed the valley without seeing it. He locked his targeting pod on tango alpha. The laser system would see through the cloud cover and guide the bomb automatically. He armed the bomb.

"Coach, Mop Maid. Ingress vector three hundred ten. Toss at angels ten."

Psycho increased his speed to five hundred knots and began his climb to ten thousand feet. After he threw the bomb, he would climb like a rocket on his afterburners. The bomb would travel eight miles from release to target. He'd be at twenty thousand feet long before detonation. He'd have a personal, safe view of the mushroom.

The warning came as he climbed. It came calmly from the Hawkeye. "Bogey. Repeat, Mop Maid. Bogey. On your eight at angels eight and twenty miles. Five hundred knots closure."

A bogey? A radar contact? Who else was out here, flying toward a target in the middle of nowhere? Psycho cursed and turned to three hundred ten. He increased his power and pulled his stick into a steeper climb. In his head he calculated that the bogey's position would be near ground zero. The bogey was dead unless Psycho aborted. His orders didn't call for an abort, not in any contingency.

Psycho kept his right hand on his stick and maintained his climb. With his left hand, he set 340 kilotons of tactical nuclear bomb for ground burst over Crash Site Alpha Bell Tower.

* * *

One hundred miles south of Crash Site Alpha Bell Tower and strapped into the left seat of the C-130 Hercules, Putin lost sight of his horizon. It happened instantly. The green carpet was replaced by thick, low clouds. He gave the controls to Chernov, keyed his radio, and radioed Rykoff.

"Dugout, this is Team Bus. We are fifty miles south of you. I'm looking at pea soup."

The voice that answered sounded South African. "Roger, Team Bus. We'll bring you in on ILS." ILS was a computerized radar system for bringing the plane down in zero visibility.

"That's a big roger." Putin took the controls back from Chernov and scanned his friend's face. "You worry too much." He waited for Chernov to crack a smile, but saw none. Putin felt a presence at his back. It was the North Korean, Park.

Park leaned over Putin and Chernov and locked his eyes where there was nothing to see but dense, gray cloud. Putin lifted his right headphone and spoke to Park. "Lots of bouncing ahead. You'll do better in the back."

Park said nothing. He looked through the cockpit glass a long time, turned, and left the flight deck. Chernov watched Park leave. "Did you see the look in his eyes?"

"No." Putin replaced his headphone.

"He's scared, just like when he was watching the penguins."

"He's the wrong man for this job."

"No, Putin. It's more than that. He knows something. Something terrible."

"Shut up, Nikolai. And help me fly this bird."

* * *

Inside the service module, Rykoff stood immobile at the backs of his technicians and scanned the monitors for the tenth time in ten minutes. Most of the systems were back online. The icons for the emergency barriers that separated isolation were tagged "system error." That was what Rykoff wanted. The barriers were manually engaged and locked, immune to electronic manipulation, even from Bell Tower.

"Dugout, this is Tower." Bulldog's voice buzzed in the field phone Rykoff held in his hand. Rykoff jammed the receiver to his ear and heard Bulldog say that radio contact was established with Putin. Team Bus was on approach and needed ILS.

"Turn on your radar and bring him in," Rykoff answered. The nearest technician heard him.

"The silence is ended," the technician muttered. "The American spy satellites will read the radar signature of the ILS. They will know we have…"

"They already know," Rykoff said. "But now they will have proof. Unfortunately for them, it is, as Americans say, the final minutes of the game."

Rykoff used his field phone again, ordered the virus specimens moved in their dewars to the landing strip. He looked at the screens. The relay from the crater camera showed that Bell Tower was motionless. He looked a long time before he noticed something was different.

Bell Tower's skin was growing dark. Rykoff told himself he was imagining it. He started to reach for the nearest keyboard and zoom the crater camera. He didn't get the chance. The field phone buzzed in his hand. On the other end, Bulldog was yelling.

"Radar's picked up a bloody bogey."

"Where?" Rykoff shouted back.

"Southeast. Moving in at high speed and climbing like a son-of-a-bitch. I read it as a jet."

"The Americans!" Rykoff snapped. "Malone!" He thought for a second and gave an order. "Shoot that bastard down."

Rykoff started to lower his field phone. A frightened shout brought his attention back to the monitor banks. He found the nearest technician staring at the feed from the crater camera, his face beaded in sweat.

"It changes."

Rykoff turned to the screen and froze. The object was changing. It was growing darker by the second, and its shape seemed different. It was flatter, growing flatter by the second. Around it the dry ice that lined the crater floor was vaporizing and melting.

Chapter Twelve

"There isn't enough time, Doc." Malone coughed.

"Never tell that to a scientist." Doc finished tapping on the steel compartment hatch, rolled the 9mm bullets in his palm, and looked at the ceiling vent. He ripped the ceiling vent from its hinges and examined it. The vent blades were angled but he looked satisfied with them.

"You tell her, Doc." H.I. pointed to April. "She needs to know."

Doc ignored him, eased himself on to the bunk next to Malone, and retrieved a single 9mm bullet. It was a hollow point, open like the peak of a volcano at its business end. It was cold steel and copper, nine by nineteen millimeters, about the size of a ballpoint pen cap. But Doc wasn't planning to do any writing. H.I. thought he knew what Doc had in mind, but he knew there simply wasn't time. April needed to know what was coming.

"Dammit! What's going on? I want an answer," April insisted.

"The answer is irrelevant." Doc began jamming bullets into the vent blades and forced a wink at Dr. Kay. She tried to wink back, but couldn't. Her hands were trembling. In spite of his pain, Doc worked with a surgeon's hands. He spoke to April without looking at her.

"Do you look at the traps when you hit a golf ball?"

"I don't play golf, Doc. You don't, either."

"If you did you'd forget the trap. It doesn't affect anything. You'd just hit the shot."

"Stop it!" April hollered. "This isn't about golf. I want to know what's going to happen!"

"Just let the man work, Baby." Dr. Kay's hands trembled more. She wiped the wet out of her eyes and watched Doc slide a fourth bullet between the blades. She fought tears, composed herself, and reached for April. April stood her ground.

"I'll answer," Malone said. "Mop Up is three hundred forty kilotons of plutonium-based nuclear warhead dropped on our collective ass, courtesy of the United States Navy and the CIA."

"They didn't need to know," Dr. Kay muttered.

"Sure they did." Malone's response was a cold whisper. "So they'll shut up and let the man work." She watched Doc fit a fifth bullet into the vent blades.

"This nuke is coming soon, isn't it?" April looked at Dr. Kay.

"Real soon," Malone answered. She wiped sweat from the delicate bones of her forehead. She looked pale. From pain, H.I. was sure. Malone wasn't afraid of dying.

April continued, "And even if Doc's contraption opens the hatch, and even if we somehow get out of this complex..."

"Not somehow," Doc said. "We will get out through isolation. No one's back there."

"No one alive," H.I. gritted his teeth. "The air's frozen in nitrogen vapor. It's loaded with the Bell Tower lifeform."

"Only the lab air, as far as we know," Dr. Kay interrupted. She wasn't trembling any more. "Maybe Node Two is okay. We can get out through the bottom hatch."

"Fine! We get out." H.I. looked Malone in the eyes. "We still don't have time to get to minimal safe distance, do we?"

Malone checked her watch, narrowing her eyes to green slits over fine cheekbones. She looked away. H.I. wouldn't have expected that from her. She was a practiced liar, the kind who could look you right in the face. This time she didn't.

"I have another way out," H.I. told Malone. "We can still make it to minimal safe distance."

"I'm all ears. Everything else hurts." She winced.

He told her about the deal he'd cut with Bulldog, and the lie he'd told him to get that deal. He told her about the swap, software worth money in exchange for a ride out. And VanRensburg, the South African who'd tortured them on the runway, had pulled H.I. aside to let him know the deal was still on.

Malone shot back a sarcastic look. "Got his phone number?"

"No. I've got his address."

"Where?"

"The tower on the airstrip." H.I. told her what incentive he was going to give Bulldog to go for the deal now.

"And why will he believe you?"

"Because he already doesn't believe Rykoff. Anyway, not that crap about Bell Tower being an experimental aircraft."

"Doesn't mean he'll believe you."

“I think he already does.”

“Why?”

“Because he didn’t throw me out of his Huey back on the river. Because he chose to believe me instead of Rykoff.”

“Or neither of you.”

“He’s in this for the money. Said so. He’s not getting paid to die. Said that too.” H.I. paused. He had Malone’s attention. “So I give him both incentives, tell him…”

“That Bell Tower is a new energy source?”

“Yeah. Worth billions.”

“Except that’s there’s now a technical emergency,” Malone was catching on. “It’s about to go critical?”

“Exactly! I tell him it’s the kind of critical that makes another big hole in the rain forest and makes everything glow in the dark.” H.I. studied her face for doubt. He didn’t see any. “He flies himself out of here while he can. He takes us with him.”

“Because you’re going to give him technical discs worth money.”

“Damn right.” H.I. looked at Dr. Kay. “All we need is a couple of doctored discs that show Bell Tower’s technology. It just has to look real.”

Doc fit a sixth bullet in the vent. The pattern was parabolic with the curve toward the ceiling. Malone glanced at his work and turned back to H.I. “If you’re wrong about either bastard, we won’t get another chance. I say we run.”

April joined in. Her eyes were blue storms. “No way you can run. You can’t even walk.” She pushed Dr. Kay toward the laptop. “Do what H.I. wants.”

The screen was black. Dr. Kay turned on the power. H.I. said a prayer. The machine booted. A central box appeared, asking for her password. Dr. Kay punched in five characters that registered as x's.

"Your password is *April,* isn't it?"

"Her father named her." Dr. Kay's voice cracked. "Knew he wouldn't be here for the birth." She wiped away tears. "I was two weeks late with April. So she didn't come in March like we expected. Her father picked the name ahead of time, knowing she'd be born in April."

Doc jammed the last of the bullets into the vent and inspected his work. Then he and H.I. eased Malone out of the bunk and removed the mattress. Doc used a piece of broken metal from the security camera strut to rip the mattress open. He began cutting the stuffing into strips.

Dr. Kay worked fast at the laptop. "Score one for our side. System's back online." She jammed in a floppy and opened an official file, *BELL TOWER APPENDIX A, SECTION ONE.* Dr. Kay began to alter the file, changing the title to *ENERGY SOURCE SITE CONTAMINATION.* She scrolled to real data reflecting the energy of the brief spikes produced by Bell Tower. A summary read *SINGLE SOURCE POSITRON SOURCE,* gamma strength 511,000 electron volts. That number registered in H.I.'s head.

Malone checked her watch again. "We're about out of time."

"Just a thought," he said. Actually it was a worry. "There's no reason to believe you can nuke away Bell Tower. I mean the thing entered our atmosphere at 150,000 miles per hour. Should have burned up at least partially, but it landed completely intact. Hit the ground at the same speed. Can you imagine the energy it sustained? Should have been pulverized to dust and vapor from impact! But it came out intact and with the lifeforms inside intact."

Dr. Kay nodded.

"Probably hit with the energy of a million nukes. There should have been earthquakes all the way to Texas. The Earth should be buried in clouds. We should be having the equivalent of nuclear winter."

"Didn't happen, did it?" Dr. Kay stared at her screen. "Just left a tire rut in relativistic terms."

H.I. thought of the physics involved. The energy of any projectile increased with the square of its velocity. Gun makers knew this fact. That's why modern weapons hurled little bullets at big speeds, not big bullets a little speed. That's why a little bullet at high speed would pulverize a target. He thought of Bell Tower traveling at 150,000 miles per hour and hitting the Earth. Where did the energy go?

"Had to be consumed somewhere, didn't it?" Dr. Kay kept doctoring the disc, trying to make it look like a report on an energy plant. She clacked the keyboard at high speed, then stopped to pop in a second disk. For a second she seemed relieved. "It's not back. It's not in my computer."

"What's not back?" Malone asked.

"Bell Tower," Dr. Kay said. "It's been in my computer, doing things."

"EMP stuff," H.I. told Malone.

"Small potatoes," Dr. Kay added. "Throwing an electromagnetic pulse through the air, locking on to the metal parts of anything in its path, creating a secondary pulse, and disrupting electronics. That's no big trick. Malone, I'm sure you have weapons that can do the same thing."

"Can't say." She checked her watch for the third time, and H.I. understood what she was doing. She was doing the same thing as Doc and Dr. Kay, pretending that there was time and that they had a chance. She was talking to keep her own mind occupied.

"Sure you can say," Dr. Kay said. She was keeping up appearances for April's sake. "But I don't meet the criteria of need-to-know, do I Malone?"

"Can't say, Dr. Waterstone. I'm just a public servant, not a policy maker."

"Right." Dr. Kay changed discs again. "I already know what you've got. But your stuff can't break into a system without a connection in order to probe and manipulate data. You can't send a signal through the air that will find access to a hard drive not meant to receive it." Dr. Kay finished working. "Bell Tower can."

"I don't believe it." Malone shifted positions painfully. "If that were true, Rykoff would want it from Bell Tower, just like he wants the virus."

"Rykoff is almost smart enough to know what he can and can't have."

"Almost smart enough?" Malone leaned against a wall.

"What he thinks is a virus is an alien crew. Intelligence on a microscopic level, probably a collective intelligence."

"Right! Little space commies." Malone winced badly. She held her breath and struggled out of her fatigue pants. Her calves and thighs were covered in bruises and cigarette burns.

"What bastard did this to you?" April applied a wet towel to Malone's wounds.

"Our host." Malone flinched. "Doesn't matter a damn now. He's a dead man, and he doesn't even know it. Won't even know it when it happens." She let April apply more compresses. "Neither will we."

"Don't be negative, Malone. It's a real turn-off. " Doc had finished cutting the strips from the mattress stuffing. All were of equal length.

"What's that?" April pointed to the strips.

"Flash substance to heat the bullets. Made of mattress stuffing. Combustible as hell. Good reason not to smoke in bed."

"What are you going to use for a fuse?" H.I. asked.

"Something manufactured to a standard so that all units burn at the same rate." He pulled a crumpled pack of cigarettes from his pocket. H.I. remembered seeing them on him at the airstrip, remembered wondering why. Doc separated out ten and began to cut sections.

"Science marches on." Malone lay her head against the steel wall.

"Back to the nuke," H.I. said to Dr. Kay. "I don't think it will kill Bell Tower. The physics doesn't add up."

"Who gives a damn about the physics?" April watched Doc work.

"I can't get my mind around the impact and all of that energy. It should have destroyed Bell Tower completely," H.I. said. "To survive impact, Bell Tower would have to be incredibly dense. And if it were that dense, it would have gone right through the planet and out the other side, like a bullet through a melon."

"It's not dense. It's hollow." April interrupted.

"But it doesn't act hollow. It acts dense. And if it were that dense, it would have fantastic gravitational strength.

Enough to compress the Earth into a ball bearing and flatten it like a pancake against Bell Tower's surface."

"It didn't happen," April said. "And it doesn't matter."

"It does matter. I think the energy went somewhere else." H.I. felt the hairs on the back of his neck go stiff. He remembered the number floating in his head. Bell Tower's energy spikes reading 511,000 electron volts. The number was almost a magic number of sorts. He remembered the dream he'd had on the flight into Villa Lobos.

It came back to him all at once. He'd dreamt of a long journey and something big traveling light years while feeding on something that was everywhere in space. The object was large and silver and changing form. It was always hungry. It was always feeding. It was always traveling. In the dream there'd been Marsden whispering the warning. The warning was still with him. It was about the end.

"The number 511,000 electron volts is a well-recognized signature, isn't it? For an antimatter and matter collision? A small collision?"

"Don't even go there," Dr. Kay said.

"Wherever Bell Tower came from, it brought antimatter with it. If there's antimatter in Bell Tower's core, and if gets nuked, then..."

"Then what?" April asked.

"Then it could be the end of everything."

"Everything what?"

"The universe. Everything."

"Done." Doc inspected the vent. The bullets were arrayed in a parabolic pattern, their casing ends wrapped in strips of mattress stuffing and fixed to cigarette sections. Doc moved to the hatch and found a small lever recessed inside a vertical well, same as the handles in doors on aircraft. Doc fixed his bullet-loaded vent to the lever, the bullets arrayed to impact around the lock.

"What's the energy of impact, H.I.?" Doc asked.

"I need to know the mass and velocity of the bullet."

"One hundred forty-seven grain, nine millimeter hollow point," Malone chimed in, "has a muzzle velocity of one thousand ten feet per second. Energy is three hundred three foot-pounds. Times ten is three thousand foot-pounds."

Something small moving at high speed was the same as something real big moving at low speed. H.I. did that part in his head. "About like a five-hundred-pound wrecking ball on a chain moving at four miles an hour."

"Take cover." Doc turned the bunk bed on its side and used it to bury the hatch and his device. He buried it further in the two mattresses.

"They have to all go off at once." Malone limped to the far wall.

"Piece of cake," Doc said. He lit the cigarettes.

"Modest son of a bitch, aren't you."

"He's confident," Dr. Kay admitted. "I like that in a man."

All of them huddled on the far wall. April held her mother. The air filled with blue smoke and the stale smell of tobacco. Doc counted the seconds under his breath.

"Something I have to ask, Doc."

"Go ahead, Malone."

"What's H.I. stand for? It's not in the files."

April answered sarcastically, "Hypocrites Isaac."

"You stuck your kid with that name?" Malone asked incredulously.

"A physicist and a physician. Two of my heroes," Doc whispered, still counting. He watched the smoke curl against the ceiling. He signaled heads down.

"You knew?" H.I. whispered to April.

"I always knew," she whispered back.

"Why didn't you tell people? All the time you were so mad at me, why…"

"I figured you had enough shit in your life," she replied.

"Head down, Baby." Dr. Kay's voice was a plea.

All of Doc's bullets fired at once. One continuous ear-shattering boom mixed instantly with the splatter of metal against metal. The echo vibrated from four steel walls and went on forever, drowning out the backward trajectory of the spent casings. H.I. felt the casings slam the mattress like rain on a tent. Then nothing except the acrid stench of burned powder. The hatch swung fully open on it hinges. Where there had been a latch and lock, there was a gaping hole the size of a lunch kit.

"What do you know?" Malone coughed. "Son of a bitch worked."

"Too bad, isn't it?" H.I. spoke up. "We're out of time."

Chapter Thirteen

In the tower at the edge of the steel mesh field, Bulldog watched the solitary blip on his radar scope accelerate and climb. Above his head a rectangular dish rotated on the metal roof of the tower's open scaffolding. He froze the dish on target. The blip was still moving fast, probably on afterburners for maximum thrust. Bulldog knew what that meant. But Danalov, the nearest Russian, beat him to saying it.

"Is going to toss bomb!" Sweat ran down Danalov's face as he moved to the two metal boxes of the fire control system and struggled with the transmitter. He adjusted the pulse width.

Bulldog twisted an ear skyward. "Bugger won't be climbing for bloody long."

"Azimuth one hundred sixty-five," Danalov read the data

Bulldog picked up his field phone and spun his head toward the Avenger vehicle stationed one hundred fifty feet away. He reached over Danalov and jammed the send button on the data link. The vehicle's twin missile pods rotated to the coordinates Danalov had input. The vehicle's infrared sight followed. Bulldog yelled the order into his field phone.

"Fire."

"Is too far," the voice from the Avenger vehicle's gunner came back.

"He's going to toss a bloody bomb. I ordered fire."

Twin puffs of smoke exploded from the missile pods, expelling the five-foot stingers from their prepackaged tubes. The stingers coasted in mid-air for a fraction of a second while their fins unfolded and their infrared guidance systems locked on target. Thirty feet from their launch pods, their motors ignited and pushed them out of Bulldog's sight at twenty-two g's and twice the speed of sound.

* * *

The warning light alerted Psycho seconds ahead of the voice yelling in his headphones. "Mop Maid, Mop Maid! Surface-to-air-missile radar on your zero!" A split-second later, the voice came back louder. "Jesus, he's launching! He's launching!"

Psycho was already looking for his tracking warning light. It was cold. That meant the incoming missiles had been pointed his way via radar but were using an internal infrared to lock on to him. He surrendered to his trained instincts. He aborted his bombing approach and used his stick and pedals to slam his F/A-18 into a turn inside the arc of the SAM radar. In the same instant he activated his infrared jammer, a strobe that began sending out pulses of heat to confuse the sensors of the incoming missiles. But he was too late.

The proximity alert was sudden and loud in his helmet.

He had maybe three seconds. He did two things simultaneously. He dropped heat flares as a second decoy and hurled the F/A-18 into a ninety-degree turn. As he did he ticked the seconds in his head. The Klaxon continued. The flares failed. He had one trick left.

Psycho rolled the F/A-18 inverted, watching the sky replace the ground. He hung by his harness as the twin smoke trails streaked toward his right wing. He opened his speed brakes and pulled his stick backward. The F/A-18 angled its nose toward earth in a dirtied-up, inverted dive. The g-forces pushed him into his seat. Earth rushed toward him.

The smoke trails shot over his belly and entered into a turn beyond his left wing. The two missiles were angling to come back. But at twice the speed of sound, their energy was high and wide. For a second the Klaxon was silent. Then it was back. So were the missiles as they completed their turn. Psycho held his dive. The Klaxon raged in his helmet. The forest was in his face.

At the last second he jerked sharply on the stick and used his rudder pedals to throw the sky over his canopy and the treetops under his wings. The Klaxon went silent. He turned his head over his shoulder, threw the F/A-18 into another ninety-degree turn, and searched the sky. Both smoke trails ended in the forest where their Mach two turn had taken them. Their contrails were breaking into little puffs in the wind.

Psycho realized he was drenched in sweat and piss. He was out of breath. He'd gone through the entire maneuver with his nuke armed. He recovered and contacted the Hawkeye.

"Coach, this is Mop Maid." He controlled his voice. But the voice that came back in his helmet was not so composed.

"What the hell is going on, Mop Maid? This is supposed to be an exercise."

Psycho ignored the question and fired back a question of his own. "How many radar sites do you have on your radar homing and warning?"

"Only one, Mop Maid. A pulse radar originating at the Tango Alpha."

"Strangle the parrot, Coach. I'm going back."

"Say again, Mop Maid."

"Say again. Jam the bastard. I'm going back." Psycho checked his position on GPS and interfaced with his targeting pod. Twenty-five miles south of Target Alpha Bell Tower, he began a climb. The radio voice from the Hawkeye became garbled in his helmet. Or maybe he was concentrating too hard to hear it. He heard the second warning from the Hawkeye at five thousand feet when he almost collided with another plane.

The other plane was a Hercules C-130 bearing USAF markings. It was headed toward the target when the two of them barely missed each other. Psycho made a break turn and then a circle. He passed over the Hercules while climbing. He had not misread the markings. They read USAF, NEW YORK AIR INTERNATIONAL GUARD. Psycho cursed and told himself the mission was coming apart badly. For a second he thought about using his radio to talk to CAG and ask for instructions. But he rejected the option immediately. His orders had been specific. He was not to abort under any circumstances.

At thirty-five miles out, Psycho dropped to the deck and began a wide arc back.

* * *

"Is the American down?" Rykoff's voice was loud in Bulldog's field phone.

"I don't know yet." Bulldog kept his eyes on the scope. He saw only one blip, and it was on approach from the South. He assumed it was the C-130 Hercules. The stinger blips had converged on the American bogey, and the bogey had plunged beneath radar. But there was no way to be sure that the American bogey was down. It was just as possible that the bogey had performed an evasive maneuver. Bulldog watched the screen knowing that Rykoff was waiting for an answer. But Bulldog's answer didn't come from his radar screen. It came from his radio.

"Dugout, Dugout. This is Team Bus." The voice of the C-130 pilot crackled in Bulldog's ear.

"Copy, Team Bus." Rykoff's voice carried across the radio.

"Bandit just blew through. Say again, we were just overflown by a bandit."

"Did you get a look at him, Team Bus?"

"That's affirmative, Dugout. He looked like an American F/A-18."

"Shit!" Bulldog swept Danalov out of the way and took over the radar transmitter. He still had only one blip, the inbound C-130. Bulldog adjusted his dish using the C-130 as a centroid and concentrating on one sector of his radar envelope. As Bulldog did so, he felt VanRensburg arrive next to him. Together they saw a continuous train of target blips suddenly appear between his dish and the C-130. Beside him VanRensburg let the cigarette in his mouth dangle unlit and closed his Zippo. Both knew what they were seeing.

"We're screwed." VanRensburg said it for both of them. The train of blips meant his radar dish was being fed pulses that created false target echoes. It meant they were being jammed.

"See if we can burn through." Bulldog adjusted his radar transmitter, opened his receiver input, and waited to see if he could distinguish the bogey through the noise created by the jamming. But the effort failed. He saw nothing but noise.

"Team Bus, this is Dugout. Stay on approach." Rykoff's voice carried through Bulldog's radio. "Say again. Stay on approach."

"This is Team Bus. Roger that."

"Negative, Team Bus! This is Tower!" Bulldog yelled onto the open frequency. "Say again, this is Tower. Abort your approach. Say again, abort your approach. Back off and await instructions."

Bulldog's field phone whined immediately. Bulldog crammed it to his face and heard Rykoff acting unsettled for the first time. "Tower, what are you doing?"

"The American bogey is not down. And we are being jammed."

"Are you quite sure?"

"No bloody time for a discussion!" Bulldog started to slam the receiver into its cradle. But as his eyes swung back to the radar screen, he forgot all about Rykoff. Next to him both Danalov and VanRensburg were seeing the same thing. The three of stood frozen and stared.

The scope was empty. Not even noise. Bulldog swung the dish through a 360-degree arc. As it rotated southwest, the scope filled with expected noise. As it swung back toward the bogey, it went blank. The bogey had to have flown wide and restarted its approach from the far side of the crater. In that direction there were no signatures on the scope. There was nothing at all.

"I've never seen anything like this." Bulldog cradled his phone. Then he retrieved it and rang up the gunner of the Avenger vehicle. "Bogey is inbound. We're jammed. Pick him up and fire on infrared."

Bulldog cradled his field phone. As he did he noticed his sweat was cold. Middle of the tropical rain forest and his sweat was as cold as the coldest night on the Veld. How could that be? His muscles began to tremble involuntarily, and he realized it wasn't just a little cold. He fixed his gaze on the Avenger and waited for the twin pods to fire. They didn't. He picked up the field phone again and yelled at the gunner. Why hadn't the idiot fired? The gunner said he had nothing on infrared. The forward monitor read almost as if its sensor were aimed into an empty, night sky in Siberia. But only almost.

Pointed over the crater, radar and infrared were seeing nothing at all. That was impossible.

* * *

Inside the command module, Rykoff saw his breath in the air and realized it was getting colder. He tried again to raise Bulldog but got no answer. He turned to the nearest technician to give him a hand radio to carry to the tower.

But the technician was no longer watching his own equipment. He was staring with all of the others at the screens receiving from the cameras inside the crater. Bell Tower was changing.

The dome shape was gone, replaced by a something formless. It was black as outer space and spreading like liquid. Its substance was dull, as if it were a hole in the universe. Or perhaps a hole into infinity, Rykoff thought. He stood motionless as he watched it spreading across the crater floor. In its path the fog was vanishing. For the first time he could see the crater walls. Lights danced from them, ice forming in thousands of places. Sensors read the data, but the data was impossible for Rykoff to believe. The temperature in the crater was falling below the sensors' ability to register it. That was inconceivable. One by one, the cameras died. The one closest to the compound kept transmitting. That was unbelievable, Rykoff knew. And all at once, Dr. Waterstone's words flooded back into his consciousness. He remembered her lovely face filled with fear, but not fear of him.

You don't see it, Rykoff. You don't see the truth.

He'd asked her what truth, and she'd tried hard to tell him. But he'd dismissed her. Still she'd persisted, wanting desperately for him to believe as she did. There was a harsh truth about the beings who'd piloted Bell Tower to Earth. The second time, he'd listened only to dismiss her again.

The alien crew is dead, dear Doctor Waterstone. They were killed by an alien virus they could not control. We've seen what that virus can do.

His own truth had seemed so self-evident. The virus had annihilated the alien crew by digesting them in their own biologic juices. Their self-consumption had been complete, leaving no trace of their presence. That made the virus a weapon that could be contained only by him. And unlike the alien crew, he'd found a way to keep that virus docile under his control.

No, Rykoff. The alien virus is the crew.

Maybe she'd been right. And if she was right, then Rykoff could be sure he was seeing nature's perfection. Maybe eons ago in the frozen primordial substance of some distant nebulae, intelligence had evolved on a microscopic level. That intelligence would have to be collective, each microbe containing a bit of information that served a mind existing only in the sum total of all of its bits. On that grand scale, it was all at once an organism, an intelligence, and a race. But only as the collective whole could it be a thinking and doing entity. And once it had achieved its sum, it had had built a spaceship in the image of its most elemental form, a single microbe. As such, the spaceship was both homage to self and also a machine of its creation. In building its spaceship, that microbial intelligence would have elevated itself to a grand scale and achieved the means to transport itself to distant worlds. On those worlds it would follow the purpose of all life, consume that which it could consume and lay waste to everything else.

"Radiation spikes!" The yell snapped Rykoff's attention back to the monitor bank.

"Danger level?" Rykoff searched the screens.

"No."

Rykoff turned back to the crater camera. In that instant he saw the light pulled from the sky, leaving nothing but night over the crater. Beneath the night, the impenetrable, dark horror was spreading across the crater floor. It was surging like a tide. If Dr. Waterstone were right, then that tide was Bell Tower taking on a new form. A spaceship coming to reclaim its crew, a microscopic life form that had traveled across immense time and distance for a purpose. That purpose was to bring about the end of the world.

"Radar is still dead."

Rykoff ignored what he was told. The radar had been dead for more than five minutes already. Its dish was still fixed to the crater's azimuth and angled parallel to the crater floor. Its sweep sector was narrowed to receive only Bell Tower's blip. But the blip was gone. The scope was empty. There was nothing, not even noise from the walls. But the camera near the rim of the crater was still transmitting. On the screen the flattened black substance that had previously been a silver half sphere was expanding faster, moving up the crater and bringing with it probably billions of lifeforms dwelling within.

Rykoff turned and saw the panic gripping his technicians. The one nearest the air lock was already starting to open it. Others looked like they might follow him. Rykoff raised his pistol in a two-handed grip and shot twice, hitting mid-body mass both times. The technician at the air lock took a full ten seconds to realize he'd been shot. Then he crumpled in a heap, dead before he hit the floor. The remaining technicians froze in their tracks.

"Back to your stations," Rykoff said softly.

None of the technicians moved. Rykoff kept his gun aimed with both hands and both eyes open. Everyone in his sights was expendable. The ground phase of his operation was close to completion. He had substantial numbers of Bell Tower lifeforms held dormant in liquid nitrogen. He had those in his control. Soon he would have transportation for them. The power within them was unparalleled in hands willing to use them.

"We are in control and close to success." Rykoff sensed his own calm. He was not afraid. The others in his pistol site must sense his own power, he knew. He watched them. They were in his grasp.

"Main bus is overheating. I have a power drain."

"Where is the source?"

"The crater cables."

"Uncouple the connection," Rykoff ordered. "Take them off-line. Do it..."

Rykoff's voice was lost in the echoing boom that rocked the module walls. For a second there was darkness. Then the batteries activated the emergency lights, throwing red shadows across the equipment and turning Rykoff's face to a macabre mask. Flashlights clicked on immediately, all of their shafts eventually pointing toward the air lock and escape. But no one moved. Rykoff had his pistol raised.

"Stay where you are and listen. What you heard and felt was one of two things. Either an American jet on approach was shot down or it dropped its bomb. Either way, we are still intact. We will complete this operation."

At first no one moved. Then came a single voice from a technician deep in the dark. "That was not a crash or bomb. It was the loss of negative pressure in isolation. Isolation has been breached. The air is filling with the hot agent."

* * *

H.I. was inside Node 1 when the explosion vibrated through the circular walls. The boom was louder than thunder. It shook the foundation and echoed into a pitch dark that lasted an agonizing few seconds before the emergency lights activated. H.I. knew it wasn't Mop Up. Had it been that, he would not still be alive. And he would not be seeing Dr. Kay's breath visible in the red emergency lights. H.I. thought of another possibility, an even worse one.

"That was a sudden breach in isolation," he said.

"No." Dr. Kay moved toward the other side of Node 1 and found the hatch that interfaced with the safe lab. She found the battery-driven LED pressure gauge. "The pressure on the other side is still negative."

"Was it the bomb?" April stumbled over her words.

"No, I think it was the generator," Dr. Kay answered.

Malone limped toward opposite hatch and looked through the glass port into the service module. She leaned in next to Doc. "They're all still in control. How do we lock the hatch from this side?"

"We can't," Dr. Kay said.

"Will the system sound an alarm on battery power if the isolation hatch is opened?" Doc asked.

"Yes."

"Good. Once they hear that alarm, the last thing in the world they'll do is open this hatch." Doc pulled away from the glass. "They'll lock the hatch from the other side and push positive pressure into control."

"So we go the other way," Dr. Kay said. "We move to Node Two."

H.I. understood that to get to Node 2, they'd have to move through the safe lab. They'd be assuming isolation had not been breached and that it had not contaminated the safe lab. They'd be basing that assumption and their lives on whether the pressure gauge built into the hatch was still functioning properly. It still read negative pressure on the other side. Once they got to Node 2, they'd have hazmat suits and access to a floor hatch. They'd have a way out, assuming they still had time to beat Mop Up.

H.I. watched Dr. Kay check the pressure gauge again. Then she reached for the crank to open the hatch. As soon as she touched it, she withdrew her hands with a jerk. On the door her handprints were frosty. Her breath was more visible in the cold air. She was shivering.

H.I. opened the hatch for her. The Klaxon sounded immediately, and H.I. felt the pain lance into both of his ears. The pressure in Node 1 was bleeding rapidly into the safe lab. At his back he heard the hatch to the service module locked down.

"Knew they'd lock us in," Doc said.

Doc joined H.I., and they both peered into the safe lab. Inside, the red emergency lights threw shadows along the scientific gear racked on the walls. Air pressure bleeding inward was blowing papers into the air. The hatch to Node 2 was twenty-eight feet away. And beyond Node 2 was isolation, where the dead bodies of Steiner and his team were entombed in air filled with frozen nitrogen and loaded with the Bell Tower lifeform.

H.I. pulled away from the hatch and let the others have a look. His mind raced elsewhere. It raced toward Mop Up.

Chapter Fourteen

Psycho pulled back sharply on his stick and increased power, taking his F/A-18 into a climb. He kept one eye on the green target diamond as it traveled across his heads-up display toward the place where it would merge with his target indicator box. Both turned red, and beeping started inside Psycho's helmet. He released the bomb, pulled into a straight vertical climb, and engaged his afterburners. His F/A-18 shot skyward on the forty-four thousand pounds of thrust generated by its twin General Electric turbofan engines. The g-forces grabbed him, but the compressed air forced into the bladders inside his G suit kept him from passing out.

The bomb left the wind in a graceful upward arc, sunlight absorbed by its dull gray casing. Eight miles from Alpha Bell Tower, it reached the top of its trajectory. A guidance system jacketed to its midsection selected the nearest of twenty-four Navstar Global Positioning Satellites and received three-dimensional location information. Inside the steel jacket, an inertial measurement system instantly knew its velocity and destination, sending instructions to the motors in the tapered tail assembly. Vertical fins angled left, pointing the nose two degrees northwest. The bomb yawed with the precision of an Olympic diver. It aimed at Bell Tower.

Psycho fought the g-forces that crushed him into his seat and watched his vertical climb indicator max out. His altimeter passed eighteen thousand feet. He sucked oxygen into protesting muscles. He lowered his visor and watched for the flash at the edge of his vision.

The bomb fell without noise. Inside its one-piece steel center case, the detonator was protected to allow ground penetration to six meters before exploding. The firing switches would ignite a jacket of high-energy, plastic-bonded explosive. The force would compress plutonium into a supercritical configuration that would instantly become the fission trigger. Atoms would split in a chain reaction, superheating the secondary lithium-deuterium fuel. Atoms would fuse, unleashing the force of 340 kilotons of TNT. The fireball would reach the temperature of the sun, fusing earth into glass and vaporizing everything within hundreds of meters. With a ground burst, the earth would tamper the force, but the destruction would still be total out to five miles, burn flesh and start fires at ten miles, and be visible at fifty miles.

At two thousand feet, the guidance system made its last correction. Horizontal fins pitched down the nose, and the bomb pointed into the bottom of Crash Site Alpha Bell Tower.

* * *

Tower at his back, Bulldog ran with VanRensburg toward the tarmac. They ran for the only Huey Bulldog knew to be fueled. Its crew was on standby in the cargo bay, as was the routine demanding that a Huey crew be ready on rotation at all times. As he closed on the Huey, Bulldog began yelling and gesturing with his hands. His gesture was one hand raised and spinning with a single finger raised. Ahead of him the Russian pilot saw the signal and shouted to his crew.

"Run faster, my china." Bulldog ran only steps ahead of VanRensburg, but he asked himself if he would wait should VanRensburg trip. He knew he would. Men who left their mates were no better than animals. And he was no animal.

Ahead he saw the blades begin to spin and heard the engine increase its rotations per minute. He let VanRensburg catch him, and they reached the cargo bay together. The crew was already in position. The pilot and copilot were ready. Bulldog ordered the pilot to take off and fly north at low altitude. He watched the pilot engage his collective and universal. Underneath his boots Bulldog felt the machine come to life.

"Told you, my china. We're going to make it out of here."

* * *

Klaxon in his ears, H.I. was more concerned about what he was seeing than what he was hearing. He flattened against the wall just inside the safe lab and beneath its security camera. Doc was already out of Node 1 and way ahead of him bolting across the safe lab toward the hatch of Node 2. The hatch window was opaque with frost. When he reached it, Doc tried to clean it with his shirt sleeve. His effort was useless. The other side of the hatch window was opaque from frozen vapor.

H.I. bolted after Doc with Dr. Kay and April following on his heels. H.I. turned to look over his shoulder only once. Behind him Malone was still inside Node 1 and collapsed against its steel wall. Her breathing was shallow and fast. She didn't look good.

"What's inside Node Two?" Doc asked.

"Hazmat gear," Dr. Kay answered. "The floor and ceiling of Node Two are both hatched to the outside. We get out through one of them if the seal between Node Two and the safe lab hasn't failed."

"One of us opens the hatch," Doc said. "The rest wait in Node One."

"So which of us gets the short straw?" H.I. asked.

The overhead Klaxon stopped. Doc looked back toward Node 1 to make eye contact with Malone. Her breathing seemed easier. She was looking at her watch. She shook her head. Doc turned to H.I., then to Dr. Kay and April.

"Go back to Node One, close the hatch, and wait."

"No way, Doc," H.I. said.

But Doc shoved him toward the open hatch to Node 1 and Malone. H.I. felt movement at his back and figured Dr. Kay and April to be following him. There was no question in H.I.'s mind about what Doc was about to do. He was about to be a test animal. If Node 2 were contaminated, Doc would die violently. And the others would be spared from Bell Tower. But they would not be spared from the bomb. They would wait without options, freezing in the cramped dark of Node 1 until Mop Up. That was no way to die. Or maybe Doc had another plan. Maybe if he lived long enough he could seal isolation back down, raise the air pressure inside Node 2, and then vent its contaminated air to the outside by opening the hatches. It was a gamble that might give the others time to don hazmat suits and escape. But it would take two to get the job done in Node 2, one for each hatch. And Doc might have trouble with his hatch. He had broken ribs and wouldn't be able to use both arms. So maybe it could be done by one person, one with two good arms.

H.I. told Doc what he had in mind. Doc shook his head. "We're all waiting inside Node One together."

H.I. nodded in agreement, then picked up his pace to get to the hatch ahead of everyone else. With one hand he found the vertical lever on the hatch and jammed it into the lock position. He stepped aside to let everyone else pass, but Doc got in his face.

"Did you think I didn't see that?"

"I'm not letting you do it, Doc."

"I'm not doing anything. We're all waiting together."

"Right you are, Doc." H.I. put his weight into his left fist, ramming into the ribs on Doc's right side. Doc buckled in pain, and in the same instant, H.I. gave him a two-handed shove into Node 1. Just as fast H.I. slammed the hatch closed. It was locked from his side. He turned back toward Node 2 and found himself looking at April. She was on his side of the hatch. Not what he wanted.

"Let's do it." She was shivering. "I'm not going back in there."

Behind his back, H.I. heard the pounding coming from inside Node 1. A shadow moved across the peep glass.

He couldn't tell who was moving inside. It didn't matter. There was no way to keep any of them at bay while shoving April back inside. He spun back toward her, but she was already halfway to Node 2.

"You hold your hatch locked! I'll open the other one!" She shouted as she ran.

He caught her just as she reached the hatch lever to Node 2. He grabbed her wrists, but she refused to let go. Instead she looked him the eyes and shook her head determined. He gripped the lever with her, hoping she would change her mind but knowing it wouldn't matter. There was no alternative. Together they began to pull.

The rumble that stopped them came from the ground, rising into the steel structure in the roar of a thousand claps of thunder that echoed without end from everything metal. In that instant everything around them became airborne. The red emergency lights blinked out, followed by the whine of metal against metal. Then came the sickening crunch of steel and concrete piers that supported the complex as they broke apart underneath, snapping like twigs.

The module left the ground and H.I. felt himself hurled through the dark. Then he felt nothing at all.

Chapter Sixteen

The blast was a thousand times as bright as a bolt of lightning.

Psycho didn't watch it directly. It reflected from his helmet visor as he climbed past twenty thousand feet. He waited for the shock wave and the ball of incandescent air that would rise to thirty-five thousand feet. But his controls remained smooth, and he knew something was wrong. He banked the F/A-18 into a gentle turn and looked down over his left wing. His blood turned cold.

The clouds were open across a fifteen-mile hole in the sky, swirling outward at the edges and breaking into gentle wisps floating over green. Psycho saw what stood in the center. He raised his visor, dropped to ten thousand feet, and ripped his oxygen mask from his face. He sucked the air and looked down.

Some trees were still standing, partially shrouded in a faint haze. There were no fires, no scorched earth, and no ugly mushroom cloud.

Impossible!

Psycho made himself think, then he knew what he was going to do. He enabled his cameras and made one pass over the target. Then he opened radio communication, hoping whatever had knocked it out earlier was gone.

"Coach, this is Mop Maid. Do you copy?"

"Roger, Mop Maid. Do you copy? What the hell's been going on?"

"I am on egress, Mop Maid." Psycho blinked. His mind was racing, mulling the debriefing that lay ahead, the things he would say that would not be believed. The unexplained loss of radio communication and radar. The image on the infrared. The 340-kiloton, tactical nuke that had detonated but had not raised a mushroom cloud. The nuke that had not ravaged the Earth and had not destroyed the target.

He tried to focus on flying, kept his voice steady. "Okay, Coach. Set me up for the fuel tanker."

* * *

Just above the jungle, Bulldog had a closer view of the blast.

Heat and wind burst through the Huey's open cockpit windows. Even as Bulldog heard himself scream, the Huey was spinning in the shock wave, then falling like rock and spinning faster. He heard VanRensburg's scream from next to him on the bench. It lasted a microsecond before it was lost in the wind that smashed the cockpit glass and surged through the open bay.

The force pulled the air from Bulldog's chest. But Bulldog didn't hear the sound because his eardrums ruptured. His arms flailed in space for only seconds before the earth slammed the undercarriage and hit his back with the force of a dozen hammers. He wasn't sure how long he lay crumpled in his seat. He forced his eyelids open and tried to see through the lights that still burned in the backs of his eyes. The Huey had come down through trees, losing its rotor and smacking the ground on its undercarriage. Van-Rensburg was crumpled in his seat, head hanging limp on a broken neck. He was dead. The rest of the crew who'd been with him in the bay were nowhere to be seen. The pilot and copilot were painted in blood. They were dead.

Bulldog unleashed his harness and fell out of the wreckage. The pain in his back lanced into his legs, and he staggered into sunlight. Overhead, the sky was ripped open in a swirling hole that pushed clouds to all horizons. The earth lay gutted apart, dozens of cracks spreading out of dust that hid the complex and crater. The tower and radar dish were gone, uprooted at their foundation and collapsed in crumpled steel. The Avenger vehicle was turned on its side.

He wandered without purpose. Slowly his hearing returned, first the whistling through holes in his ear drums and then the noise. The listening hurt. Somewhere in the wreckage he heard a shrill buzz. He staggered toward it, fell to his knees in the mud, and found the field phone. He sat in the mud and cradled it, wondered if anyone was alive on the other end.

* * *

In the service module, Rykoff watched flashlight beams sweep across equipment and monitors. The beams mixed with shafts of light diffusing into the compartment through its glass ports. All of the ports were cracked. The compartment was still upright. Rykoff swept blood from a painless gash in his dead face. His fingertips touched cold, rubbery skin, and he tasted his own blood with the live part of his tongue. He ignored the bleeding, stepped to the nearest wall, and rolled an eye up to a glass port. Outside the hull there was nothing but swirling dust.

"Is dead." The nearest Russian technician cradled a broken arm. "All equipment is dead."

"We were hit by an EMP." Rykoff lied with conviction. He touched his cheek. The bleeding was less. "The pulse penetrated the module wall and fried the hardwired equipment. It followed the hardwires to the emergency batteries and fried them as well."

"Explosion," the Russian answered. "Big explosion."

"To trigger the EMP," Rykoff lied. "The bogey fired an EMP weapon before it went down. The attempt to disrupt this operation failed. Survey your hand-held equipment."

The flashlights, the hand radios, and the portable sensors were intact. Rykoff began to believe his own lie, that an EMP had truly hit the complex, been absorbed by the wall but not jumped the air inside the module. An EMP from where? A weapon dropped by the Americans? Not likely! If not the Americans, then Bell Tower? He shoved the thought from his mind.

"Radiation?" Rykoff asked.

"Is okay." Two technicians answered as Geiger counters swept the darkness, emitting low crackling noises.

Rykoff grabbed a flashlight and swept its beam toward the hatch of Node 1. The peep window reflected his beam back into his face. He remembered that the containment alarm had sounded just before the explosion. Dr. Waterstone and the others would be on the other side of the hatch, sealed in air contaminated by Bell Tower. They were unsalvageable, Rykoff told himself. He pictured Dr. Waterstone's exquisite face and felt a loss.

He shoved her out of his mind, realizing that if the hull were breached by the explosion, the air outside of the complex might also be contaminated. Rykoff turned to the nearest Russian technician. "Go out through the air lock. I want a damage report. Lock and pressurize before you crack the outer hatch."

"Da." The man did as he was ordered. Rykoff picked up the field phone and hand-cranked the generator. The line was alive, its mechanical generator and plastic components immune to EMP. He rang up the airstrip and got the South African.

"Outfield, this is Dugout. What is your situation?"

"Bloody bad. We got hit by something bloody big." Bulldog's voice was shaky. "Tower's gone. Radar's gone. Avenger's bloody on its side."

"Is the airstrip intact?" Rykoff asked.

"Lots of buckled mesh."

"What about the fuel and the salvage containers?"

"Pissing drums everywhere, but I don't see any bloody spills." The South African said he didn't know about the containers holding the Bell Tower specimens. He did not know how many of his helicopters could fly. The ones on the ground had sustained damage. He didn't know how bad. The ones in the air were simply gone. He was still taking a head count on his mercenaries. Unless the some of the helicopters on the ground could be repaired enough to fly, they were going to have a long pissing walk home.

"Run the bulldozer over the strip. Flatten it," Rykoff ordered.

"There ain't no way that will work. I'm seeing uprooted ground. It'll bloody blow the tires on the landing gear. You'll splatter that pissing Hercules from here to bloody Peru."

Rykoff looked at the luminescent dial of his watch. "Do it. You've got ten minutes. I'm going to bring in Team Bus on visual flight rules." He cradled the phone before the South African could protest. He picked up his hand radio and changed the frequency.

* * *

At fifteen thousand feet, Putin kept the Hercules C-130 in a steady turn, holding a ten-mile radius around the coordinates where blinding light had stung his eyes right through his aviator glasses. The flash was gone. In its aftermath, the packed clouds were blown apart in all directions, as if the Earth's surface had given birth to a second sun. Beneath the parting clouds, Putin saw endless green jungle. He flew with his gaze frozen, forgetting about his low fuel. He watched the dust settling in the middle of a hole blowing the clouds to all horizons.

"Mother of God!" Chernov muttered from the right seat and raised an earphone away from one side of his head. "What is that?"

"That is what we came for." The Korean said, suddenly standing behind Chernov.

"I want to know what this is all about." Chernov spat his words. Putin cut him off and asked for the fuel reserves.

"We are way down." Chernov scanned the instruments. "We have to commit or find someplace else. I figure the nearest airstrip is..."

The radio crackled in Putin's ear. The reception was weak. "Team Bus, this is Dugout. Do you copy?"

"Two by two, Dugout. What's your situation?"

The voice on the other end ignored the question. "Do you see the airstrip?"

Putin dropped to five thousand feet and put the Hercules into a narrow left turn that took him across the hole in the clouds. The airstrip came out of nowhere, snaking across a clearing in the jungle. Steel drums were scattered across one end. A handful of helicopters were airborne below. Others were smashed on the ground. A big vehicle was rolling slowly down the center of the airstrip.

"I don't like it." Chernov covered his mic and spoke to Putin. "Let's punt."

"No. We have to land," the Korean said.

"Not down there, comrade. Not unless I have a good reason," Chernov snapped.

"I'll give you a reason," Putin interrupted. "If we don't land, we don't get paid."

"We have to land," the Korean said. "It's waiting."

"What's waiting?" Chernov spoke louder. "I want to know."

"Both of you shut up." Putin tensed his fingers on the yolk and keyed the microphone in his headset. "Dugout, this is Team Bus. Get the vehicle off the runway. We are coming in."

* * *

A thin shaft of dull light entered Node 1 through the peep window in the dorsal hatch. The light fell on displaced equipment racks and dangling wires. There were no sparks. The wiring was dead. Malone limped through the wreckage. She thought she knew what had happened, but she knew what she thought was impossible.

"April! H.I.!" Dr. Kay shouted. She pounded the hatch to the safe lab a fourth time and tried the locking lever. It wouldn't budge. The window was blocked by something black as night, something that almost seemed to move. She put her ear to the cold steel and heard a noise that made no sense. Some sort of heavy liquid was in motion, dripping and thumping slowly on the steel.

"Frozen or broken?" Malone limped to Dr. Kay.

"Probably both." Doc interrupted as he stepped around Dr. Kay, pounded the hatch, and placed his ear against the steel. No knock came from the other side. The steel and glass were freezing. They shouldn't have been. He quickly scanned the other axial hatches. The peep holes were all blocked by something black and fluid.

"You hear it?" Dr. Kay asked. "Like something dripping."

Doc didn't answer her, just placed his ear to the glass. Dr. Kay heard her voice crack. "The kids are on the other side. They're…"

"We should all be dead," Malone interrupted, coughing with pain.

"Agreed," Doc said. He worked his palms up and down the hatch surface. The steel was freezing cold. It should have been molten fragments. So should he and the others.

"The explosion?" Dr. Kay asked. "Was it the nuke?"

"It must have malfunctioned," Malone answered. "The weapon would have been set for a ground burst. Most of the energy could have gone into the earth and the crater walls. But we should still be ashes. Maybe the fission primary fizzled and didn't trigger the fusion fuel." She nodded her head nervously, agreeing with herself. "Yeah, that's it. Maybe all we got was a smaller blast from polymer-bonded explosive and some of the primary fission before it sizzled out. At a mile we could survive that."

"No," Doc said.

"What do you mean, no?"

"Your stuff works. This one worked."

"How do you explain the fact that we are alive and holding this conversation?"

"Somehow Bell Tower absorbed your nuke," Doc answered. He put his weight against the hatch. "Some of the energy from the fission-fusion blast went into the ground, like you said. The rest, the mega-energy, the heat, the radiation, all went into Bell Tower."

"Three hundred and forty kilotons worth of fission-fusion bomb? No way!" Malone said. "I may not be a physicist, but I know…"

"That nothing short of a black hole could absorb the energy."

"I don't know black holes from holes in the ground. But one mile from ground zero, we ought to be atoms."

"Shut up! Both of you!" Dr. Kay launched herself at the hatch. She tried the mechanism, but it wouldn't work.

Malone said, "The force of the explosion must have jammed the hatch."

"No, not the force." Dr. Kay began to sob. "It's the safety locks. They automatically enable if the seal on the mating adapter is broken. They seal to prevent an accidental depressurization. Seal if the..."

"If the connection is broken?" Malone muttered.

"Yes."

"You're saying the safe lab is..."

"Gone. I'm saying it's gone. " Dr. Kay pressed her face against the hatch. She pounded it and listened for a signal from the other side. She heard someone crying and realized it was herself. She sank to the steel floor. Doc wiped tears from his eyes, put his arms around her, and looked toward the hatch to the service module.

* * *

"What's our situation?" Rykoff used his hand radio to talk to the man he'd sent outside. The static was getting worse by the second.

The voice came back garbled. "Am moving under service module. Air is thick. Is colder than winter night in Moscow. Ground is broken. Piers are cracked, but holding. Lab module is gone. So is living module and tunnel." More static interrupted the transmission. The voice came back briefly. "Crater is..."

"Say again," Rykoff ordered. "You are breaking up. Say again."

There was no answer. In flashlight beams, Rykoff saw a half-dozen Russian faces staring at him and staring at the air lock. He tried the radio again. He listened.

"Crater is gone. I see black water." Sharp static split the Russian's radio voice apart. "Black water. Cold." The transmission ended in a scream.

Then there was nothing but static.

Chapter Seventeen

H.I. woke up in the dark. The air was freezing, and it hurt to breathe. He was on his stomach on a cold steel surface, his head rolling below his shoulders. The steel sloped downward into nothing. He had no idea how long he'd been lying there, had no idea where he was.

"April?" He winced as he called her name. He got no answer.

He tried to climb to his knees. The angle was too steep. It pitched him forward and slammed him back against the steel. He rubbed his hands, got some feeling back, and used them to feel his way forward. The surface was grated with plastic runners to prevent slippage. He put all of his strength into his arms and reached. His fingers found a hand rung. He knew it had to be near one of the hatches. But he didn't know whether he found a rung near the hatch to Node 1 or Node 2. He pulled himself upright and felt for the hatch window. It was freezing when he found it. He put his ear near the glass and heard a noise coming from the other side. It sounded like liquid slurping against the glass.

"April?"

He didn't get an answer. On his belly he inched away from the hatch and followed the sloping floor downward. In the dark he couldn't determine the angle. But he guessed it was somewhere between thirty and forty-five degrees. The lab module was twenty-eight feet in length. He could make his way downward an estimated half-foot with each move.

In the first few feet, something swiped at him. He swiped it away in the dark. It came back and hit him a second time. Then he realized what it was. Wires dangling from a dead equipment board. He crawled through more wires as he descended. The cold got worse by the inch. He could feel a draft coming from below. He knew what the draft meant. There was a breech between the safe lab and isolation! The breech would be moving air mixed with frozen nitrogen inward. That air would be loaded with the Bell Tower lifeforms. They would be thawing.

He inched down. Something flapped in the air around his head, touching him like the wings of bats. He knew it was papers moving in the draft. He felt one of them bite into the flesh of his arm. That couldn't be correct. Papers did not bite. He felt blood run down his arm, hot and sticky. He reached for the wound and was bitten a second time. Whatever bit him was still biting him. He tried to pull it out of his arm and felt it bite his finger. It was a shard of glass. He pulled it free, held pressure, and waited until the bleeding seemed to stop. Then he moved deeper until he touched something soft, warm, and smooth. It wasn't moving.

"April?"

She didn't respond. With numb fingers he slid his hand from the slope of her cheek to the place where he could check the pulse in her neck. No good! His hands were too numb to feel anything. He brought his head close to her face to feel for breathing.

"Don't move, Tech. Don't make a sound."

"Are you okay?"

"Shut up. There's something in here with us."

"We need light."

"No. It'll see us."

He found a matchbook in his pocket, the matchbook Doc had used to light the fuses on the device he'd made to break the door back in the habitat module. The first two matches he lit did not burn in the draft. He cupped a third in his hand after striking it. It flared in April's soft face. She was looking wide-eyed beyond him.

Only a few feet away, the hatch to Node 2 was open. The match light flickered against hanging hazmat suits and threw shadows across the far hatch that connected Node 2 to isolation. The far hatch was solid glass. On its other side, a bald man with the thick glasses seemed to be standing. But then H.I. realized the bald man was dead.

The dead man hung suspended by an air hose attached to an overhead track. The flesh of one side of his face was eaten down to his skull. The other side was blackened mush, eaten to muscles that had tightened his mouth into a twisted smile. Blood and bits of his flesh smeared dozens of cracks in the hatch glass. Through the cracks puffs of gray vapor were steaming into Node 2 and the safe lab. H.I. knew the puffs were loaded with

Bell Tower lifeforms and mixing with the air they were breathing.

The match burned to H.I.'s fingers. He dropped it into the darkness. The dead man's half-eaten face was the last thing that blazed in his vision.

Chapter Eighteen

"We have to get out now!"

"What did that to him?" April refused to budge.

"I don't know." H.I. felt for the rungs where April held a death grip. They were spaced in parallel tracks at intervals meant to accommodate an astronaut ambulating in zero gravity. He peeled her hands free and forced her around to point her up the sloping metal floor. The hatch to Node 1 was twenty-eight feet away, he told her. Doc, Malone, and her mom would be waiting behind it.

"No. They're dead. Otherwise they would have already been here for us."

"I think they're okay. I'm going to light the way. Get ready for another match."

"No! I won't look at him."

"Don't. Just keep your eyes pointed uphill."

The match took. The compartment flickered into view, a steel floor angling upward into shadows littered with hanging wires, wrecked electronics, and broken glass. April blinked at the wreckage. She asked if it had been caused by the nuke.

"I think so."

"Why aren't we dead?"

"I think Bell Tower absorbed the energy."

In the light from the match, the hatch to Node 1 seemed a mile away. Its window was dark. The sound of gurgling came from the other side of the hatch. H.I. stared until the match burned his fingers and he dropped it. The dark became total.

"You hear it?" April whispered.

"Don't think about it."H.I. inched his way upward, pulling her with him. The noise became louder, liquid gurgling against metal like water running and dripping in a steel sink. It slushed at intervals, slow and rhythmic. He thought about turning the two of them backward. But he knew the air bleeding into the safe lab from Node 2 would be loaded with Bell Tower lifeforms. Inside the safe lab, the air would be warming, and the lifeforms would become active.

"Tech, did you see his face?"

"Keep climbing."

"What did that to him? The virus?"

Not a virus, H.I. told himself. It was an alien lifeform smaller than bacteria and technologically more advanced than humankind. The lifeform could think and act collectively. It could plan and kill. Dr. Kay's laptop data had been clear. The lifeforms entered through skin, penetrating pores and hair shafts to find the places where the only thing between a human and the world was a single layer of cells. By that time the lifeforms would have also traveled in air droplets to find the slightest breaks in the soft tissues of the nose, mouth, and throat. Some would go even deeper, down to the tiny air sacks of the lungs, where entry into the bloodstream was a thin membrane away.

"We have to climb faster!"

He shoved a fallen equipment rack out of the way, pulled April behind him, and reached for a hand rung. It was too far. He settled for a foothold in broken wiring. The wire pulled out of the wall, and the two of them slid backward into another tangle of wires. They hung in the dark. April angled a foot against a wall and tried to untangle herself. She fell against him, heart pounding.

"It's okay, April. Don't look down."

He lit another match and looked down. Below, he could still see deep into Node 2. On its far side, cold vapor was spewing faster out of the cracks in the glass hatch that closed off isolation. Beyond the glass, the bald man seemed to be mocking them, a twisted smile frozen across his half-eaten face.

"I'm loose." April braced herself against a wall and extended a hand.

He gripped her hand, and the two of them were free. The two of them climbed. But his mind went to bad places. Inside humans the alien lifeforms penetrated cells. They crossed membranes and cytoplasm to find the cell's nucleus and its genes. There they would redirect the instructions, commanding the cells to do horrific things to themselves.

"It's cold." April stopped climbing.

"Does anything hurt? Skin, chest, throat?"

"I can't tell." She sounded out of breath. "I can't tell. Everything's numb."

"Numb is okay, as long as there's no pain."

"No pain. Why are you asking about pain?"

"Just want to make sure you're okay."

"Don't bullshit me, Tech."

"Climb, April."

She leaned her weight on his back while he pushed with his legs. He grabbed and pushed on anything that would hold, wires or fallen racks or anything. His muscles burned. He managed to move close enough to grab a hand rung. He felt her weakening.

"Does anything hurt?"

"No. Just getting tired and out of breath. Nothing hurts."

Pain was the first symptom produced by the alien lifeform. But the pain came after bad things were already happening and unstoppable. By that time the lifeforms had already attached to genes and unleashed commands that made cells build enzymes that digested flesh, toxins that burst blood cells, and poisons that interrupted nerves. Pain meant living things were about to turn themselves to mush with their own juices.

"I have to rest," she said.

"We can't."

He positioned himself under her and raised her up on his back as he pushed with his legs. She grabbed onto something to support her weight long enough for him to find a new foothold. Then the two of them repeated the maneuver.

"I can't feel my hands."

He lit another match and looked. Her fingers were blue. He rubbed her hands between his. He asked her if it hurt to breathe. She said it didn't. He reached for another foothold and positioned her on his back again. She collapsed against him.

"How long does the virus take?"

"It's fast. If you had it, you'd already be dying."

"How can something from space do this?"

"Ask your mom in a minute. She's waiting on the other side of the hatch."

He pushed the two of them higher up the sloping floor. He wanted to believe what he was telling her. He told himself that Dr. Kay and Marsden should have met. She'd have told him things, told him that maybe the Bell Tower lifeform and Earth life were all part of the same genetic continuum. Maybe all life began in one faraway place, maybe some distant nebulae. Maybe life was seeded onto planets and allowed to evolve. Maybe Bell Tower and life on Earth had the same ancestor. Or maybe the same creator. Perhaps humans were not only the planet's most advanced lifeform, but also a living genetic repository for all that had gone into their creation. Perhaps all of life, from microbes to humankind, had been genetically planned and coded somewhere far away and high above. By a creator perhaps. And maybe at the apex, humans carried the genetic roadmap for their entire evolutionary pathway. And for all other Earth life too. For all proto-forms and for all forms yet to arise. All pre-coded and set in place and waiting. The work of a grand plan maybe. One that created Bell Tower as a repository too. Maybe Bell Tower could bring both extinction and new life though all of the genetic pieces already set in place.

"We're moving," April said.

He felt it and knew she was right. The whole module was moving down. Noise grew against the walls. It sounded like liquid hitting metal. There was only one direction in which the module could be moving down. That direction was into the crater.

"Climb." He tried to pull her arms around his waist and find the next hold. She tried to help him. But her head rolled against his back.

"We're going to die, aren't we?"

"No. It's not going to kill us because killing is a dead-end for viruses. Successful viruses never kill their hosts. And Bell Tower is intelligent."

"You've got it all wrong." April coughed.

H.I. knew hearing her cough was bad. He tried to convince himself that she was coughing from the cold in the compartment. But he knew better. She coughed deeper, and her voice trailed off.

"It's just another cruel thing that exists to kill, isn't it?"

"No, April. I don't believe that."

"This isn't a virus." She coughed. "The virus is only the how."

He had one match left in the book. He peeled off his shirt and draped it over a hanging wire. The shirt caught fire with the last match and threw out warmth. It lit the way to Node 1's hatch, only five feet away.

"The virus is only the how. Bugs don't think." Her eyes were half-closed as she said it. Her face and her forehead were beaded in sweat. In the cold that shouldn't have been possible. He shook her. She barely moved.

"You hear it?" Her whisper was no louder than a breath.

"What?"

"Sounds like water moving in a brook. You hear it? It's all around. We're moving. Can you feel it?"

He pulled her with him and slammed his back against the hatch. The locking lever was jammed. It wouldn't budge. The sound came on all sides and all at once, like a wall of water crashing on a roof. The compartment began to move downward. He knew it was going into the crater. He braced himself and locked his arms around April. Below them the last strip of his shirt began to burn to embers. The last flicker of light fell on broken equipment and April's sweating face.

The pain began everywhere and all at once. It hurt to breathe, hurt to swallow, hurt to move. It surged like fire though his hand. He grabbed that hand with his other and felt his skin come apart like dead flesh. He felt it bleed and slough down to strands of nerves and vessels. He tried once to yell, but instead he coughed. The cough surged through his chest like fire. It splattered his face and neck with his own blood and tissue. He tried once more, but his one word died a whisper in his throat.

"April?"

She was gone from him. With his last reserves, he rolled his head to look down the sloping, steel floor. As he did an explosion erupted from far below, blinding him as it sucked the air from his scorched lungs and hurled him to his side. The bones of his arms and legs snapped. And then he was sliding without any fight, down into the form moving up toward him through the freezing vapor. His last vision was eyes, thousands of eyes. They were coming up to meet him.

Chapter Nineteen

"It won't open." Dr. Kay wrenched her hands from the lever underneath the single emergency light still functioning inside Node 1. She slammed her slender body against the steel that separated Node 1 from the safe lab. Nothing happened. "The auto lock is enabled on our hatch. That only happens if the hatch seals are broken. That means the safe lab is gone."

"No," Doc answered. "It just means the shock wave ruptured the seal."

"The safe lab is gone." As she spoke Dr. Kay saw Malone move to the hatch on the other side of Node 1. With her small body, Malone blocked Dr. Kay's view of the hatch window that interfaced with the service module. Dr. Kay turned to Doc. She felt the tears filling her eyes. "If the safe lab is gone, the kids are gone."

"We don't know that yet." Doc winced as he moved, but he steadied himself with one hand holding pressure on his ribs. He tried the hatch lever himself, but it wouldn't budge. He turned to Dr. Kay. "We'll have to go out through the service module.

"I can't let you do that!" Malone moved between the two of them and the far hatch. She cradled her own broken ribs.

"Get out of my way, Malone." Dr. Kay tried to move around her. But Malone positioned herself against the hatch. Dr. Kay saw that Malone didn't have a weapon. And with her broken ribs, Malone wouldn't be much able to fight. Dr. Kay reached out to grab her shoulder. But Malone wouldn't budge.

"I told you I can't let you do that, Doctor. Rykoff is on the other side of that hatch."

"It's not up to you, Malone."

"It is up to me. Rykoff still has Bell Tower's lifeforms ready for transport. But you're the only one who knows enough to control them. That means without you, he can do nothing. So my job is clear."

"Our kids are out there. They might be dying."

"And if Rykoff succeeds, the death count might go up into the millions. I'd call that a really bad trade."

"How are you going to stop me, Malone? Kill me?"

"Not just you. All of us." Malone opened the palm of her good hand. She was holding the knob to the lever on the hatch that interfaced with the service module. "We're going to sit here together and wait for the air to run out."

"You're not thinking, Malone." Doc moved toward her.

"Is that right?" Malone winced. "Are you telling me that you're going to take it from me because you're bigger than me?"

"I'll do what I have to." Doc brushed Dr. Kay aside.

"This doesn't work that way, Doc." Malone looked him in the eye. Without a struggle she handed Doc the knob. It was metallic and barrel shaped. It was hollow in the center where the interfacing nut screwed in place. Malone watched Doc examine it. The nut was gone.

"Where's the missing piece, Malone?"

"I don't know, Doc. You're the doctor. I swallowed it about a minute ago. So you tell me where it is. Is it in my stomach? Is it in my intestine?"

"You psychotic bitch!" Dr. Kay launched herself at Malone, putting her slender weight and the strength of her long legs into an unpracticed right hook. Malone didn't raise a defense. She took the punch full in the chin and spit blood as she slid toward the floor. Dr. Kay's rage took full hold of her. She screamed as she felt her leg swing by itself into a kick.

Doc pulled Dr. Kay backward. The kick connected with air. Spinning toward Doc, Dr. Kay collapsed on his shoulder sobbing. "You're crazy, Malone."

"No, Ma'am." Malone stayed collapsed against the hatch. Her mouth was bleeding. Her eyes were green slits filled with surrender instead of fight. "I'm just doing a shit job that someone has to do. I'm sorry. I really am."

Dr. Kay sobbed until her strength was gone. Then she looked up into Doc's face and saw that he still had determination in his eyes. He hugged her with one arm, rolled the broken knob in his hands, and started toward the hatch. Stepping over Malone he pounded the hatch window. Malone made no move to stop him.

"They can't hear you, Doc," Dr. Kay said. She saw that Malone almost looked regretful. "The glass is thick on both hatches, and between them there's a vacuum."

Doc backed away and found the grate belonging to a small air vent. He spoke softly to Dr. Kay. "Bet you didn't know that first communication lines on ships were just pipes that ran from the bridge to the engine room. They were low tech, but they always worked." He began tapping the grate.

"That's no good, Doc." Malone eased herself away from Doc's legs. "Even if they hear you, Rykoff won't open the hatch. He won't take the chance that Node One is contaminated."

Doc ignored her. He concentrated, tapping the way he remembered.

* * *

In the service module, Rykoff heard the metallic pings first.

"Silence!" He transferred his pistol to his right hand and grabbed up a flashlight with his left. He swept the walls looking for the place where he heard pings originate. In his beam the faces of his Russian technicians were pale. He ignored them and concentrated his effort. But the pinging stopped.

Radio static filled his ears as one of the technicians again tried to raise the man Rykoff had sent outside. But Rykoff had already reasoned that the effort was useless. The man had broken contact. That meant he was dead. Rykoff ordered the radio be shut off.

The pings resumed. Rykoff traced their origin to his left and pinpointed a hand-sized ventilation port in the floor. He stooped to listen but kept his eyes and pistol on the technicians. The pings came in a pattern that brought back memories from his boyhood. He understood them.

"Open the hatch to Node One."

* * *

Malone realized too late what Doc was sending. She told herself her brain was fuzzy or she'd have stopped him earlier. She launched herself at him anyway. But by that time the hatch was already opening from the other side, and flashlight beams were already invading the semi-darkness.

"Put your hands above your heads and freeze." The voice was eerily calm. Hearing it Malone stopped in her tracks. Raising her hands sent splinters of pain into her ribs and doubled her over. Doc caught her in his good arm.

"Who sent the Morse code?" Rykoff stepped into view holding an automatic pistol. "It was kind of fun."

"I sent it," Doc said.

Rykoff ignored him and moved his flashlight. Malone was blinded as he shined it directly into her eyes. "I was hoping it was you, Malone."

"Bite me, Rykoff."

Rykoff swept his flashlight across Doc and Dr. Kay. "I see you're not all here."

"Bastard!" Dr. Kay moved fast, but not fast enough to keep Doc from restraining her. That was too bad, Malone told herself. Rykoff might have shot her and ridden himself of the only scientist who might have been able to control Bell

Tower as a weapon. This time Dr. Kay was holding back her tears. Maybe that was a good thing. Maybe given a chance, Dr. Kay would have another go at him.

"I want to make a deal, Rykoff," Doc said.

"I'm listening."

"Isolation is breached. You don't have a way out."

"Cut to your proposal."

"I take a radio and go outside. I find you a way out."

"That's been tried. We've not heard back from the man we sent."

"He probably ran away. I won't."

"Why is that besides your touching concern for Dr. Waterstone?"

"Why is because of the other part of the bargain. I find you a way out. You let me look for the kids."

"The way out comes first."

"Agreed." Doc took the flashlight handed him.

"Keep in mind that I'm not feeling patient just this moment. If I don't hear from you very, very shortly, I'll shoot Malone." Rykoff angled his flashlight into Malone's eyes again. She closed them and shot him the finger. She waited for him to start shooting. Instead he remained calm. "I won't shoot her all at once of course. I'll do it in pieces. And then I'll do the same thing to Dr. Waterstone."

The flashlight left Malone's face. She opened her eyes in time to see Doc enter the air lock.

Chapter Twenty

When Doc had been outside only five minutes, Rykoff lowered his hand radio and looked at Dr. Kay. "How long does incubation take?"

"It can take a while," she lied. "Let me talk to Doc."

Rykoff hesitated, then handed the radio to her. She cradled it against her face, and yelled. "Run! Find the kids. Find the…"

Rykoff put a hand over her mouth and wrenched the radio out of her hands. He twisted her arm enough to make her squeal with pain, and as he did, he pressed the send button on the radio. "Are you still with us, Dr. Tech?"

"I'm here. I want to know that Dr. Waterstone is okay."

"She's fine for now." Rykoff turned to Dr. Kay. "Let's try it again. How long exactly?"

Dr. Kay looked at the floor. She felt Rykoff hover over her. His voice was calm again.

"Your own team was in the crater twenty minutes before they began to die. We can assume they were not contaminated before the crater. So contamination and incubation and death was between zero and twenty minutes." He raised Dr. Kay's chin in his hand. He was rough. "I'll wait twice twenty minutes just to be safe. That will delay things for your children, won't it?"

"Five minutes." Dr. Kay spat the words at him. "My guess is five minutes."

Rykoff let go of Dr. Kay's face. He used the radio. "Are you still at the air lock, Dr. Tech?"

Doc answered affirmative. Dr. Kay listened for any sign in Doc's voice that he knew what was coming. She did know what was coming because she understood how Rykoff did business.

"Move due east toward the landing strip," Rykoff ordered.

"That wasn't our agreement." Doc's voice mixed with static.

"Move east, Doctor. Or I begin shooting."

Dr. Kay watched Rykoff raise his pistol toward her face. But in an instant, he changed his target to Malone. She heard him cock the hammer.

"Moving east." Doc's radio voice sounded distant.

"What do you see?"

"Blasted earth. All of the fences are down. So is the microwave array. I can see some of your people ahead, alive and moving. There's what looks like a C-130 Hercules parked the airstrip."

"Right on time." Rykoff lowered his pistol, then his radio. He took a sigh of relief, handed Dr. Kay the radio, and walked toward the hatch. She fumbled with the send button, then jammed it open.

"Doc! Can you see the safe lab module?"

There was no answer.

"Doc?" Dr. Kay pleaded.

"It's gone." Doc's voice sounded further away. "I don't see any wreckage. It's just gone. The crater is gone too, like it never existed. Looking southwest, I see nothing but flat earth. In places the soil is fused to glass."

Dr. Kay dropped the radio and shook with sobs. She felt Rykoff touch the top of her head, and she launched herself at him. This time a technician caught her in his grip.

"You already knew it was gone, didn't you, Victor?" Malone spoke up.

"I lost a man finding that out."

"You're a bigger bastard than I thought."

Rykoff ignored her and turned to Malone."Get up, Malone. You've got some walking to do."

Ten minutes later Dr. Kay, Doc, and Malone sat under guard beneath the left wing of a C-130 Hercules. The rain pounded the Russian guarding them. The downpour was hard enough to shroud what was left of the Bell Tower complex. Just above the sound of the shower, Malone heard the distant crackle of automatic weapons fire. She glanced north toward the jungle and saw a weapon burst in the dark between the trees. Then silence. Malone knew what she was seeing. The airstrip was under attack, but from whom?

Looking at Dr. Kay and Doc, Malone told herself that for the first time, the two of them looked old. It wasn't in their bodies. It was in their eyes and faces. It wasn't her first time seeing the look, and the two of them weren't the first she'd seen bear it. It was the kind of look that came from knowing you were beaten and had no choices left. Malone didn't plan on ever looking old like that. She didn't plan on running out of options.

She studied what she could see of the C-130, starting with the left cockpit window. The pilot's shadow was moving just inside the glass. She reasoned that he was going down a check list. Every now and then, the pilot's shadow shifted, and she could follow the direction of his attention toward the Russians rolling fuel drums to the plane one by one. Fuel was being pumped into the wing tanks. Malone studied the aircraft decals. The red markings on the tail and the blue markings on the fuselage were visible. U.S.A.F. was clearly visible. So was NEW YORK AIR INTERNATIONAL GUARD.

The plane was stolen, Malone told herself. She knew that the New York Air Guard flew in and out of McMurdo station in Antarctica. That meant Rykoff would be flying south, across the Antarctic to McMurdo. Then he'd fly north to island hop the Pacific to Asia. Malone did the math and told herself that Rykoff would have to land and refuel at least once between Crash Site Alpha Bell Tower and McMurdo. He'd probably refuel in Tierra del Fuego, where he could pay the officials to look the other way. In McMurdo he'd have to play it straight.

In McMurdo Malone would have a chance.

And if not in McMurdo, she'd have another at the next stop. She did the math again and came up with New Zealand, where Christchurch was the southernmost landing field. She'd have a second chance in Christchurch. But then where?

More automatic weapons fire reached her ears. This time it came from the jungle toward the south. Malone saw the pilot's shadow frozen against the cockpit glass. His head tilted to hear the distant shooting, followed by a pause. She asked herself again who was drawing the gunfire. The answer came to her instantly. It had to be the Jivanos! At the sound of more gunfire, the pilot's shadow left the cockpit window.

Malone considered her options. She'd have to make her break in Tierra Del Fuego, have to reach a phone, and have to make one call to a very private number in D.C. Destruction of the C-130 in the air would follow. It would have to be total. It could be done over the Antarctic, where temperatures would keep the contents away from humans and frozen all year long. Malone liked what she was thinking. There was still a chance she could get her job done.

Sudden mechanical noise interrupted Malone's train of thought. The rear cargo hatch of the C-130 lowered to the ground. A tall, blond man in a U.S. Air Force flight suit descended and turned toward the wing. His eyes were hard. Malone knew those eyes well. His accent was flawless midwestern America.

"Hello, Malone."

"Hello, yourself, Putin. I see you're still keeping bad company."

"Bad company pays better." Putin shrugged and took cover under the wing. A Korean followed behind him. The Korean was nervous, as if he were waiting for something. The something arrived a minute later, crates marked "Medical supplies, perishable, and fragile." Malone knew that what was in the crates was neither perishable nor fragile.

"After you, Malone." Rykoff was suddenly standing over her and gesturing. He held a pistol.

Malone limped up the ramp ahead of Doc and Dr. Kay. The cargo bay was subdivided into compartments, the most aft of which was fitted with double rows of airline seats. Just inside the massive rear hatch, the Korean was bent over the crates and removing their covers. Inside the crates the tops of the steel dewars were visible, all shrouded in frozen water vapor. The Korean closed the crates. Putin's men moved them forward into what Malone guessed was a storage compartment. Bulldog climbed up the ramp and talked to Rykoff.

"The job is done," Bulldog said. "Where's the rest of my bloody money?"

"In the bank you chose."

"There aren't enough copters left to fly everyone out." Bulldog eyed the rows of airline seats.

"Some of you will just have to travel on foot."

As if on cue, another burst of automatic weapons fire reached Malone's ears. This time she counted several weapons being fired. The gunfire mixed with distant shouting.

"Here that lovely sound, my china?" Bulldog moved close to Rykoff. "The bloody wogs got out of their little prison in the dark. They've been harassing the boys and doing a bang-up job of it. Who's supposed to stay behind and end up with a shrunken head, eh?"

"That's your decision. It's why you get paid the big bucks."

Bulldog smiled and unslung his weapon. He departed the cargo ramp as the Korean said something in Russian to Rykoff. Rykoff nodded his approval and raised the rear hatch.

Five minutes later the C-130 was airborne. Malone was seated in the aft compartment with Doc and Dr. Kay. All of them were handcuffed to their seats. Noise from the rear hatch made it difficult to talk, but Malone was sure it was not the noise that was keeping Doc and Dr. Kay silent. She knew nothing would ease their pain.

Beneath Malone's window flat and scorched earth stretched toward the distant forest. She checked her landmarks. She was over the Bell Tower crater. But the crater was gone. In places there were shimmering reflections where the earth had fused into glass. The C-130 passed over it quickly and reached the forest. And just as quickly, the forest disappeared beneath clouds. The sun was on her left. Malone was satisfied that the plane was heading south. She thought of Tierra Del Fuego, her escape, and the phone call. Her left hand was free. She tested the cuff that held her right. Picking the lock would be easy.

She told herself she had lots of time, probably hours until Tierra Del Fuego. The opposition would be tired. She counted their numbers in her head. Putin had a copilot, the Korean, and three other men. Rykoff had two additional men, both Russians. Hopefully they'd all be tired, and she'd be rested. Malone changed her mind when Rykoff entered the aft compartment accompanied by one of the Russians. The tray in the Russian's hand held one syringe, a vial, and a tourniquet.

"I regret this." Rykoff filled a syringe and milked the needle. "But I can't spare anyone to watch you. And I can't have any problems. I'm sure you understand."

No one answered. Malone cursed under her breath. Rykoff turned in her direction and tightened a tourniquet around her arm. Her brain screamed at her to resist, but she felt the Russian's pistol against her head.

"You're first, Malone. Pleasant dreams."

Chapter Twenty-one

For H.I. consciousness came and went. Images floated in his brain. There was a steel surface and terrible cold. He remembered dying with his skin rotting off and his lungs exploding outward through his mouth. April was gone, but he had not been alone. A thousand eyes had been with him, alien eyes probing him.

It had to be a bad dream. His brain said it was. Dreams were like that. Things came and went without logic. But in dreams there was no real pain, cold, or touch. Yet he'd felt all of those things. So it couldn't be a dream. And maybe it didn't even matter. The steel was gone. So were the cold and the pain.

Something soft and pliable rippled under him as if he were floating. It was warm underneath him, pleasant and rippling like the surface of a pool reflecting golden sunshine. The warmth touched his skin like the air of a summer day. He wanted it to go on forever.

His brain told him it was the first day of vacation.

He kept his eyes closed. He was twelve years old, and he was lucky that falling asleep on a raft in the backyard pool had not gotten him drowned. He noticed he had gotten water in his lungs. When he breathed he felt the liquid spew out of his mouth. He should be choking, but he wasn't. That didn't make sense. And anyway, he didn't really remember that he'd ever fallen asleep while floating in Dr. Kay's backyard pool. Maybe he was living it all over again. He was twelve and floating while waiting for April.

Only April would not be coming. Neither would Dr. Kay. It would be Doc coming to talk to him. He would be coming to tell him things that no twelve-year-old would want to hear. Doc and Mom would be calling it quits. But it would all be for the best. There would be summers with Mom in New York, and academic years in Bethesda with Doc. But learning the news of his parents' divorce wouldn't be the worst thing that would happen to him in that pool.

April would begin to come to the pool less often, because more and more she would be in the house on the phone. Or she would be at the end of the driveway leaning into a car window talking to a guy old enough to drive. There would follow more than one guy at the end of the driveway. And all them would be making the same mistake, thinking she was older than she actually was. She would grow to have the height and the curves, and maybe they would not even care how old she was. Maybe each of them would just want to see how lucky he could get. But she would never get in the car with any of them. That would be a violation of the rule Dr. Kay would make for her. But neither the rule nor her behavior would matter. The rumors would start anyway. The guys would tell stories. Each would be privately mad at her because he would know his own story was a lie but would think everyone else's was true. And the girls would believe everyone. They would grow to hate her, and they would conspire to spread even more stories behind her back.

Meanwhile H.I. would treasure every second April would give him. But it would only be a matter of time before they would both be fourteen. Then they would be together in the pool one last time. That day they would splash, and he would chase her. This last time he would catch her, and she would slip into his arms with their faces only inches apart. He would look into her soft face and liquid eyes and think of an angel. Then he would kiss her, and she would let him without kissing him back. Instead she would look at him with eyes red because of what she would be telling him. Things weren't going to be like this between them. He was her best friend, and he would always be her best friend.

Their best friendship would be with them in name only until a day at the water fountain that would arrive a year later. She'd turn and see him with the others, and the hurt would be in her face. And for once she would not shoot the finger at the crowd pestering her. Instead and for the first time in her life, she would run away crying.

And sometime long afterward, Vernon Clayfield would pull him into the headmaster's office and order him into the hot seat facing all of Clayfield's autographed photos taken with senators and congressman and the Beltway powerful. Clayfield would be smiling while telling him that he was no longer welcome at Adams Day School. Clayfield would be unwilling to understand that it was all Doc's doing. Not that H.I. would care about Adams Day. But he would care very much that he would no longer be anywhere near April Waterstone.

H.I. floated in oblivion and told himself life was all a dream. Everything with April was a dream. So too were

Raymond Marsden, 1999 RM, and Object Alpha Bell Tower. None of them existed. All of them were the product of a dream he was having after falling asleep in Dr. Kay's backyard pool. He was twelve, and the life he had ahead of him was not the one his brain was remembering. He was twelve and floating in a pool and waiting for April.

He felt her slip into the pool and climb onto the float next to his. He smelled her hair and tanning oil, sweet and close. He opened his eyes and reached for her.

There was no April, and he wasn't twelve.

Formlessness stretched into infinity. He shut his eyes and tried to make it go away. It had to be a nightmare. But nightmares went away when you opened your eyes. And nightmares did not come with real pain.

The pain came back to him instantly, fire tearing through every inch of skin with the pulsing of every heart-beat. He reached for his face and touched raw bone. Dead flesh peeled off in his hands. The bellow that reached his ears was terrified beyond all rational thought. It was his own.

Consciousness went mercifully away.

But somehow H.I.s thoughts continued. As if in a dream. The Bell Tower lifeform was a micro-life. Its intelligence was collective, spread across billions of viral-sized creatures, each carrying its own bits of information and each helping the whole intelligence to process thought. The Bell Tower lifeform built a spacecraft that mirrored its own form. Their spacecraft carried it across the stars, so it could farm life and pull weeds on far-away worlds.

H.I. knew that he was dreaming. And in his dream, he saw April. Not the April he'd always known. This April was in the full of womanhood and more beautiful than ever, eyes filled with wisdom and courage. Her eyes were behind glasses and leveled on a gathering of great leaders and great learned. Some were listening. Some were not. And suddenly all of them were gone. Just as suddenly, she was young again. She was dressed in shorts and t-shirt. She stood dirty and angry from the ordeal in the rain forest. Her voice echoed over and over in his head.

Bugs don't think. The virus is only the how.

H.I. watched the end of the dinosaurs. Their end came with the massive object that impacted the narrow finger of land between the great northern and southern continents. The shock wave took away the sky and filled it with floating bits of earth and billions of Bell Tower lifeforms. The dinosaurs died with their skins eaten from their bones. Their remains were consumed and recycled into the smaller, smarter lifeforms that were already changing. Some sank deep, where they would compress into the fuel. They were making way for humankind.

It was all part of a plan. Every step staged. Like the birth of the universe itself. Out of something other than chance had come time, matter, energy, and the forces that had them form worlds. Life had followed, its building blocks complex and precise and complimentary. Not merely the collisions of random molecules. All linked by common genes. Brought into existence with purpose. Nothing by chance.

Bell Tower's tiny creatures were elemental and advance life all at once. They were not the why.

Not the why but the how.

More likely just a part of the how. Maybe they were collectively a wandering farmer. Maybe visiting worlds to pull weeds and tend life. Or maybe like humans they were arrogant and forgetful of their place.

H.I. understood. Marsden came to him and led him to other scientists crowding a blackboard. The others were arguing and calling each other names. Marsden shook his head, raised a finger to his busted face, and smiled through broken teeth. Sharp bone pieces poked through the skin of his hands. H.I. followed Marsden's gaze to the blackboard and the same words scribbled over and over.

Extinction. Evolution.

Life could not have evolved on Earth, a bald scientist with thick glasses argued. The Earth was too young, only 4.5 billion years old. The time between the Earth's own birth and the appearance of one-celled life was too short to be explained by evolution. Evolution began in outer space, he insisted. A second scientist with a pocket calculator said life evolved on Earth from a primordial soup, new genes arising by accident and building new lifeforms. Marsden told them both they were wrong, told them they weren't even scientists.

The blueprint for all life and evolution was already in place in a grand genetic code, Marsden said. Evolution happened as the need arose. Genes for evolutionary change were already conceived and in place and waiting. They were not random. They were not an accident. They were part of a grand plan.

Einstein stepped beside Marsden. It was the same Einstein who looked over H.I.'s observatory from a wall poster. Same crazy hair and worn-out sweater and tired eyes. He stepped out of the poster and looked into the substance of genetic codes and proteins. He looked at atoms and then subatomic particles. All the while he scratched on the blackboard playing with the calculations thought to explain the locations of the smallest bits of matter in existence. But the calculations predicted chaos instead of the reality he could clearly see. Reality was not chaos. It was the harmony of the cosmos. He put down his chalk. He was humbled. He spoke what he felt.

God doesn't play dice with the world.

Einstein and the others vanished. The blackboard faded into stars, and Raymond Marsden stood healed. His injuries were all gone. He was young again, his eyes filled at last with peace. He looked in H.I.'s direction and went away forever, into a place more beautiful than H.I. knew he could ever imagine.

Consciousness came back a second time.

The pain was less this time, just a dull ache. H.I. sat up and hollered at the top of his lungs. All he heard was a whisper. He touched his face with trembling hands and he found intact flesh. He pried his eyes open.

A milky haze stretched across the dark.

Brilliant particles diffused back and forth in liquid streams, some misting down and feeling warm where they touched him. He looked at his hands. The dead tissue was replaced by large stretches of healing skin, pink-red and glistening in silvery sweat. The same silvery liquid hung as a vapor in the mist.

He realized it was hard for him to think. He found the pulse in his neck but muddled the rate while trying to count it. It was over a hundred and fifty. He forced his brain to clear and tried to figure where he was. For sure he was not in the lab module. He was sitting on a soft surface of some sort. The surface was sloped, but he couldn't figure the angle. His head was still spinning.

A moan came from his back. He turned and found April.

She was asleep on her back with her arms outstretched above her head as if welcoming the world. Her face and throat were healing in pink patches. She was still wearing the T-shirt that she'd bought from the old Indian in Villa Lobos. It read "I love New York" with a big heart. How long ago had that been? H.I. didn't know. He watched her almost stir. Then she sighed and slipped back into serenity, lids relaxed and breathing soft.

"Come on, Baby. Wake up." He nudged her gently. "Come on, Honey."

Then he stopped himself. Had he actually called her *Baby* and *Honey*? He had no right. She'd hate him for it.

He nudged her again, stroking the side of her face.

"Wake up, April. Open those angry blue eyes."

No response. She was still deep asleep. He leaned his face against hers and whispered into her ear. He shook her harder. Still nothing. And then he began to kiss her cheeks, her hair, her neck. He placed his face against hers and held it there, then kissed her full on the mouth. He kissed her until he felt her move.

"What are you doing, Tech?"

"I'm just kind-of waking you up." He hated the sheepishness he heard in his voice.

"Really? Is that what that was?"

"Yes."

"Well, I'm awake now. So you can stop."

"Okay." He knew he sounded even more sheepish. He looked into her eyes expecting blue storms. But no storms were there. He started to pull away, but she reached up and cupped both of her slender hands around his face. She pulled him back to her and kissed him. He kissed her too—for a long time.

"Do you know where we are?" she asked.

"No." He had a very good idea where they were. But it wasn't time to share it yet.

"Do you remember anything?"

"I remember us being in the safe lab module. I remember the pressure door to isolation blowing open and then horrible things."

"As in pain and your skin rotting off while you watched?"

"Yeah, that too."

"And thousands of eyes looking down on you?" She shivered. He didn't answer her. She continued, "You thought it was just a dream, right?"

"It had to be just a dream."

"Wrong. Look behind you."

He turned to see that the soft floor underneath him sloped into the dark. Above him it climbed into a misty light. The light penetrated walls, all of them gelatinous and moving. Inside the walls silver liquids pulsated though tubules.

"You and I both know where we are," she said.

"We can't be sure."

"I'm sure." She massaged her head, like she was in pain. "We're in Bell Tower, aren't we?"

He nodded. She massaged her temples. Watching her, he worried about a head injury, asked her if she was okay. She answered, "It just felt like electricity going right through my skull."

"I felt it too." He lied for her sake.

The surface underneath them seemed firmer. They stood, and April leaned into him with her arm around his naked waist. They started to climb. Suddenly the surface under them became terraced into steps. They climbed more easily until April suddenly shook again, this time almost collapsing. H.I. held her up.

"That felt like I was putting a finger in a socket."

"Do you still feel it?"

"No. But there were two jolts that time." She added, "My head really hurts."

"Just lean on me."

They climbed the steps to the top of a crest that opened inside a big chamber. The walls were transparent. Inside them luminescent fluids of every color he could imagine seemed to be pulsing. The fluids were transporting something he thought. Squinting, H.I. thought he could see particles swimming as the fluids pulsed. They were being fed into a plexus of massive silver membranes in the center of the chamber. The plexus of membranes changed shape constantly as if it were flesh. And all at once, H.I. knew he'd been wrong. April had said all along that bugs don't think. But no one had listened to her, not him, Dr. Kay, or Doc. All of them had been wrong. April was right.

"Bell Tower isn't a spaceship, is it?" April massaged her temples.

"No. It's not a spaceship."

"I know what it is." Sweat formed in silver beads on her face. She turned to face him. "Bell Tower itself is alive."

The lidless eyes came from nowhere, in clusters on all sides of them. They were unblinking and ovoid. They were alien.

Chapter Twenty-two

"Don't move."

"Not going to," April answered.

The eyes were impenetrable. Plasma fed into them from the walls. The plasma was filled with something small and particulate and moving. H.I. knew he was seeing the alien's flesh. He knew that the something moving within the tubules was its blood, brilliant colors in some tubes, but mostly silver and metallic. Dr. Kay and the others had seen but hadn't understood. The swarms of spheres they'd observed under the electron microscope had not been viruses. They'd been blood cells, blood cells that could carry out the will of their alien organism.

"Why aren't we dead?" April whispered.

"I don't know."

He was telling the truth. The alien blood was now inside them. Of that he was certain. The alien blood could have killed them already, infiltrated their human cells, unlocked dormant genes, and turned them to mush in a mix of every digestive enzyme and toxin found among Earth life. That's what it had started to do to them. But instead it had taken away the pain and begun healing them. Why was truly unknown.

H.I. looked at April. The pink healing areas in her flesh were becoming smaller at an accelerated rate, in essence healing as if there had never been injury. They were both healing – being healed actually- at an impossible rate. He looked back into the alien eyes and sensed that he and April were also being studied. H.I. stared back with equal intensity as he considered what he thought he knew.

The alien lifeform called Bell Tower was carbon-based like Earth life. Its blueprint was DNA, like Earth life. But Bell Tower could feed on cosmic rays, mix them with anti-matter in its gut, and produce energy. It could navigate between stars and alter its form. And somewhere in its form was an intelligence and purpose that could manipulate the genes of any lifeform in its path.

Bell Tower had absorbed the energy of the nuclear weapon. It had gutted the lab module like a tin can and dragged the wreckage into the crater where it reached inside to pluck April and him out and reverse the damage its blood had started. It had other plans for them.

April suddenly wobbled. He held her and told her to stay still.

"I can't. My head's wrong. Like little shocks."

"It'll go away."

"No. It's starting to really hurt."

The alien eyes clustered and focused on her. Flesh moved toward the two of them, flowing in a slow wave like liquid. H.I. began inching the two of them backward.

"We get out slowly," he said.

He looked over his shoulder. The passageway was gone, replaced by moving alien flesh. There was nowhere to go. The alien flesh tensed into ridges and began to absorb the luminescent mist. All that remained were its eyes, inhuman in the dark, like a zoo at night.

"It doesn't make any noise." April was starting to lose her footing, and H.I. realized she was dizzy. Her voice drifted and her eyes closed. "It doesn't have a smell. Maybe it can't hear."

The alien's flesh tensed again, then relaxed slowly. It inched closer on all sides, extending tentacles. The tentacles were smooth and formless. They snaked forward.

"Freeze." H.I. held her. "Don't move a muscle."

Their reflection came back at them from the glassy surfaces of the alien's eyes, and H.I. saw himself and April holding each other powerlessly. The first tentacle touched H.I.'s leg and began to slither up it. A second tentacle touched April and curled around her. She didn't look down.

"It's touching me, isn't it?"

"Don't move."

The tentacles were cold and formless. The alien flesh constricted until it was only feet away. The pulsations became more rhythmic. Each pulse sent fluid through eyes fixed on April. And then she had her first seizure.

Her eyes rolled back in her head. Her limbs and body thrashed. H.I. held her and tried to keep her from hurting herself. She sank her teeth into him, frothy saliva mixing with his blood and dripping silver-yellow down his arm. April thrashed for less than a minute, then lay unconscious in his arms.

The alien eyes watched her.

H.I. thought of pounding its eyes with his fists. They shifted toward him for a second, and underneath them alien flesh opened into vertical cracks like the gill vents on a fish. The cracks enlarged as tall as a human and sucked air inward through fine horizontal filaments.

"Make it stop." April rolled her eyes half open. "It's in my head."

"Do you know where you are?" H.I. expected her to be disoriented and confused.

"In Bell Tower!" She wasn't confused.

He hesitated to ask the next question, but he needed to know. The victims of grand mal seizures were prone to become incontinent. He asked her.

"What? No!" More silver-yellow sweat formed on her face. Her breathing seemed fast.

He told he'd seen her lose consciousness, thrash, and salivate. In essence, he'd seen her have a seizure of some sort. That meant aberrant electrical activity in brain cells. But seizures like hers only occurred when the activity fired across large networks of cells including the networks the controlled continence. Hers hadn't. Hers had been selective. It had been purposeful.

"This thing did this to me!"

The alien vents vibrated. Its eyes watched her. H.I. tried to pull away a tentacle. It tightened. He turned to face April as tentacles pulled her toward the eyes. Once more her eyes drifted back in her head, and she collapsed in the alien's grip. She seized a second, third, and fourth time.

"Leave her alone! You'll kill her."

Beneath the alien's eyes, the human-sized vents opened still more and then vibrated. As they did so, April woke again, but wasn't strong enough to stand. H.I. reached as far as he could, barely able to touch her with the tips of his fingers. She choked, "Electricity. It's going on and off like a light switch."

Her words echoed in his memory, bringing to mind something he'd once seen. An experiment of some kind, he thought. But the mere thought of April being subject to an experiment drove him to frenzy. With all of his strength, H.I. dug his thumbs into the tentacle gripping his legs, twisting it in rage as he might the head of a snake from its body. The tentacle broke his grip, tightened, and slithered around his trunk. It squeezed, and the wind left his lungs. Lights danced in his graying vision, and he felt the world going away. He collapsed in the alien's grip, as just out of his reach April went into another seizure.

She continued thrashing. He had no strength left to reach for her. Somewhere at the edge of consciousness his mind began to flood with images. There were men in uniforms administering electric shocks to prisoners to break down their resistance and make them talk. The shocks were measured and meant to extract information. As such the shocks were a form of communication, a form of questioning. The shocks were either on or off.

"Electricity. It's going on and off like a light switch."

The words repeated themselves in his head as he watched her from the edge of blackness. More images flooded into his brain. A war was raging. On one side, a young German was building machine that could store memory in the form of either a yes or no displayed in lights. Relays were either open or closed.

The tentacles relaxed their grip. Air surged back into H.I.'s chest. He tried to lift his head but couldn't. He grappled with what his mind was trying to tell him. But it was beyond his reach. April was beyond his reach too. She wasn't seizing anymore. She was lying inert in the Alien's grip. She seemed a million miles away.

Another image invaded his brain. The war came back. He saw an estate in the English countryside. Men and women in uniform hovered around metal panels packed with cables and switches. They called it Colossus. It talked to them on paper. Its internal switches were either on or off. H.I. tried to drive the image out of his mind. He was going to die while April seized just out of his reach, and his mind was flooding with images from the science channel and the history of computers 101. He fought to clear his head. And then he knew what his mind was trying to piece together.

"Binary language, it's binary language. It's fricking zeroes and ones like computers use."

"I know what binary language is." April was conscious again.

"It's trying to talk to you."

"I'm not a damn computer."

The alien's flesh moved closer. Its eyes turned black and cold. H.I. tried to peel the tentacle from his belly. But another one slithered upward to his throat and squeezed enough to make him stop. April seized again and crumpled into the alien's grip. The tentacles held her out of H.I.'s reach.

"Breathe, Baby!" H.I. yelled at her. "Please let me see you breathe."

"H.I.," she moaned. "It didn't hurt that time."

"Hold on, April. I'm coming for you." But she was out of his reach. More tentacles rose around his chest. But they let him breathe.

"H.I.," she struggled to speak. "It talked to me."

"Did it use words?"

"No, not words. It talked in pictures." In the dim light, her eyes almost seemed black. There was terror in them.

"It's pissed. This thing is very pissed!"

Chapter Twenty-three

Rykoff glanced across the cold tarmac of Tierra Del Fuego a last time. The refueling was nearly complete. He left Putin in the cockpit of the C-130 Hercules and slipped through the crew's quarters. He found the North Korean, Park, standing at the locked hatch to the right forward storage compartment. Park asked the same question he'd already asked twice. "Are you sure they are dormant?"

"Completely." Rykoff tried to control his impatience. He swept Park aside and looked through the hatch window. Ten steel dewars were locked inside and lined in rows angled ninety degrees from the bulkhead. From the compartment hatch window, they almost looked like milk cans. But the biohazard labels made that comparison impossible.

"The temperature is minus one hundred ninety?" Park asked it again.

Rykoff didn't answer. He stared at the water vapor beading on the sides of the dewars. Slope-faced cryo-cell units were fitted on top, numbered and positioned so that their LED data could be seen from the hatch window. But their visibility was mere backup. The primary data relay went by telemetry to a laptop sitting on a secured table in the crew quarters behind the cockpit. The temperature inside the dewars was minus 190. At that temperature no biochemical processes could occur. Life was frozen in state.

Rykoff avoided Park's gaze. It made Rykoff angry that his battered face seemed not to affect the North Korean. "Are you satisfied, Mr. Park?"

The Korean took a turn at the hatch window. "Yes."

"I'd tell your people to be damn careful how they test that virus, Mr. Park."

Park ignored him and counted the dewars while whispering to himself. He muttered, "ten."

"Nine," Rykoff corrected him coldly. "The tenth is mine."

Park jerked his head away from the window. Rykoff addressed him slowly. "I'm not going to sell the tenth. I'm going to use it."

Blood left Park's face, and Rykoff could tell he was trying to process the full meaning of what he'd just heard. Seeing the shock in his face gave Rykoff a pang of pleasure. Putin entered the passageway before Park could answer.

"We're refueled," was all Putin said.

"Contact the tower and take off," Rykoff answered.

Rykoff moved aft by himself. He passed the lavatory and shot a glance at the special metal case waiting on the floor. The contents of the case would bring pain, but only temporarily. The pain would always be part of him. He moved beyond the galley and stepped into the tail portion of the converted cargo hold. The air became cold and wet. Rykoff knew it would get colder.

Beyond the double rows of airline seats, twenty feet of naked steel stretched to the massive vertical hatch. Even at sea level, the steel was beaded in water vapor. At twenty thousand feet, and in spite of the pressurization, the steel would give off a bitter draft. And the vibrations would be loud. But Rykoff didn't expect his passengers to be comfortable or talkative. He moved to the first row and studied them.

Malone lay crumpled and motionless with her unconscious face tilted toward the ceiling. Dr. Waterstone lay in the same condition with her head on Malone's shoulder and half of her face buried in black hair. Both women were handcuffed to their seats. Dr. Tech was across the aisle, moving unsteadily in his seat and already recovering from the injection. His gaze met Rykoff's for a second, but his eyes were unfocused.

Rykoff had expected the man to metabolize the drug faster than the women. In a way it was a mercy. Dr. Waterstone had things she wouldn't want to remember. And Malone had things she wouldn't want to anticipate. Rykoff gripped Malone's inert face in his hand. He considered changing his plan.

Maybe it would be better to open the hatch at five thousand feet and throw the two of them out. Malone would go first and then Dr. Tech. But Rykoff knew Dr. Tech was important to Dr. Waterstone. That made him the leverage that would be needed to make the very moral Dr. Waterstone do very immoral work for the North Koreans.

Rykoff thought of the two of them together, Doctors Waterstone and Tech. They were colleagues. But he knew they were also intimates. And the mere thought of them together sent rage surging through every muscle in Rykoff's body. But Rykoff knew he needed Dr. Tech alive. So he targeted his anger elsewhere.

He looked at Malone.

His hand slid down her face to her throat. He fought the urge to squeeze. Back in his bunker in the compound, he'd almost told her things about himself. Almost told her things she wouldn't believe, things no reasoning person could believe. He'd stopped himself short, felt his rage at being weak enough to talk to her, and punished her for almost hearing him. Then after the questioning conducted by Bulldog, he'd let her live.

Malone had value. The same people who were buying the virus would be very interested in talking to Malone. And before they were finished, she'd have a lot to say.

Rykoff let go of Malone's neck and let her head slip back against Dr. Waterstone's shoulder. As he did, two 4050 horsepower Allison turboprops thundered against the airframe on the right, joined within seconds by two more on the left. Putin's garbled voice spewed from the intercom.

"Tower's given us permission to take off. There's chop until about fifteen thousand feet, so fasten in."

Rykoff buckled himself in the second row, his eyes on the slumped heads of his passengers. As quickly as it had come over him, his rage was gone. Dr. Waterstone was part of the Bell Tower sale, Dr. Tech was leverage, and Malone had her own value. It was all just business. Rykoff smiled only inwardly. His nerve-dead face remained flaccid.

The C-130 began to taxi. Two Russian mercenaries entered from the galley and sat armed with .45 cal pistols. Seeing them, Rykoff reached for his face and found only rubbery, cold flesh. The move was instinctive, even after all the time that had passed.

Time! He'd almost told Malone how much time. That would have been a mistake. She wouldn't have believed him anyway. No one would.

Rykoff felt the C-130 taxi slowly and make a turn onto a runway. Wet, gray landscape slid passed the tiny windows. For a moment there was the sea, harsh, gray, and violent even in the Beagle Passage. Then the C-130 turned again, and outside of his window, the sharp, craggy peaks of Tierra Del Fuego, the land of fire, rose out of sight. He touched his face, and the hated memory came back like a torch.

They'd caught up with him in Sarajevo the day after the job. There'd been four of them, only one of them a Russian like himself. The other three had been Cossacks. The Russian had done the talking.

"This is a bad business, Victor."

The Russian had been soft spoken, almost restrained. The Cossacks had not been. In their baggy suits, they'd looked like chained attack dogs. They'd waited for the Russian to finish talking. "This is a very bad business, Victor, your people killing the Austrian and his wife."

"They ignored the recall."

"You ignored the recall, Victor. You pushed your people to do thc killing."

"Kids and fanatics don't need a push."

"You pushed them, Victor. You were supposed to be eyes and ears. Only eyes and ears! But you armed them with guns and bombs. You pushed them to do it." The Russian's eyes had been downcast, almost ashamed. "The Austrian's wife was pregnant. Did you know that?"

In fact Rykoff had not known. But knowing wouldn't have changed anything he'd done. So he hadn't answered the Russian.

"This business will go far beyond Belgrade and Vienna. We will all suffer."

Rykoff had answered with a smile. That had been the last mistake of his former life. The Russian had nodded to the Cossacks, and they'd produced lead pipes.

"I'm not going to kill you, Victor. I want to send a message. I want your face to be seen. It won't be handsome anymore. Your voice won't be persuasive to willing ears."

The Cossacks had stepped in with their lead pipes and done their work. Rykoff had expected lots of pain, but there'd been very little. He passed out in the first minutes. The pain had come later, lots of it.

Rykoff felt the pain every day, and he remembered.

The C-130 made a last turn and strained against its brakes as the engines roared in Rykoff's ears. The brakes were released and the plane began to lumber like an elephant, slowly picking up speed. Rykoff glanced at the Russian mercenaries. They sat impassively, as if their part of the job was over. That was a mistake. No job was ever over. There could always be repercussions.

The men who'd beaten Rykoff were long dead. Regretfully they were not dead by Rykoff's hand. So their descendants would pay. For the Cossacks paying would mean the obliteration of a village on the Don. For the Russian the retribution would come to a village in the Urals. In the old days, the world would never have known. But that was the old days. What Rykoff planned would probably be seen in real time on CNN. All over the world, there would be fear tampered by official lies. The real fear, the stone cold terror, would be only for those select few who knew the truth. Those few would be the occupants of small rooms in Washington and smaller rooms in Pyongyang.

Rykoff took his eyes off of the Russians. The C-130 left the runway at a shallow angle of climb. The big plane banked and turned gently south, throwing the city of Ushuaia under Rykoff's window. Streets lined with low structures climbed steeply from the rough bay, blending into mountainsides that rose to jagged, snow-covered peaks on three sides. All vanished as the plane climbed into the first layer of violent gray clouds.

At twenty thousand feet the plane leveled. Rykoff left his seat. In the forward passage, he stepped around Park. The Korean was still pressed to the cargo window, a notepad dangling in his hand. Rykoff made sure the lock on the compartment door was secure and stepped through the crew quarters into the cockpit.

Beyond the pilots and controls, an endless cloud bank hid the earth. The sky was brilliant blue. In the left seat, Putin lifted a headphone from one ear and turned to Rykoff. "There'll be questions in McMurdo. I don't think..."

"We aren't landing in McMurdo." Rykoff cut him off. "We'll refuel at Halley."

"Brits," Putin muttered. "That's a lousy little research station they have on the ice. Probably they'll have fuel, but I don't think they'll part with it."

"They will when I've talked with them." Rykoff told Putin what he planned and watched as Putin shrugged at the audacity and the simplicity of it.

Rykoff left the cockpit and found his way to the lavatory. The steel case and its contents were still waiting. He stared at the contents a full minute before beginning his work. He knew the pain would come on slowly, but also knew it was necessary. Rykoff reached for the first syringe.

Chapter Twenty-Four

The gunfire came from both sides in controlled bursts. Bulldog kept his head low and cursed Rykoff. The bastard had taken what he'd wanted from the pissing crater and left those who'd done the job for him to face the wogs. He wondered if worthy oriental gentleman was even a fit term for the bloody Jivanos Indians picking at his men from the woods. Didn't matter. He thought about Rykoff.

"Pissing back-stabber!"

An arrow whistled within an inch of Bulldog's ear and thudded into the Russian standing next to him. Gunfire followed as a half-dozen MP5s and one squad automatic weapon raked the jungle, hitting nothing but impenetrable green.

"Hold your bloody fire." Bulldog dropped to the mesh tarmac and crouched behind an empty fuel drum. "There's no pissing targets. Hold your fire!"

The order was ignored. The gunfire was joined by a volley of rocket propelled grenades that exploded inside the first line of trees. The dull booms echoed in Bulldog's ears and splattered the jungle with shrapnel. Bulldog yelled through the smoke. "Cease your damn fire!"

A last burst of automatic weapons fire erupted somewhere behind Bulldog's back. Then silence. He raised a radio to his ear and contacted the Cobra gunship hovering overhead. "Cop, this is Outfield. Can you see anything?"

"Nothing, Outfield."

Bulldog glanced at the Russian who'd fallen a meter away. The primitive arrow had hit the Russian in the shoulder but left him twisted and inert on his back with saliva foaming in his mouth. His face was blue, eyes open and glazed. The arrow was poisoned.

"Cop!" Bulldog barked into the radio. "I want you to lay down incendiary on the east edge of the strip. Cook the jungle."

"Copy, Outfield." The pilot's voice broke up in static. Bulldog knew there should not have been static. He was about to use his radio when an electronic hum rose in his ears and turned to a shrill whine.

Bulldog's first thought was that he was being jammed again, that the American jet was returning. He tilted an ear skyward and listened for the sound of jet engines. For a second he heard nothing but the rotors of the Cobra gunship. Then the shrill electronic hum came back. It went through Bulldog's ears like an ice pick. It heated the radio casing in his hand and singed his fingers. He dropped it.

The hum died into nothing and was drowned out by the blades of the Cobra gunship. Bulldog stared at the radio that was still too hot to hold. His first thought was that he'd been hit by an electromagnetic pulse of some kind. But from where?

The Cobra gunship roared overhead, giving Bulldog a brief view of its sleek fuselage, bubble canopy, and tandem pilots. A series of long, dull booms split the air, followed by a wave of tremendous heat as incendiaries lit the jungle. Bulldog shielded his face with a raised hand and moved east along the stacked drums.

The wall of fire swept across the entire eastern perimeter. At the drums the heat was intense. Bulldog kept low and ordered the Russians to do the same. He tried to hold the radio again. It was like holding something from a stove. He considered his position.

The wogs, the escaped Indians, had bloody positioned themselves on the high ground where they'd hidden in the bush. They'd already picked off four of the Russians. The thought of it filled him with rage, wogs with blowguns and bows picking off men with state-of-the-art automatic weapons! How many times in his life had Bulldog seen the same thing? The answer was a dozen different times in a dozen different third-world toilets. In the bush a wog was bloody invisible.

He peered east along the drums. The heat and the acrid smell of napalm stung his face and nostrils. He tasted it in his mouth, felt it on his skin. The wall of fire was a hundred yards away, and still it felt like it was in his face. That was good. His east flank would stay secure. So would the north and south, protected by the stacked drums. The west was open across two thousand feet of airstrip, creating a large killing ground if the wogs tried to come from the west. But Bulldog knew the wogs would bloody well not come.

The wogs would wait. Wogs had no sense of time. A wog measured life by the sun, the moon, and the season, and by the hunger and thirst in his belly. So the wogs would bloody wait. And their wait would be for nothing.

Bulldog told himself his evacuation would be over by nightfall. By then he would be drinking warm beer over the border in Columbia. He told himself he'd run the evacuation in shifts, move the Russians in groups to the east and cover them with the gunship. He'd fly them out in shifts using the one remaining Huey. The other Hueys were out of fuel or they'd suffered damage from the American bomb and the collapse of the crater.

Scattered bursts of gunfire came from the west end of the landing strip. Bulldog flattened and pressed binoculars to his face. He could see a half-dozen more Russians crouched among the wreckage of what had been five Hueys and a control tower. The Russians were firing wildly. Bulldog yelled, knowing he could not be heard.

"Stop! You'll hit the good Huey!"

He tried to the radio again. It was cooler to the touch. But as he raised it to his face, the static erupted in high frequency bursts. Bulldog dropped it and held his ears. He was sure he was being jammed. The static rose to a high-pitched whine, and the radio casing looked like it would crack open. The whine ended.

Sweat ran in rivulets down the hollow of Bulldog's back. Another electromagnetic pulse, he told himself. And no approaching jet to explain it. He stared skyward and saw his Cobra gunship hovering unsteadily over the west end of the strip. He told himself their avionics had to have been affected.

Another burst of gunfire erupted toward the west. He jammed the binoculars to his face and cursed as he saw the muzzle flashes on the west end of the strip. None of the distant figures were holding a radio. All of them were shooting at nothing.

The electronic hum came back. But another noise also rose in Bulldog's ears. In the distance the Cobra engine sputtered and died. Without power its blades slowly chopped air. Seven tons of machine fell to the Earth like a brick. The Cobra crashed on its fuel tanks, instantly crushing them, compressing and sparking their internal liquid-vapor interface. The Cobra went up like a bomb, showering the one remaining Huey and the Russians crouched underneath with flaming debris and engulfing them in dense black smoke. In the same instant, the Cobra's rocket pods went off like a fireworks display, smoke streams screaming into the jungle on all sides. The ammo joined in, banging like firecrackers.

Bulldog hugged the mesh and watched one of the Russians break clear of the smoke, flailing and screaming and running east toward Bulldog's position. The Russian dropped in his tracks, arrows protruding from his back. At his back the wreckage of the Cobra and the last Huey vanished in ugly black smoke.

We'll have to bloody walk out, Bulldog told himself.

Near his hand, his fallen radio began to whine again. Its internal antennae and melted circuitry were absorbing another electromagnetic pulse. The same pulse was surging through every metal in range. It rose to a series of high-pitch beeps that went like needles through Bulldog's ears. He slapped both hands to the sides of his head and tugged at the grenade ring he wore as an ear ornament. It was absorbing the energy. It was scorching his flesh.

The grenade ring heated like a poker and transferred the electric shock into the side of his head, twisting his face west. Bulldog writhed on the mesh, his muscles twitching from the current. He rolled his head in the direction where the crater had once been. There the flat ground that had replaced the crater began to move. It began to come apart in seams and angle upward like the edges of a popcorn package cooked on the stove. Wind came all at once and blinded him.

Then his vision cleared, and he saw what was rising out of the earth. He watched it climb into the sky and begin coming directly toward him. He held his ears, screamed, and heard nothing.

Chapter Twenty-five

H.I. saw that hundreds of alien eyes were fixed on April. The tentacles released their grip. In an instant they were all gone, as if they'd never existed. April let out a muffled cry, kicking and swiping at nothing.

"Is it gone?"

"No." The tentacles released H.I. and vanished. He reached for her, calling her name gently. She turned toward him, her eyes aiming at nothing and her hands wandering. She was blind.

"I've got you," he whispered.

"I can't see you. I'm seeing things in my head. Pictures."

She was calm as she spoke. Her face wandered but pointed nowhere. Beyond her the alien's eyes bunched in clusters. She smiled. The smile gave H.I. a chill.

"It's found a way to talk to me," she said.

He watched the alien eyes cluster like the eyes of an insect. He understood, or thought he understood. The alien had found the common denominator of higher animal brains on Earth. Higher animal lifeforms could see their environment. Visual images were a common message.

What was the first book given a human child regardless of its language? The answer was a picture book.

"Why me?"

"I don't know."

But H.I. did know, or hoped he knew. He remembered the images on Dr. Kay's laptop, photos of mother and daughter merged into one. Maybe Bell Tower sensed Dr. Kay's presence through her data entries. Maybe it sensed Dr. Kay's progeny was April. Or maybe it saw the two of them as one being.

"Oh, God! Something's changing."

"What, April?"

"It's so angry." Her face twisted with fear. "I feel things. Bad things. April hugged herself tightly. Her eyes wandered blindly. She stammered, "Violence and destruction."

"Why does it feel those…"

"No, H.I! It's not what it feels. It's what it sees." She sobbed, tears flecked with silver film. The alien blood was in her tears. It was in her blood and brain. It was manipulating her cells to release her own chemical transmitters and make pictures.

She continued, "It sees those things in us." She spoke a sudden calm. "It's moving. It's taking us."

He started to ask where. Where was a scary possibility. Where could be light years away, infinitely beyond their life spans. He thought of their dead, preserved bodies on display to a race of Bell Towers on some far away world.

"We're out of the crater." Fine silver sweat beaded on her forehead. "I see Russians on the ground everywhere. They're shooting. They're…oh, God!" She shut her eyes, buried her head in H.I.'s shoulder, and sobbed violently.

"What, April? What are you seeing?"

* * *

Bulldog ran without his weapon. He ran without crouching, leaving his torso fully exposed above the protection of the fuel drums. It didn't matter about the Indians and their poisoned arrows and darts. There was no room in his brain for them. In his mind there was only room for running from the thing. At his back the others were shooting at it.

The gunfire died before he reached the end of the fuel drums. A popping sound echoed from the fuel drums, and sparks stung his eyes. Another electromagnetic pulse. This one was massive, surging through every shred of metal within its range. It transmitted though the grenade ring in Bulldog's ear once more, heat searing his flesh, electricity contracting the muscles in the side of his head and twisting his neck sideways. It froze his arm before he could claw the ring from his ear. It knocked him to the ground.

He landed skidding and twisting in the mud and unable to move. The electricity went away and left him wailing at the top of his lungs. From a hundred yards away, the heat from the incendiaries stung his skin. He ignored it. His eyes were just above the mud, seeing what he did not want to see.

The Russians were all down, writhing from the burns inflicted by the massive pulse that had surged through the metal parts of their weapons and into their bodies. MP5s, M16s, and squad automatic weapons were scattered on the ground, metal parts red-hot, ammo clips and chambers firing rounds from the heat. Bullets whined across the landing strip and pinged into charred metal fuel drums. Grenades on belts exploded, hurling debris and bloody limbs skyward. Beyond the carnage Bulldog saw the thing coming from the sky.

It was shrouded in an ugly black cloud that moved ahead of it like a wind. It approached from where the crater had been. It moved like a huge living thing, hurling wreckage into the jungle and cleaning the face of the Earth. The shear angry force of it sucked the wind from Bulldog's lungs, dropped the air pressure around him, and ruptured the vessels in his nose and ears. Blood poured down his face. The pain howled in his head and went through his skull like an ice pick. Beyond the roaring inside Bulldog's head, the thing inside the cloud made no noise. It just hovered. It was silver and massive, and it was searching with thousands of eyes.

Bulldog's brain screamed at him to run, but his body wouldn't obey. He lay in the mud and waited for the end.

The silver thing hovered inside the black cloud, immune to the force it was unleashing against everything in its path. It reached the west end of the strip, and its skin began to expand. Silver-yellow mist descended to the earth and spread to the edges of the jungle. The mist rolled forward as if driven by muscle.

Bulldog pulled himself upright. Every muscle in his body fought him. He staggered backward toward the heat, trying to pull his eyes from the thing. It hovered as around it the black cloud began to send down rain. The silver mist spread faster, groping the earth as if it were alive and crawling across the terrain.

Bulldog ran harder, each of his steps sinking ankle-deep in mud. He hollered and put all of his remaining strength into his legs and lungs. He veered north away from the incendiaries. At the edge of the jungle, he heard the screams and turned.

The mist swallowed the airstrip to envelope the Russians writhing on the mesh. One of them staggered into view, screaming in agony. His head was buried in gloved hands. His hands fell away, and Bulldog saw blackened flesh drop off the exposed bones of his face.

Bulldog's shriek came by itself, rising in his throat and going beyond his pain. He sank into the mud and landed facing the sky, knowing his legs would no longer run. He waited his turn to die.

The howling stopped.

A new noise approached from the west, a soft sound, the gentle whir of air brushing around something big. Another sound joined in, wind compressed and moving through some sort of tunnel. It stirred the mud around him, making ripples in the water, brushing him with vapor. He looked skyward and watched the silver thing flatten and expand until it filled the sky. It floated like something gossamer, all of it silver and huge. It expanded as it absorbed the silver mist back from the earth.

Bulldog waited for the pain of his own skin rotting from his body. It never came.

The tunnel noise rose higher than the scream of a jet engine. It rose until he thought his head would burst. And then the thing was gone. It moved south and out of his vision. It accelerated into the sky, moving out of sight with the power of a rocket.

It left Bulldog alone and alive. The jungle noises came back.

Bulldog heard his own laugh rise to a hysterical pitch. The spasms carried into his chest. He was alive. He lay in the mud and let the laugh go on by itself, let the ordinary jungle noises take over his mind. Swarms of brilliant white birds moved into the trees. Their squawks joined the chirping of millions of insects and tree frogs. The smell of flowers and damp earth reached him. He was alive. He'd get out. The money from Rykoff was waiting for him.

Bulldog never heard their approach. He felt it, the hairs on his neck rising, the muscles in his back tensing with his little remaining strength. They were around him before he could move. Their squat brown bodies were naked except for loin clothes. Their round faces were painted to look fierce.

Every muscle in Bulldog's body froze. The terror rose in his chest. Stories echoed in his brain: That the Indians took the heads of enemy warriors killed in battle because the taking of heads was magic. That the magic would be celebrated with a feast of monkeys. That the Indian believed that the waking life was false and that the shrunken head of an enemy warrior would trap the warrior's avenging soul forever, giving power to its owner.

The darts made barely a sound as they came from all directions. Bulldog felt them bite his skin. Then nothing.

* * *

"It's taking us away."

April's eyes darted, driven by the images Bell Tower was putting in her brain. She hugged herself into a ball, rocking and trying to shut away something only she could see. Then she settled, face frighteningly calm, blue eyes empty.

"Where, April? Where's it taking us?"

"So many worlds." Her voice was soft. Silver tears ran down soft cheeks. She smiled and cried at the same time. "Thousands of beautiful worlds, all waiting. I can see them."

"Stay with me, April. Concentrate. Think."

"So beautiful." Her eyelids slid half-closed. "I can hear them singing. Can you hear them?"

"No, and you can't either. You can't hear shit." H.I. spun toward the alien. "Leave her alone. Get away from her."

Alien flesh quivered. April began to drift off. "Bye."

H.I. put his face against hers. "Fight it. Focus and listen to me."

April began to hum, and the alien quivered again, absorbing sounds and probably isolating every tone that came out of April's mouth. It was trying to make sense of human language.

"Leave her alone."

April's voice rose higher. Her face floated in the semi-dark, serene and angelic and framed in blonde hair. Alien skin vibrated with every sound she made. It quivered as it sent April's voice climbing like a soprano's.

"Get out of her head. You'll kill her."

The alien eyes locked on her, its skin vibrating faster. Her voice split the air, sustained itself in a note that emptied all of the air out of her lungs. The alien let her breathe. She collapsed against H.I., heart pounding in her throat.

Fine moisture formed around her lips, all of it flecked with silver.

"You've got to listen to me!" he yelled. "Concentrate on what I'm telling you. Push it out of your head. You have to."

She made babbling noises, baby-talk that drifted aimlessly. The alien listened with pulsating skin and drove her voice faster, then slower. Her face twisted painfully, then settled empty, as if nothing was left inside.

"Listen to me!"

Just empty blue eyes and more humming and rocking. Then her face twitched and broke into a sweat. She seemed to sense her surroundings.

"April, can you hear me?"

"Yes." Her eyes darted aimlessly. She was still blind. "I saw things, heard things."

"I know."

"No, you don't know. It's not in your head." She slipped her hand into his. Beads of alien blood formed on her skin. "The stuff in my head is what Bell Tower thinks of life on Earth. All life kills and feeds on other life. At the top, humans kill their own kind."

Evolution. Extinction.

H.I. looked into the alien's eyes. They were cold. He shifted toward April. "You've got to show it the other side of humanity. Fill your mind with images from your own life. Let it see what we are."

"It's already seen my life. It's seen yours too. It knows us better than we know ourselves. And it senses the same dark things everywhere. Even in you and me there's violence and destruction."

H.I. tried to think of a response. He couldn't. There was nothing he could say. All of humanity was two-sided. Even the kindest individuals harbored dark corners. No one was all good.

"This thing is going to do something." April's face was an inch from his. "It's going to do something terrible."

She turned her head unsteadily, maybe sensed the alien's eyes. By the hundreds they melted back into its skin. Two eyes remained. They were the size of angry headlights. They focused on April. Her head wandered aimlessly. "We're moving fast over the jungle."

"Where's the sun?"

"It's on our left."

"That means we're heading south."

"It's taking us where there is only cold."

Chapter Twenty-six

Rykoff sensed the violence even from twenty thousand feet. He imagined all of the forces that spun the planet from day to night and back again coming to bear on just six hundred miles of sea at the bottom of the world. The Drake Passage bore the combined weight hurled against it by both the Pacific and Atlantic. But it fought back. Like Rykoff, it would always fight back. It was perfection.

Rykoff pulled his face from the fuselage porthole, and for a second he saw a wisp of his reflection. The deep vertical scars were almost invisible. Ten minutes earlier, he'd injected them with collagen and then saline, filling them until they blanched. Without the injections and without the devices, his face was formless and crisscrossed by deep scars that retracted skin to crushed bone and fascia. The collagen swelled the creases outward, and the saline turned them to fine white lines. They were barely palpable under his fingertips. The saline effect would last only a day. More injections would follow.

He felt no pain from the long spinal needle. The skin of his face would never feel pain, never feel touch of any kind.

Not so with the crushed bones underneath. They always hurt, always felt as if the beating were still happening. They hurt worse with the devices. But the hurt drove him and gave him purpose. It made him better than others.

Rykoff stepped back into the lavatory, clicked the door shut, and faced the mirror. His hair was dyed blond in most places, steel gray in others. The contact lenses turned his eyes black, hiding his pupils. The effect was power and cruelty. He approved.

The black case was still open on the lavatory floor. He removed the prosthetic abductor devices and placed them on the counter next to the sink. The first one was small and made of two nearly identical parts of titanium coated with silicone. Each slid into what had once been a nostril. He inserted them without pain and saw a nose where there had been collapsed flesh.

He hesitated with the other devices. Under the skin and soft tissue of his mouth, they would create artificial cheeks, give him a jaw and the appearance of human teeth. They would even allow him to chew solid food. But the pain would be deep and continuous, hurting his crushed bones with every move.

He turned on the tensor lights and lifted the first device. It went inside his face like a precision-tooled part. The deep pain came immediately, and sweat formed down the small of his back. His chest and neck blushed with heat, and his pulse pounded in his head. He distracted himself thinking of the far greater pain he would inflict on the world.

He thought of the alien virus thawing from the tenth steel canister and sweeping through two villages, eating the flesh from the descendants of the men who'd broken his face. He thought of the North Koreans holding the other nine, a smoking gun they had not fired and could never fire. That realization gave Rykoff a wave of pleasure.

He studied his face, felt the stubble of his beard with the back of his hand. In another few hours, the white stubble would begin to bury the blanched scars. He told himself he would dye his beard steel gray just before landing.

Rykoff closed the black case and opened the clothing bag crumpled next to it. He put on the cheap gray suit and stained white shirt. He left the knotted tie loose, as if he'd been living in those clothes for days. He slipped his new identification into his pocket, the credentials identifying him as Smith and linking him to the CIA. The identity and appearance would be necessary.

Rykoff stepped into the passage and found Putin waiting for him just outside of the door. Putin looked tired, but he showed no reaction to Rykoff's altered appearance. He just shrugged and spoke. "Park says we've got a storage problem, but I think it's bullshit."

Rykoff nodded and stepped around Putin.

"I think he's posturing to get a better price," Putin added as he followed.

"Better price on what?" Rykoff made his voice nasal. It sounded like he was from Brooklyn.

"On whatever techno bullshit you're selling." Putin let the words hang in his mouth and waited for an answer.

Rykoff gave him none. He entered the crew cabin ahead of Putin and addressed the Korean. "What's the problem, Mr. Park?"

"The temperature in the storage compartment is falling."

"You think there's a leak to the outside?"

"Not sure."

"You think the compartment is depressurizing?"

"That's impossible," Putin interrupted. "The storage unit was pre-fitted for the space and assembled in place." Putin explained that the walls were aluminum stainless clad in four inches of polyurethane insulation, tested to stimulate an altitude of two hundred thousand feet. A leak was impossible, and if the impossible occurred, the leak would equalize with cabin pressure.

"You heard the man, Mr. Park," Rykoff said. "There's no leak. The goods are locked tight."

The Korean didn't answer. Rykoff turned toward Putin. "How long before we get picked up by Halley station?"

"Depends on when we tell them we're coming." Putin shrugged. "I'd like to do that in thirty minutes."

"They have radar?"

"They have weather radar for sure, but not anything that will pick up aircraft." Putin shrugged again toward the cockpit door. "Thirty minutes give or take. I'll want to call them, check the weather, and see about the ice."

Rykoff shook his head. "Do it on approach. I don't want them making any calls to McMurdo. I want just enough time to tie them up with the landing. On the ground I introduce myself as CIA and tie them up more."

Putin said nothing. Rykoff moved aft and checked the storage compartments. Only the right was in use. Beyond the glass the ten dewars were internally cooled to minus 190. The compartment was pressurized to one atmosphere and a temperature of 68 degrees. Rykoff touched the glass. It was cold. That was impossible. Maybe Putin was wrong.

Maybe there was a leak to the outside. He checked the hatch lock. It was secure. He told himself he'd have the fuselage checked in Halley.

Rykoff moved aft to the passenger hold. He stepped around the two Russians armed with .45 cal pistols. He maintained his Brooklyn accent. "Rest well, Doctor Waterstone?"

He watched her blink, but saw she couldn't answer. He shifted his gaze to Malone, stared at her with black eyes. "How about you, Malone?"

Malone had been awake for a half hour. Rykoff figured that she'd already surveyed her surroundings and realized she'd missed Tierra Del Fuego while drugged. By now maybe she was even resigned to the fact that for her there would be no escape. He met her gaze with his new face.

"How's that new face feel, Victor? You hurting, Baby?"

"You won't provoke me, Malone."

"Why Baby? You want to play again later?"

She was mocking him with her smile. But Rykoff knew better than to play the game by her rules. He gazed at her with his new eyes, black and impenetrable. At his back he sensed the Russians watching her. Rykoff knew what Malone was doing. She was distracting them all to keep their attention from the someone who was about to make a move.

"Tell me something, Victor. Have you ever been with a woman without drugging her? Have you, Baby?"

"You're a real piece of work, Malone." Rykoff kept his voice cold and calm.

"You do it with corpses too?" Malone said. "That your deal?"

Rykoff caught the glance Malone passed across the aisle to Doc. Out of the corner of his eye Rykoff saw that Doc was fully awake. Doc was sneaking glances at his porthole.

Probably he was overthinking what he was about to do. Probably he was even calculating the physics in his head, estimating the mass of his handcuff and the force he could apply backhanded to break the porthole glass and depressurize the plane. Rykoff laughed inwardly. With only ten inches of chain separating his cuff from the armrest, Doc couldn't generate enough arc to break the glass.

"You should save your strength, Doc." Rykoff took a seat behind Malone. "Where you're going, you'll need a lot of strength."

Rykoff saw Doc study the nearest Russian. Probably Doc was asking himself what kind of rounds the Russian would have in his pistol. For a second Rykoff considered telling him that both Russians were using bullets especially designed for aircraft. They would break apart on impact without penetrating the fuselage. He decided to let Doc wonder. Even if Doc managed to get a gun and fire a round, the round would fragment on contact without punching a hole in the fuselage. But it would punch a hole in the porthole. That was another question, but Rykoff decided to let Doc waste his time grappling with it.

"Are you hungry, Dr. Waterstone?" Rykoff saw that Dr. Kay was now awake.

"I'm particular whom I eat with."

"You'll eat with much worse before this is over."

A Russian entered rolling a food cart. He served Rykoff first. Between painful bites, Rykoff spoke to Dr. Kay. "The viral harvest was smaller than I planned. Enough to send a love note to the good people of two villages in the former Soviet Union. I have to thank them, you know, for what they did to my face."

"I'd like to thank them too, Victor." Malone said it.

Rykoff took another bite. "The amount I'm selling the North Koreans will really wet their appetite, but they'll want to grow more. So you're my product support person, Dr. Waterstone."

"You're a really sick puppy," Malone interrupted.

"I didn't mean to leave you out, Malone," Rykoff answered. "The North Koreans are just dying to talk to you. And before they're finished, you'll be just dying to talk with them."

The Russian tried to serve a food tray to Kay. She batted it onto the floor. Malone accepted her tray and glanced at the dinnerware. Rykoff watched her focus her attention on her tray. The tray was metal, but there was nothing she could do with a tray. He shifted his gaze toward Doc and saw that Doc was looking toward the rear cargo hatch. Rykoff knew that meant Doc had by now figured that even a gunshot through the porthole wouldn't bring down the plane. Bringing down the plane would require an explosive depressurization. Rykoff took his eyes off Doc and reclined in his seat.

"Bathroom," Doc muttered.

Rykoff nodded ok to the nearest Russian. The Russian tossed Doc the key and kept his distance. Doc unlocked the cuff from the seat and stood with his back to the porthole. Rykoff watched Doc's amateurish attempt to pretend to rub his wrist while eyeing the distance between his handcuff and the porthole. Pathetic, Rykoff told himself. Even amusing, allowing Doc to give it a try. But before Rykoff could let Doc try his move, Putin burst into the cabin.

"The Korean wants you now. He says the temperature in the specimens is rising."

Chapter Twenty-seven

H.I. looked for a way out. There wasn't one. Alien walls surrounded the two of them on all sides, twitching like liquid muscle. H.I. could sense gravity. He could definitely tell up from down. But he couldn't sense motion. April could. Bell Tower's blood fed the images directly into her brain.

"Sun's rising on the left. Jungle's underneath. We are moving fast."

"That means we are still headed south. Are we climbing?"

"I don't know."

H.I. tried to think of something he could use for a weapon. He needed something that would inflict pain and maybe make Bell Tower expel them. The idea was useless. Bell Tower would respond by reducing them to mush.

"Where's it taking us?"

"Some place dark and cold where there are lots of stars."

Her teeth chattered. H.I. touched her skin. It felt like ice. But H.I. wasn't cold at all.

"It's in your head, making you think it's cold."

"It is cold." She shook harder.

Beyond her the alien eyes were lidless, deep and streaming with liquid. Beneath them gaping vertical slits narrowed and constricted. They vibrated every time April spoke. And suddenly H.I. understood.

"It's listening to you, April."

"I want it out of my head. Make it go away."

"I can't." He moved closer to April and whispered, "You have to let this happen. If Bell Tower somehow deciphers one human language, it could use it as a data entry point. Use it to understand and..."

"Use it to know more bad things about us." Her eyes wandered aimlessly, like eyes do in a dream, driven by things that exist only imagination. "It just talked to me."

"You heard a voice in your head?"

"I heard my own voice, but not words I would use."

"It's playing with your brain cells, and you interpret what it does as words."

"Not words I use." She shivered. "Gamma meal and gamma food."

"The nuke," he told her. The data from the disc he'd seen en route to Villa Lobos aboard the jet came back into his head. He remembered a graph generated by an oscillation scintillation spectroscope aimed at Bell Tower's tail as it had approached Earth. It had recorded a gamma emission spike at 511,000 electron volts, a signature for a matter-antimatter collision. It meant Bell Tower ate gamma rays and interfaced them with antimatter to make more energy.

Irony hit him. In his race to extract a biologic weapon, Rykoff had missed something infinitely more powerful than Bell Tower's blood. Bell Tower could confine antimatter. How?

The answer was extreme cold. University types generated antimatter in high-energy particle accelerators. Then they stored it in a vacuum cooled to just above absolute zero so that any air molecules that had escaped the vacuum pump would stick to the walls and miss the antimatter buzzing about the core. Magnets held the antimatter in the core. Basic storage was just a big, magnetized thermos bottle.

"I can't do this." April interrupted his thoughts.

"But it chose you."

She nodded, still shivering. "It was sick and dying and bleeding until the nuke provided it a gamma meal."

"Why was it sick?"

"It's too horrible!" April screamed, shut her eyes, and jammed her hands over her ears. Her eyes darted wildly under closed lids. "Get out of my head."

"What are you seeing?"

"Darkness and cold. Stars. There are lots of stars. They're so far, so cold."

"Is that where it's taking us?"

"No. It's where it came from." She said she saw Bell Tower living and traveling in space while feeding on gamma rays the way whales traveled the ocean feeding on plankton. Bell Tower fed on gamma particles, mixed them with antimatter to generate energy, and pushed itself through space. Its structure tolerated radiation without breaking into radicals and destructing. It carried its DNA to far-away worlds and farmed life. Maybe it was even farming life on Earth. Or maybe it was just making a stop on a long journey.

Maybe Earth was just a stop where Bell Tower was injured.

Maybe it had done what any injured traveler might. Maybe it had built a shelter and looked for food. In Bell Tower's instance, dug a crater and made its surroundings as cold and cozy as home. Then it had searched for a gamma meal. And had found its meal courtesy of Malone's nuke.

But what had injured Bell Tower in the first place? And why had Bell Tower remained in a crater for six months and killed all life in its surroundings? And what had brought it to such a remote spot when it could have chosen any spot on the planet? H.I. asked April.

"It meant to come here."

"Can you see its arrival? Feel it?"

"No!" April's screamed painfully. "I don't want to see!"

"You have to."

"Terrible heights and falling and nothing to hold." She shook her head, shut her eyes, then pried them open. She flailed at the air. He grabbed her arms.

"It's not real. It's just a picture in your head."

"It is real, was real." She stopped struggling. "The night it arrived it met fire in the sky, streaks of fire coming from below and rising to meet it."

All at once H.I. understood. "Do you still see it?"

"No. I see clear sky. The sun's on our left. It's so cold and so far away. We're over the sea. It's cold. I see ice."

"Do you see anything else?"

"A plane. One plane."

Chapter Twenty-eight

"What kind of temperature rise?" Rykoff asked.

"Enough to upset the Korean."

Rykoff disappeared into the passage. Putin followed. Doc stood under guard and waited until they were out of sight before glancing across the aisle at Malone. He saw she was bending to drink coffee from her left hand, which was cuffed to her seat. The cuffed hand and coffee almost hid the slight movements in her right hand. Doc caught a flash of something metallic under her fingers, and he knew Malone was trying to pick her lock with her fork. She didn't return Doc's stare. She remained bent and sipping coffee.

Doc took a last look at Dr. Kay. She sat next to Malone, sobbing with her face in her hand. Doc turned to the Russian guarding him and spoke loudly. "Toilet!"

The mercenary nodded and motioned with his .45 pistol. Doc walked slowly toward the passage and tried a last time to make eye contact with Malone. She didn't acknowledge his gesture. Twenty feet beyond her, the rear cargo door was beaded in condensation, vibrating almost imperceptibly. Doc was still looking when the guard gave him a shove with his empty left hand.

Pain lanced into Doc's injured ribs. He stumbled into the passageway and passed the galley too fast to look for a weapon. He slowed his pace, walking stiffly as if his legs were weak and cramped. The Russian didn't react, just followed with his gun leveled beyond Doc's reach. Well trained, Doc thought. Well trained but not thinking or anticipating. Doc's job was to even the odds and give Malone a better chance at the second Russian and the rear cargo door. Her job was simple. Open the door and depressurize the aircraft.

Doc knew breaking a window wouldn't depressurize the plane fast enough. But opening the rear cargo door would depressurize the C-130 almost instantly. The altitude would determine everything that followed. At thirty-five thousand feet, it would take about fifteen seconds for everyone to pass out and die. Holding one's breath wouldn't help because the low pressure would pull oxygen right out of the blood. If the plane were on autopilot it would continue on its way until the fuel was gone. Then it would fall out of the sky and come down somewhere in Antarctica, frozen and lost forever, including the alien specimens.

"Stop," the mercenary ordered.

Doc froze as the mercenary clicked open the lavatory door and backed away. Doc side-stepped into the lavatory. The mercenary blocked the door with his body and kept it open with his weight. He pointed his gun at Doc and muttered, "You go."

Doc faced the toilet and kept the calculations running in his head. At twenty-five thousand feet, there'd be about a minute and a half of consciousness, plenty of time for the pilot to make an emergency descent to five thousand feet. No one would die. Then it would be just a matter of closing the door, repressurizing, and climbing again. So Malone would have to break the door somehow. If the door couldn't be closed and if the plane couldn't be repressurized, the C-130 would be stuck at five thousand feet. Its cruising range would be sharply reduced. It would have to turn back, maybe even ditch in the Drake Passage.

"Finish," the mercenary ordered.

Doc nodded and flushed the toilet. His ribs hurt as he moved. He turned toward the sink, his eyes scanning every inch of space for a weapon. Doc washed his hands and smiled in spite of himself. Finding the weapon and picking it up under the mercenary's view was easier than Doc thought.

* * *

In the crew quarters, Rykoff looked over the Korean's shoulder at the laptop screen. Two graphs were displayed. Beside the laptop a notepad was filled with scribbling. Rykoff shrugged. "What's the problem, Mr. Park?"

"The heat is exchanging between the dewars and the chamber," Park answered. The graphs showed it. The chamber temperature was down twenty degrees, and the dewar temperature was up.

"A tempest in a teapot, Mr. Park."

"I want to go inside the chamber." Park didn't look up. "I want to check the instruments directly."

"My friend." Rykoff thickened his new Brooklyn accent. "Once we're on the ground at our destination and once I know I've been paid, you can do any damn thing you want."

Rykoff glanced at his watch and turned to Putin. "Take over up front. Raise Halley Station. You know the story."

Putin nodded toward Chernov, who nervously followed him into the cockpit. Rykoff watched them until the cockpit door closed. Then he spun, left the Korean at his laptop, and entered the passage. He stopped at the porthole of the storage compartment. The outside surface of the glass was beaded in water vapor. Rykoff wiped the glass with his fingers. The cold stung him. Through the frost he could see inside the sealed chamber and count the ten neatly aligned dewars. Rykoff felt the Korean's presence at his side.

"You can look, but don't touch." Rykoff warned.

"The pressure in chamber should not be falling, but it is." the Korean said.

Rykoff wiped the glass a second time. His fingertips almost stuck to the glass. He peered at the dewars again. For a few seconds, he could see the sharp red blossoms that were biohazard warnings. The glass fogged again.

"The dewars are leaking," Park said. "They're losing frozen nitrogen."

"Not possible, Mr. Park," Rykoff lied. He told himself that maybe the force from the explosion at the complex had loosened seals on the dewars. It didn't matter. The chamber would stay cold. The virus would stay contained.

Out of the corner of his eye, Rykoff saw movement. He turned and saw Doc step out of the lavatory and into the passage. He saw that Doc's Russian guard was keeping the appropriate distance, weapon out of Doc's reach. Doc raised his hands over his head. Did so painfully because of his injured ribs and was unable to fully raise his right. Rykoff watched the two men move aft, and he almost turned away.

But something caught his eye. Something odd about Doc's hands. Exactly what eluded him. He watched Doc slow his pace as if his ribs were hurting worse. Then Doc seemed to stumble and fall against bulkhead. The Russian reacted professionally, immediately backing further out of Doc's reach. Watching the Russian's move, Rykoff relaxed.

"To seat now."

Between Rykoff and Doc, the Russian raised his pistol in a two handed grip. In that instant Doc propelled himself from the bulkhead and popped open his palms. Watching it happen, Rykoff realized a microsecond too late what Doc was hurling into the Russian's eyes. It was soap powder.

* * *

Putin was in the left cockpit seat when he heard the first gunshot. He glanced toward the right seat and saw that Chernov had heard the shot too. Chernov flinched and locked one hand on his yoke. With the other hand, he raised his headset from one ear. A second gunshot echoed through the steel. A third followed immediately.

"Special rounds! They won't penetrate the fuselage!" Putin yelled at Chernov. "Concentrate on flying and let Rykoff worry in the back."

Putin and Chernov both scanned the instrumentation. They both saw that cabin pressure was intact. But something else was very wrong. The backup analogue instruments were working, but the computer-driven glass instruments were not. The CRT screens were frozen. All of the computer instruments were stalled.

Chernov shouted, "Something was hit!"

"Couldn't have been." Putin stared at the frozen screens and digital instruments. Instinctively he groped for his emergency oxygen bottle and ordered Chernov to do the same.

"Do we reboot?" Chernov's voice was garbled by his oxygen mask.

"We use our backup clock instruments. We don't reboot." Putin raised his headset away from one ear. He heard nothing but the engines vibrating through the airframe. He waited but heard no further gunfire.

Putin used his head mic. "Raise Halley Station and ask for the man in charge. Rykoff will be here in a second to talk to them." Putin ticked off a second in his head and then another and another. Rykoff didn't enter the cockpit.

Chernov tried to raise Halley Station on the radio. He shook his head. "Nothing but static. Lots of it. Like being jammed."

"Keep trying." Putin listened to the static then looked at his horizon. Between wisps of clouds, the sea was harsh and cold, interrupted by icebergs frozen the color of the sky. Out of the side window, something else caught Putin's eye.

The C-130's shadow moved across a cloud. Something was wrong with the shadow. Its outline was wrong.

The hairs on the back of Putin's neck stood up. He scanned his instruments in time to see his CRT screens go dark. Instantly they came back to life, filling with nonsense hieroglyphics.

"I've still got static." Chernov spoke into his headset.

"Go through the maneuvers," Putin ordered calmly. An instrument light flickered in his eye. The indicator warning light for the rear cargo door blinked unsteadily, then went dark. The door stayed closed.

"We're still being jammed," Chernov said with practiced tranquility.

"Get Rykoff up here."

Chernov tore off his headset and grabbed up his oxygen bottle in one hand. The bottle smashed against a bulkhead and bit at his fingers as he lurched into the crew's quarters. He found the backup crew flattened to the floor. Two of them were nearest the passageway door and peering cautiously around the corner.

"I don't hear any more shots!" the one on the left shouted.

"The Korean's still standing there! He's crazy!" the one on the right shouted back.

Chernov noticed that the flight crew were all breathing fine. He felt his fingers swelling from the blow from his oxygen bottle. He cursed, ripped off his mask, and dropped the bottle. The air seemed good. His hand hurt badly.

"Mr. Park!" One of the backup men on the floor yelled into the passageway. "Get down."

Chernov leaped into the passage in a full run. He almost collided with the Korean who stood at the window to the storage compartment. A smell stung Chernov's nose, the smell of burning plastic. Chernov's first thought was that there was a fire, and his first impulse was go back for his oxygen bottle. He ignored his instinct and ran toward the aft cabin.

* * *

The first gunshot exploded in Doc's ears long before he felt the pain. The force spun him sideways in mid leap even as his momentum carried him toward the Russian. Two thumps followed within a split second, as the round ricocheted from a bulkhead and entered a seat. Doc's lunge from the bulkhead carried him into the Russian before the Russian could tighten the aim on his second shot. Doc hit him in the gut, bending him in half and deflecting the second shot toward the floor. It ricocheted from the floor and into another seat.

In the passageway, Rykoff reacted immediately by dropping into a crouch as he drew his weapon. He fired two handed. His subsonic round whined passed Doc's ear and thumped into something soft. Malone's cry echoed from the aft cabin, and Doc heard her fall to the floor. In the same instant, the Russian near Doc pinned him to the floor.

Doc felt blood spreading across his chest and sapping away his strength. He wasn't sure if he'd been shot or reopened the wound over his ribs. It hurt to breathe. He rolled his head to see into the passenger compartment. In agonizing slow motion, he saw Malone lying on the floor and spurting blood from her calf. She was inching forward on her belly, trying to reach the cargo door. The door control panel was less than five feet from her extended arm.

The second Russian stepped toward Malone and pointed his gun at her. Doc caught a glimpse of the Russian's gun barrel and Malone's red hair. The gun never fired. Dr. Kay came from the Russian's right. Her first kick knocked the Russian's gun out of his hand and under the seats on his left. Her second caught his knee from the side and made a popping sound. The Russian went to the floor in pain.

Bleeding badly, Malone squirmed forward and outstretched an unsteady arm. She was trying to pull herself upright as Rykoff leaped over Doc moving like a big cat.

Rykoff lowered his gun to take aim at Malone's back, but Dr. Kay launched herself at him. The chain of her handcuff drew taught and stopped her short of his face. He reacted with rage, backhanding her with his gun and dropping her into her seat. Still in rage, he closed on Malone.

Doc tried to pull himself upright. He was too weak to fight the Russian pinning him down. Doc tried to yell. The effort was too great. It hurt too much to breath. He heard Rykoff laugh sadistically from the far end of the cabin.

"I like you, Malone. I really do." Rykoff laughed louder.

Malone kept pulling herself toward the panel. Her wounded leg buckled and smacked her against the bulkhead. She threw her strength into her good leg, shoved herself upright, and reached the safety switch on the panel. With trembling fingers, she toggled it. A warning light indicated that the door could now be opened. Rykoff watched.

"You need a doctor, Malone." Rykoff spit the words as stood directly over her. "Is there a doctor on board."

With her last bit of strength, Malone threw her hand toward the panel. Rykoff blocked the move and let her fall to the floor. She landed inert, face away from Doc. She was barely breathing. Rykoff stepped over her and reengaged the cargo door lock.

Doc tried a last time to make a move, but his body wouldn't obey. He felt Chernov step around him. "Putin needs you up front."

Rykoff glanced at Doc, then at Dr. Kay. She raised her head above her seat and turned pale as she saw the blood spreading across Doc's shirt. She faced Rykoff, her eyes filled with hate. She raised her hand against its steel cuff.

"Unlock her." Rykoff ordered. "See if the good doctor can render aid." The Russian unlocked Dr. Kay's hand. She rubbed her wrists and started toward Doc. She stopped beside Rykoff. "Whatever you've promised the people buying Bell Tower, I won't help. I'll see that it fails. I won't help you with anything."

Rykoff answered sharply. "In a short while, we'll be on the ice asking for fuel. And you'll be doing what I tell you." He lowered his voice, spoke softly. "If you don't, I'll have to kill everyone for that fuel. It's in your hands."

Rykoff stepped aside as a Russian handed Dr. Kay a medical bag. She bent to help Doc lean upright against the base of a seat. Doc tried to raise his face. He said he wasn't as badly wounded as he thought. Maybe he hadn't been shot but had just reopened the wound over his ribs. Dr. Kay knew instantly he was wrong. But Doc pushed her away.

"Malone first."

* * *

In the passageway Rykoff noticed the cold all at once. It was a terrible cold, more bitter than a Russian winter. It was also a wet cold, like the wind over an icy pond in some remote, dark, and terrible place where humans didn't live. Rykoff stared up the passageway.

The Korean was gone. The hatch to the right storage compartment was open and spewing air so cold that water vapor turned to fog in the passage. At first Rykoff thought the fog was gray. Then light glinted from something moving in its center. The moving thing was a silver, yellow mist.

It rolled toward Rykoff as if it were alive.

Chapter Twenty-nine

The man known as Mr. Park stood just inside the storage compartment and waited to die. Dr. Park Il-sung, as he was correctly addressed in Korea, had realized all along that his death might be necessary. He'd realized all along that he might have to destroy the materials offered for sale by Rykoff. Dr. Park stood within reach of the ten dewars and let the cold overtake him.

Sunglasses partially shielded Park's eyes from the freezing nitrogen gas escaping the dewars. The breathing apparatus discarded by the Russian copilot shielded Park's nose and mouth, but he knew his eyes were the most vulnerable to the cold. While he could still see, Park fixed his gaze on the sharp red petals that warned of dangerous lifeforms. Microbes! Dr. Park Il-sung had dedicated his life to them because he had always understood their importance.

Microbes were the first life on Earth. Microbes had made the evolution of higher lifeforms possible. And once evolved those higher lifeforms had become the prey of their own microscopic ancestors. The war with microbes was endless.

Through fading vision Park looked at the dewars and told himself that the microbes contained within were not of this Earth. He'd been afraid of them from the day he'd learned of their existence. So he had made sure that he would be the one chosen by his superiors in North Korea to confirm Rykoff's claims of their destructive power. And all along Park had known what he would do. Prevent their reaching the hands of the evil men who were his bosses and his country's so-called leaders.

Park's exposed hands burned like fire in the cold, then went numb. His glasses froze, a fine frost forming on the inside. He shut his eyes and waited. Pops and cracks exploded like popcorn inside the dewars as the specimen vials burst. They were bursting because the alien microbes were pulling heat in and expanding the frozen nitrogen. The alien microbe could not be contained. Park had known it could not be contained even back in Pyongyang when he'd first been made aware of the find.

The alien microbe was endlessly adaptive. It was born in space. It could read the genes of any lifeform in its path and turn them into its destructive tool. That the microbe would escape containment was inevitable. Park had realized that the microbe was emanating from the vessels on the plane when he'd smelled the burning plastic in the passageway. The scent meant the alien microbe had invaded the ordinary bacteria resting on the plastic seals of the atmospheric chamber. The microbe had manipulated their bacterial genes so that the bacteria could eat plastic the way humankind used bacteria to eat toxic chemicals.

Park's eyes froze shut. He took air in deep breaths and felt the acrid stench as his lungs filled with toxins from melting plastic. Park ripped the oxygen mask from his face and felt the mask come apart in his hands. It was the last thing he saw.

Dr. Park Il-sung died quietly without realizing he wasn't perishing from a microbe at all.

* * *

In the cockpit Putin felt the temperature plummet. In the same few seconds, his whiskey compass began to spin. That should not have been possible. His whiskey compass was independent of his electronics and worked off the earth's magnetic field. He banked slightly to the left so he could look up and check the position of the sun. But the sun was gone, hidden behind something hovering over him while matching his speed and direction. Its form was indistinct.

Putin banked the opposite direction and looked down trying to identify his shadow and his pursuer's on the elongate cloud bank passing below on his right. But his shadow was nowhere to be seen. It was lost inside the shade of something massive.

He eyed his instruments. He knew his flight controls and throttles would operate independently of his computer. Whatever was going wrong electronically, he assured himself that he had control of his plane. He tightened his grip on the yolk and pressed firmly on his rudder pedals.

The electromagnetic pulse came from nowhere. It surged through his headset and locked up his muscles. Just as quickly it stopped. Putin recovered and screamed for a backup copilot. No one answered. A blinking light caught his eye. The lock on the rear cargo door was disengaged.

All of Putin's instincts commanded him to descend, and to do it quickly. His hands moved almost without his will, reaching for the mechanical controls that flattened the angle on his props and extended his flaps. In the same few seconds, he nosed the C-130 down and watched his horizon. Over twenty thousand feet below, the sea was a cauldron littered with frozen ice the same shade as the heavens. Wisps of cloud shot underneath. They were white for only a glance before they vanished in the dark directly below.

The thing was still above him. Following him.

Putin glanced skyward, and it filled him with terror. He jammed the nose down steeper into a dive, thinking only of running. His hand moved by its own will to alter his prop pitch to Beta to slow the C-130 and get it away from the thing above him. A scream came from his back. Putin spun in his seat, thinking Chernov had returned to the cockpit. Putin was right. Nikolai Chernov had returned, but not the Nikolai Chernov that Putin knew.

The Chernov who collapsed against the back of the right seat was writhing in pain while clawing at the blackened flesh that was falling away from the bones of his face.

* * *

The electromagnetic pulse shot up though the metal floor while Dr. Kay was moving from Malone to Doc. The force threw Dr. Kay backward and spun her head toward the rear cargo door. As the current released her, she saw that the Russian in the back of the cabin was down. Beyond him the warning light indicated that the switch for the rear cargo door was unlocked.

"Door!" Malone muttered in Dr. Kay's direction. "Open the cargo door."

Dr. Kay gave the cargo door barely a glance. She looked into Malone's pale, sweating face. Rykoff's bullet had hit the bone in Malone's leg, and the bone had protected the muscle behind it from massive soft tissue damage. But the bullet and bone had fragmented, like they always did on impact. And a piece had nicked the popliteal artery. Dr. Kay had pulled the belt around Malone's calf tight enough to stop the arterial pumping. But it was likely that Malone would still lose her leg, and she might even die.

"Russian's down. Run to the door," Malone pleaded.

"Do what Malone says," Doc managed to gasp while keeping pressure on his chest wound. Rykoff's bullet had glanced off a rib and left him bleeding from an intercostal vessel. Steady pressure had stemmed the bleeding. Doc gasped a second time, "Cargo door."

"Shut up, Doc." Dr. Kay swept her eyes between Doc, Malone, and the cargo door. The decision was impossible. Then she saw Rykoff backing away from the passageway. Rykoff looked afraid. Eyes still on the passage, he backed into a seat and and fastened his belt. His hands were trembling. His attention was still toward the passage. He was vulnerable.

Dr. Kay glanced into her medical bag and found a dull-tipped pair of bandage scissors. She thought of April and let her rage take her. She threw Doc's hand over his chest dressing, grabbed up the scissors, and launched herself at Rykoff.

It was only Putin's taking the plane into a dive that stopped her from driving the scissors into Rykoff's throat.

The sudden drop threw her off her feet, taking the scissors out of her hand. Rykoff spun in his seat, raised his weapon, and grabbed her by the hair.

"You can't kill me, Doctor Waterstone." Rykoff thumbed back the hammer on his automatic pistol. He affected a Brooklyn accent. "We're going to die together. The virus has escaped containment."

A second electromagnetic pulse surged through everything metal, hurling sparks from Rykoff's weapon and locking his hand in a spasm. The same pulse sent an electrical charge surging through the prosthetics that gave form to his face, burning Rykoff from the inside. Rykoff seized up like a man in an electrical chair.

Dr. Kay's vision became a blur. At the rear of the plane, the downed Russian was writhing on the steel flooring, and beyond him, a red light was blinking. And just as suddenly, the rear cargo door was open.

Dr. Kay looked into open sky.

Wind blasted her. Everything not fastened down was sent flying. The air left Dr. Kay's lungs, and the force swept her like a giant hand. It swept her out of the cabin and into the sky. She fell spinning like a top in terrible cold.

Sky and sea exchanged places in the blink of an eye and then back again. Something hung above her blocking out the sun. It was something massive and silvery that she saw for only a second. The wind shot through her ears and carried the scream of metal straining against sky. She was tossed on her belly, and she saw Doc and Malone tumbling out of the cargo door far below her, the wind hurling them away like limp dolls. The two Russians followed, flailing until the strength left their bodies, the wind throwing them out of sight.

And far below them, the big C-130 continued its descent, wings moaning, smoke streaming from all of its engines. And then it was gone beneath the clouds on her left.

Dr. Kay fell toward the sea and ice twenty thousand feet below her. Her arms and legs snapped helplessly. She waited for unconsciousness and death. And then the wait was over.

Chapter Thirty

"Mom?"

At first Dr. Kay acted as if she were hearing things. Looking at her H.I. decided that her reaction was what he expected. He watched her pull herself upright. Greedily gulping air, she struggled to turn in the direction where he was standing beside April.

"April?" Dr. Kay's lips were trembling. "Baby?"

"Don't call me Baby." April blindly groped her way out of H.I.'s grip and into her mother's arms where she let herself be hugged and kissed frantically. H.I. only let it go on for a few seconds.

"Where's Doc?" H.I. asked. But Dr. Kay didn't answer him.

Alien flesh closed in from all sides. The movement was fast, almost muscular. It stopped twenty feet away and wept luminescent mist. The mist showered something moving toward H.I. from the dark. . Actually two somethings were moving toward him, emerging from an opening that closed behind them.

"Doc?"

H.I. didn't want the lead figure stumbling toward him to be Doc. That figure was bleeding from the chest. But it was Doc! And Doc looked to be in better condition than the second figure. The second figure, half in Doc's arms, looked dead.

"Malone?"

"Get over here!" Doc yelled. He added, "You okay?"

"Yeah, Doc." H.I. saw that Doc's chest was bandaged. The blood that had seeped through was mostly dried. But Doc looked pale. He'd lost a good amount of blood.

"Is this where I think it is?"

"You're inside Bell Tower, Doc."

Doc nodded and turned to Malone. She was bleeding actively. Her pant leg was soaked. So were her ankle and foot. Doc tore apart her pant leg, wadded up the bloody cloth, and guided H.I.'s hand to a gaping hole the size of bottle cap. Soft tissue and shattered bone were exposed. Her calf was swollen twice its normal size.

"Gunshot wound. Squeeze hard on the muscle. Keep direct pressure. And be careful of the bone edges. I'm going to release the tourniquet and see if there's a distal pulse."

Malone winced as H.I. took hold. She rolled her head toward him and mumbled, "Car's coming."

H.I. knew Malone was in shock and out of her head. He knew that much from hearing Doc talk about trauma and from getting his butt dragged to grand rounds at Doc's hospital. H.I. also knew bullets fragmented as they hit and that fragments multiplied the damage from gunshot wounds. Malone's calf felt like dough. That meant just as much bleeding inside as out. Malone was bleeding to death.

"Who's flying this thing?" Doc asked without looking up. "Where's the crew?"

"It doesn't exactly work that way," H.I. answered. "This isn't exactly a vehicle."

"Headlights, kid," Malone whispered through pale lips. "Lots of headlights."

"She doesn't have a distal pulse." Doc ordered H.I. to squeeze hard on the wound, applying direct pressure. He released the belt tightened below Malone's knee. Immediately blood spurted through H.I.'s fingers.

"Not good." Doc ordered H.I. to apply more pressure.

H.I. closed his fingers and thumb like a vice. The bleeding slowed on the outside but not on the inside. Her calf looked bigger.

"Kid," Malone whispered, eyes half-closed. "Get the car."

"I see the car. It's bringing help."

"Don't screw with me. Look at the headlights."

He looked where she tried to point, directly into Bell Tower's eyes. On all sides, they hovered in pairs in the alien flesh. The light pulsing into them reflected back out like torches. Beneath them slits the size of humans opened and extended their filaments, listening.

"See them coming, kid?"

"Yeah, Malone. I see them."

Beneath the eyes the filaments vibrated to each voice, all the while beading a silver-yellow film. H.I. knew it was alien blood.

"What in God's name?" Dr. Kay was suddenly standing over H.I. while holding April and fixing on the alien almost hypnotically. The eyes shifted to her as if they'd been looking for her all along. Dr. Kay tore her gaze from the alien and looked at April. But April's face was pointed at nothing.

"Baby?"

"She's blind," H.I. said. Immediately he regretted saying it with Doc's blunt style.

"Got a distal pulse," Doc interrupted. He took over for H.I., squeezing directly on Malone's wound. Malone winced again, a good sign.

"April?" Dr. Kay asked louder.

"Now I see things on the inside," April answered. "I see the things it puts in my head. Sometimes it hurts."

"Who puts things there, Baby?"

"The alien." H.I. stepped in. "Bell Tower. 1999 RM. Whatever you want to call it! It is not a spaceship." He cut to the chase. "It is alive. It is the alien lifeform. The things you thought were microbes are its blood."

"We're loaded with it." Silver tears pooled in April's eyes.

H.I. saw that the part of Dr. Kay who was the scientist and the cool problem solver was gone. She tried to speak, but tears blocked her voice. Doc pulled her from April and made her take a turn holding pressure on Malone's wound. Malone's head rolled to the side like dead weight.

"Its blood can do things," April's eyes were directionless. "We understand it firsthand, H.I. and me."

"No!" Dr. Kay shook her head violently. "You are not contaminated. You are not..."

"We are definitely contaminated," H.I. said. "Both of us are."

"It puts pictures in my head," April said in Dr. Kay's direction. "In my head I saw you pulled out of that plane and into Bell Tower."

"Tell them the rest of it," H.I. said.

"Our planet is an endless biologic war zone, survival of the meanest."

"You hear this in your head, Baby?"

"I see it."

"Those words, Baby? They're not your words. It's not you talking."

"It is me seeing things and feeling them. All life is driven to survive by killing something else. Humans are at the top. We have the ability to think and build tools. We use it to kill our own kind, to expand and conquer. But our world wasn't created to be this way. And neither were we. We live in a fallen world."

"Stop talking like this, Baby."

"I have to talk like this. It's in my head like a dream that won't stop. Parts of it are even worse."

"It's not real."

"It's very real. The alien showed me your work. It put it in my head, your computer and horrible words like *toxin* and *cell death* and *lethal dose.* Your signature is all over them."

"It's hard to explain, April."

"Try me. I'm a big girl."

"I was doing it for you because Rykoff..." Dr. Kay's voice broke. "He threatened..."

"Tell your mom the rest of it, April," H.I. interrupted. "Tell her why Bell Tower crashed."

"It didn't crash," April said. "It was shot down."

Dr. Kay seemed to refuse what H.I. was telling her. April kept talking. "I keep seeing it in my head, streams of fire coming from below. Then falling."

"Doc, are you listening?" H.I. asked.

"I already suspected this," Doc said. He didn't look up from Malone. "Back at Langley during the briefing. All of those atmospheric lights the night Bell Tower entered Earth's atmosphere. The so-called entry fire storm. I knew what it was." He changed hands on Malone's wound again. "I knew the so-called firestorm was in front and underneath Bell Tower, not behind it."

"Who fired on it, Doc?" H.I. asked. "Don't tell me. Let me guess. We all did. Every industrialized nation with a missile system of some sort took a shot. And so did a bunch of nations too poor to feed their people but rich enough and prideful enough to have missiles."

"Under the circumstances," Doc continued. "With what was known at the time, it had to be done. Hostile intent had to be presumed. Judging by the alien's actions on the ground, hostile intent was correct."

Dr. Kay looked up while holding pressure on Malone's wound. "It's the Malones of the world who made the presumption. They had the authority."

"We gave them the authority," Doc answered.

"We're all guilty, Doc."

"And now it means to end us," April quivered. "It's what we all have coming."

A muffled cry came from Malone. April broke free from Dr. Kay's grip. "I want to take a turn with Malone."

"Be careful of the bone edges," Doc warned her. "They're sharp."

"I'm counting on it."

April leaned into Malone and let Malone's broken bone edges slice her arm open like a knife. H.I. knew instantly what she was doing. But it took Doc and Dr. Kay a full second to realize what they were seeing. Dr. Kay reacted first. She tried to grab April's arm, but failed. Doc wrenched April from Malone on his second attempt. The slash in April's forearm went from wrist to elbow joint. It was muscle deep and bleeding badly. Immediately Doc applied pressure.

"Baby, what are you doing?" Dr. Kay fought tears as she touched April.

"I'm saving Malone's life." April was in pain. "I'm loaded with Bell Tower's cells. So is my blood."

Doc stared open-mouthed at April's arm. "You're not bleeding anymore. You're already granulating. That's impossible."

"But I bled into Malone before I stopped bleeding, didn't I? I passed some Bell Tower cells from my blood to Malone. It'll save her, right?"

Doc glanced down. "Malone, can you hear me?"

Malone didn't answer. Her skin was bloodless. Her eyes were half-open and glassy. Doc felt for a pulse and muttered. "Her pulse is real thready. I shouldn't have pulled the tourniquet."

"She needs a central line." Dr. Kay shook her head. "She needs volume and packed cells. And oxygen."

"We don't have those things." Doc looked hopeless.

"Oh, God. She's going to code." Dr. Kay answered.

"She'll be okay, right?" April choked with tears. "The alien blood will help her, right?"

"Even if Bell Tower's alien blood can make new red cells and heal organ damage, she still needs volume replacement."

"What's volume replacement?"

"It's basically the fluid you need to maintain blood flow to tissues. We're talking plasma made of salt water and proteins."

H.I. felt Bell Tower's walls close in. He looked at its eyes, floating in transparent liquid and watching as Malone took her last breath. She lay limp, white, and motionless. The eyes watched Doc scramble for a carotid pulse and blurt out that he couldn't find one.

"No. She can't die," April trembled as she cried. "I gave her its blood."

Doc grabbed at Dr. Kay, and the two of them began CPR. Dr. Kay pounded on Malone's chest, and Doc forced his breath into Malone's lifeless mouth. H.I. touched Malone's neck. It was still warm. He found her carotid pulse. It thumped each time Dr. Kay pounded on her chest. H.I. kept his hand in position. Dr. Kay pounded until she was exhausted.

"Check it," Doc said.

Dr. Kay nodded and stopped compressions. Without the compression there was no pulse.

Chapter Thirty-one

"She's gone," Dr. Kay said.

"No! We wrap her extremities." Doc tore off his shirt and fumbled trying to bind Malone's good leg. "Like an Emergency Room G suit. Restore central pressure."

"She's gone, Doc." Dr. Kay placed a hand on Doc's shoulder. "You have to stop."

April twisted her face blindly. "Don't let her die."

H.I. saw filaments vibrate inside the human-sized slits beneath Bell Tower's eyes. But the eyes stared unblinking. He watched April lurch to her feet, groping and maybe trying to touch Bell Tower. She cried. "Please!"

H.I. relieved Doc and began pounding Malone's chest again. Her shirt fell open, exposing the places where Rykoff and Bulldog had hurt her. H.I. felt rage. He wanted to kill Rykoff but told himself the alien had already done it. H.I. felt Doc push him aside. Doc lifted Malone's inert face into his as he made her chest fill with his air. He waited and checked her pulse again. H.I. moved his hands to do more compressions. Doc blocked him and shook his head.

"Please," April cried.

"Bell Tower isn't God," H.I. said. He felt his voice crack.

Somehow the agony of death was gone from Malone's face. She looked almost peaceful. Doc closed Malone's eyes. In the dim light, H.I. almost imagined there was color in her face. That was impossible. The burns on her skin were pale and bloodless. Malone wasn't moving. She'd never move again.

"Sorry, Malone," Doc said.

April sank to her knees, crying. Doc held her and examined the gash in her forearm. The edges were puckering inward, making the wound narrower by the minute. Bell Tower's cells were driving the repair, healing her at a thousand times the normal rate. She pushed Doc away, flew into a rage, and swung at the air.

"Why didn't you help her?" April pointed blindly, shouting in all directions. "You came here to kill all of us, didn't you?"

Doc buttoned Malone's shirt and rested her arms to her side. For a split second H.I. thought he saw movement in Malone's face, a slight twitch maybe. A postmortem muscle contraction, he knew. Anything else was wishful thinking.

"You're not God," April muttered toward Bell Tower. Her eyes wandered blindly for a second before she lay back against Dr. Kay.

"Where's it taking us, H.I.?" Dr. Kay asked.

"April knows. She wouldn't tell me."

"Tell me what you think."

"I think we're it. Maybe not all of us are it. Maybe it's just you and April who are."

"I'm not following you."

"You're following me very well. It's just that what I'm telling you is too terrible to contemplate. Those of us still alive—or maybe just you and April—are the last of all life on Earth."

"What do mean the last of all life?"

"I mean specimens from Bell Tower's experiment, life on Earth."

"We are not some damn experiment."

"Bet that's what your lab rats think," H.I. blurted, even though he wasn't sure he believed his own words. "Maybe this has all been Bell Tower's experiment. And now it's shutting the experiment down and saving a few specimens."

"I've seen it," April joined them. Her tears were gone. Her eyes were directionless. "It came to end us. There'll be nothing left but dust and water."

"Two or four humans from the whole planet is incomplete sampling." Doc looked over from Malone's body. "It's bad science."

"Or not," H.I. answered. "Maybe it just needs a sample of the final genes."

"You're wrong." Dr. Kay shook her head violently. "We're not here by accident. And we are not some experiment."

"She's right," April said. "This is not about an experiment."

H.I. glanced at the alien. The eyes looked back impassively. Filaments vibrated in their slits. The alien was processing noises, processing speech from everyone. H.I. looked at Malone, thought he saw her move. But she couldn't have. She looked cold and still. He looked back toward Doc. "Assume the alien is preparing to shut down an experiment. What makes the alien run the experiment longer?"

"An unanticipated result." Doc understood immediately. "How do we produce one?"

"We are one," April said. "We are more than the sum of our parts."

"I don't accept any of this as an experiment," Dr. Kay said. "You've left out God. The natural state of the universe is disorder. The fact that there is order is God's hand."

God doesn't play with dice.

H.I. remembered Einstein's words from his dream. He answered, "I believe in God."

"We're more than genes, much more!" Dr. Kay raised her voice.

"There's no evidence of that," Doc said.

"You're wrong. There's overwhelming evidence." Dr. Kay looked down at her daughter. April tilted an ear upward, her eyes wandering as if she was seeing things inside her head.

"I know what's coming," April said.

H.I. saw that Bell Tower's walls were much closer. He wiped away sweat and glanced at his hand. Beads of silver glinted back at him, just like the tears running down April's cheeks. April reached for him until she found his hand and gripped it. "It's listening to us."

"I know, but it can't understand language."

"It's in my head. It can feel what I feel."

"What feelings would those be?"

"For a smart guy," she said, "you don't get it at all."

The slits beneath Bell Tower's eyes closed and melted back into its flesh as if they'd never existed. The flesh began to pulsate with force. H.I. looked into April's face.

"There's something I've wanted to tell you for a long time."

"You're too late," she answered. "Game over."

The move was sudden. Bell Tower's flesh constricted like muscle, then extended a massive tentacle toward Malone's inert body. H.I. felt Doc throw himself in the way like a shield. Dr. Kay did the same to protect April. In that instant Malone was gone. Bell Tower absorbed her like an amoebae ingesting its prey. Liquid flesh held her against its inner surface for a second. Her head rolled lifelessly against her chest, and one of her eyes opened. Then she was gone from sight.

"Nobody move," Doc whispered.

Alien flesh began to close in more. H.I. screamed at himself to do something, to find something he could use as a weapon. His impulse was to strike back. But Doc must have read his mind.

"Hold your ground!" Doc yelled. His breath formed a vapor in the air before H.I. even felt the cold. The liquid on Bell Tower's skin began to frost. The flesh kept moving inward.

"We're there," April muttered.

"Where, Baby?" Dr. Kay tried to shield her. "It can't be some far-away world."

"We're not making that kind of trip. Not any of us." April tilted her ear toward Dr. Kay. "There are so many beautiful worlds out there. But we aren't going."

"Baby?"

"We're where it finishes." She shivered badly.

Up close the alien's flesh looked almost like one surface layered over another and another. Something was moving inside them. None of it mattered. Only one last thing mattered. H.I. wanted April to hear what he had to say.

"I love you. I always have."

He held her in the microsecond before Bell Tower's flesh ruptured and its substance hit them all at once.

Chapter Thirty-two

It hit like ice water. H.I.'s mind stayed alert, told him that intense heat and cold might feel the same in the first few seconds. He tensed for the pain. Pain nerves were a microsecond slower than temperature nerves. But there wasn't any pain. There was just locking April's hand in his and falling through something liquid that was either burning or freezing.

His brain raced, still scrambling for a way to survive. If humankind was the end result of some sort of experiment, then maybe humankind was the unexpected result. Humankind was more than the sum of genes. Humankind had the potential to make choices not dictated by genes. The alien had to know, had to see.

Around him, the liquid became a vortex. The force spun April and him, trying to tear them apart. He tried to pull her to him. Something slammed into him. H.I. tried to shove it away and touched a leg wrapped in a shirt. Malone! Her inert form was tumbling with them. He opened his eyes to look for her but saw only the dark. Liquid filled his lungs, and he knew it was over. The last sensation would be like drowning.

He locked his arms around April and let every other muscle surrender. He closed his eyes in the dark maelstrom. The alien had seen humankind, and it had to know it had seen the unexpected result. But knowing wouldn't change the outcome. His eyes opened by themselves, and he saw light rising toward him. Then it surrounded him. Still holding April he slammed into a frozen white surface. Noise grew to a shrill whistle in his ears. It was wind blowing across ice! But there was no cold. And underneath the ice he felt firm ground.

He lay there for almost a minute, holding April and waiting to die, but not dying. The ice flow stretched into forever. The sky was gone, shut out by Bell Tower's massive form swirling away from a single burning eye. Underneath it Doc and Dr. Kay were trying to stand. Nearby Malone was lying on her side. She was moving. No mistake about it. Malone was alive.

The wind howled without cold. H.I. stood and pulled April to her feet. He held up his hand and saw it was coated in something liquid, thin, and clear. Everyone was coated, every inch of them. H.I. wiped the stuff from his palm. Cold wind hit the exposed skin like a knife. He closed his hand to protect it. The same film hung over his eyes. It was transparent.

He looked at April. Her eyes wandered blindly. Her lips parted, and she said something he couldn't hear. Beyond her, Bell Tower's falling mist touched the ice and began to turn it to steam that expanded into fog blotting out the landscape in all directions. It surged like a tide and in less than a second swallowed Doc, Dr. Kay, and Malone. H.I. waited to hear their screams. But they never came. And then the fog reached him.

"H.I." April's voice was softer than he'd ever heard. "I can see you. I'm not blind anymore."

He looked into April's face, and her eyes wandered up into his. Her lips parted, and he found all of her mouth with all of his. Hers was soft and yielding and kissing him back. He opened an eye and took in every wonderful curve of her face. One of her eyes opened and filled with a tear. It was a human tear, clean as water. Her eyes slid softly closed, and they kissed again.

She heard the noise a second before him. They both turned to see the big eyes come from all sides. They came burning white through the fog and splitting the air with roar of gasoline engines. The fog cleared from their path, and dark figures moved between them. Radio static boomed across the ice, then human voices. They were British voices.

"Number one, this is Haley Station. Are you there?"

"Quite here, Haley. Rather afraid you won't believe what's been found."

The fog swirled away. H.I. saw the lights were not eyes. They were the headlights of a half-dozen snowmobiles perched fifty yards away on the edge of melting ice. Humans were approaching. They were carrying blankets and rescue gear.

Bell Tower was gone. The sky was clear.

Doc, Dr. Kay, and Malone were walking out of the fog. H.I. hesitated before he looked skyward. He sort of knew what he was going to find. He looked anyway.

The sky was empty to the far-away horizon. The sun was a distant, cold light. The first stars were visible. One of the stars was more brilliant than the others, moving in front of them, moving faster and faster. Then it was gone.

Chapter Thirty-three

The CNN announcer was brief, squeezing in the last bit of evening news before *Crossfire.* Senator Orton Bledso watched the television from his antique desk while holding his second bourbon and branch water in death grip. The announcer sounded bored. Good news wasn't exciting.

"Scientists in Brazil are today breathing a sigh of relief as they report there has been no radiation spread from an accident that occurred here over three weeks ago at the site of an experimental reactor deep in the Amazon rain forest. Initial reports had..."

Bledso turned away from the television and finished his drink in one gulp. "Neat, Ramsey. Very neat."

Ramsey said nothing. He just looked through the window at the capital. The view tonight wasn't pretty. The lights reflected from a murky sky and dirty snow. Ramsey closed the curtains and turned. "Would have been neater, Senator, if there'd been no reports at all."

"There always seem to be leaks."

"Always are." Ramsey was still wearing his overcoat. His right sleeve was empty and his coat was draped over his shoulder. His right arm was in a sling. A dressing covered half of his neck. The dressing needed changing.

"Your people have any ideas," Bledso fumbled with his empty glass, "about how this man Rykoff found out about Bell Tower?"

"We always have ideas." Ramsey watched the gas flames appear to consume the artificial logs. The logs only looked real. The fire and heat were very real. Ramsey cradled his right arm in the sling under his coat. If he were in pain, he didn't show it. He kept his eyes on the fire.

"Couldn't be helped, could it, Ramsey? The leaks that came after."

"No, Senator. It couldn't. Not with all of those civilian satellites up there. Our bomb sent infrareds off the scale. No way anyone could have thought they were seeing a geologic."

"None of the satellites detected any radiation?"

"No radiation. Just like it says in the president's PDB." Ramsey referred to the president's daily brief, the official report to the White House prepared each morning by the CIA. Listening, Bledso wondered whether Ramsey meant that the president hadn't been told the truth in print or hadn't been told the truth at all. Probably hadn't been told at all. This president had a very bad track record with secrets.

"Why is that, Ramsey? Why no radiation?"

"I'm not a scientist. You'll have find one and ask him. Pick someone inside the loop. Perhaps Dr. Tech."

"I prefer Dr. Waterstone." Bledso tried to smile. "I hear she's lovely."

"These days she's not talking to anyone. I'd recommend Dr. Tech."

Bledso cringed at the mention of Dr. Tech. He poured another drink and turned his head toward the television. On screen the announcer seemed perplexed. "In related news, scientists are dismissing stories of strange lights and phenomenon in Antarctica. Rumors began a week ago…"

"Nice of our foreign friends to cooperate," Bledso said. He felt the nervousness in his own voice.

"Nice," Ramsey agreed coldly.

Bledso looked at his empty glass. In a year his term was up and his career was finished. His exposure was not finished, never would be finished. "Damn cooperative of them."

"Easy to be cooperative," Ramsey answered. "They don't know about the bomb."

"It's not in the PDB either, is it?" Bledso waited for an answer and didn't get one. He took his cue. "The president has plausible deniability. I don't. Am I right, son? "

Again Ramsey said nothing. Bledso tried to make eye contact with Ramsey, but Ramsey's eyes were still on the fire. The logs were glowing, the lights dancing on Ramsey's plain, tan overcoat. Bledso thought that outside of the office, Ramsey would not be noticed. Ramsey would be another man in a gray suit and tan overcoat wandering about the capital. And no one would even remember seeing him enter or leave Bledso's office. Ramsey had arrived late, after Bledso's staff had already departed for the day.

"The president doesn't know about the bomb, does he, son?" Bledso asked.

"Which part would you tell him, Senator?" Ramsey turned from the fire holding an ornate poker in his left hand. The logs didn't need stoking. They and the poker were for show. Watching Ramsey hold the poker, Bledso felt himself begin to sweat inside his clothes.

"What are you getting at, Ramsey?"

"Would you tell him that the thing that landed in the Amazon did so because we shot it down? Would you tell him it wasn't a comet or an asteroid or even a spacecraft? That it was a living being, intelligent and ready to destroy this planet? So indestructible that the nuke we dropped didn't touch it?"

"Dropped inside a friendly country," Bledso added. He immediately regretted speaking.

"That too. Not a pretty picture, Senator." Ramsey eyed the poker, eyed the fire, then Bledso.

Bledso felt his blood go cold. He avoided Ramsey's stare and flicked his eyes toward the television. *Crossfire* was on. Bill Press and Tucker Carlson were about to start a yelling contest with one of the candidates running for Bledso's office.

"Fire's nice," Ramsey said. "It's time, Senator."

Bledso nodded and retrieved a large envelope from his desk. He held it in an outstretched hand. Ramsey replaced the poker beside the fire, strode to the desk, and took the envelope. He judged its weight and without hesitation hurled it into the fireplace.

"You didn't want to check the contents?" Bledso asked.

Ramsey laughed without answering. He stood watching the envelope blacken and crumble apart in the fire. The first ashes rose with the heat.

"That the only hard copy?" Bledso asked.

"The only one, Senator. You're the last to see it."

"No computer files."

Ramsey didn't answer. The fire cast his shadow across the room. The powerful muscles of Ramsey's shoulders and back were evident. Bledso heard his own voice tremble, "You were lucky to get out, weren't you, Ramsey?"

"That's right, Senator. Lucky." Ramsey didn't turn.

"This man, Rykoff. Do we think he's dead?"

"He went down in Antarctic waters, Senator. You don't get any deader."

"And the rest of his people?"

"Not a trace."

"I guess all of our bases are covered."

"Not all of them." Ramsey picked up the poker again. "Dr. Tech was able to isolate an alien blood sample from the Tech boy and Waterstone girl. We wanted it, but Dr. Tech wouldn't part with it."

"What do you mean he wouldn't part with it? I want to know what your people are doing about this!"

"It's being handled, Senator. It's being handled." Ramsey spread the ashes across the logs and held the poker as if it were a weapon. He turned toward Bledso, eyes burning with anger. He seemed to consider Bledso for a half-minute. He spoke softly. "Our business is done, Senator. Thank you for your oversight."

Ramsey replaced the poker gently in the fireside holder and left as quietly as he'd arrived.

Chapter Thirty-four

Hospital rounds went late. Doc took them where they clearly did not belong. He didn't pause to bait the house staff or quote obscure medical journals. Doc was in a hurry. He knew he had very little time before things hit the fan.

"This is the last one." The pediatric resident assigned to hematology/oncology was young, unshaven, and had an attitude. His name tag was big and labeled in bright colors, "Billy Bob M.D." Billy Bob M.D. wore a look of disbelief and stared at the empty bed with its mangled sheets and disconnected IV line.

"The patient is a seven-year-old boy with acute myeloid leukemia that failed chemotherapy," Bill Bob rambled. "His parents signed for the study this morning, did the informed consent, and per your protocol, lot number..."

"Cut to the chase," Doc interrupted, checking his watch.

"The study drug was administered at 0735. As of 1200, the kid's white blood cell count was ten thousand with a normal differential." Billy Bob smiled incredulously. "That's down from sixty thousand, mostly blasts. The kid's afebrile and running around..."

Billy Bob didn't finish. He was interrupted by a dark-headed, impish boy peddling by on a brightly colored three-wheel toy. The boy rang the bell on the handle bars and scooted toward a woman in her thirties. The woman was crying.

"Anyway, he's afebrile. His platelet count is..."

"Fixed," Doc interrupted again. "He's fixed, and he's the last one."

Doc turned to face an entourage of a half-dozen white-coated residents and interns stretching out of the door and into the hall. "We'll do adult oncology next. We'll boost the dose, ten units per kilo."

"Dr. Tech," Dr. Davis called from the rear of the white-coated column and maneuvered around the last figure standing in line. The last figure was a woman who Dr. Tech knew did not belong on rounds or in a white coat. But she looked as if she belonged. Dr. Tech knew it was her job to be good at blending in.

"Shit's hit the fan," Davis said loudly.

"How bad?" Doc asked.

"Bad! Someone from the institutional review board is meeting with administration now. Legal is in there, and so is the head of credentials. And from what I heard, the chief of pediatrics is on his way down here to kill you himself. He wants to know what you're doing on his ward and what you're giving these kids."

"Tell him it's Alpha-Bell-Toweran." Doc opened a box of vials. There was a glint of silver-yellow in the liquid suspensions. "Tell him I'm saving lives and stamping out disease."

Doc turned again toward the petite woman at the end of the line. The name tag on her white coat was a lie. It read M.D. With her sweet face she almost looked like a caring kind of doctor. Her copper hair was shorter than Doc remembered, but her eyes were the same: intense and green as emeralds. She bore no traces of the severe injuries she had sustained three weeks prior. Neither was there any trace of alien cells in her blood.

"You catch that last part, Malone?"

"I caught it."

"It's disease we're stamping out. It's lives we're saving."

"That's what I heard."

Doc checked his watch. The supply of Alpha-Bell-Toweran was running short, and inside the liquid suspensions the cells were not replicating. The cells would function briefly inside the patient recipients and then disappear. Doc started a mental countdown.

He had maybe an hour before he lost the assistance of his house staff and nursing. By that time a member of the review board would have advised administration and legal that he had no knowledge of Doc's study drug, and that no protocols had been presented to his committee. What would they say if Doc told them the drug was made of extraterrestrial blood? They'd say the same thing they were going to say in an hour anyway: that his hospital privileges were suspended and that he was being reported to the state board.

Doc told himself it didn't matter. He'd switch his attention to other, more important concerns. There were two humans whose blood samples still contained replicating alien cells, and there would be some not-very-nice people very interested in those two humans: April and his son, H.I. Then there was Dr. Kay, and the news concerning Dr. Kay wasn't what he'd hoped.

"Where to next?" Dr. Davis broke Doc's train of thought.

"Adult oncology," Doc answered. He told himself he'd use the samples he had left only for advanced disease and non-responders. Priority would be given to young age.

"Stairs," Doc commanded. He took the lead.

* * *

Three weeks of H.I.'s life were mostly a blur. By the first day of the new semester, he thought he could piece together the important parts.

He remembered the kiss and Bell Tower being gone. He remembered a patrol of Brits wrapping everyone in blankets and taking them to a cluster of shelters raised on stilts above the Antarctic ice flow. There'd been questions on the spot, and Malone had told him not to answer them. He'd talked anyway. But the Brits hadn't believed him, not the part about Bell Tower or Rykoff or how the world almost ended.

H.I. still thought about his own questions and answers. His all ended in *maybe.* Maybe Bell Tower somehow understood the dual nature of humankind. Maybe it saw that humans were as capable of caring for each other as they were of killing each other, and that the decision to do one versus the other was a fight waged within each and every human being without exception. Maybe Bell Tower understood that the choices humans made were not in their genes. But who was to say that Bell Tower had any concern about the well-being or morality of other intelligent creatures? How could it be that there was a universal sense of morality? Dr. Kay had offered an answer. She'd used the word "maybe" argumentatively. But by no means had she meant that there was any doubt in her mind. Maybe their survival and the survival of the whole planet had been a miracle. Maybe it had all been about God. Maybe it always would be.

Back on the ice flow, the Brits had probably thought his brain was foggy from exposure on the ice. Maybe they were right. The more time passed, the more part of him came up with natural explanations as to what he'd experienced. It was the human mind's eternal attempt to frame all of its experiences within familiar, rational boundaries. And rational boundaries did not include his experience with Object Alpha Bell Tower. So some days his mind suggested that everything had in truth been some sort of dream. But H.I. promised himself the kiss was real. If everything else was driven over time into some sort of rationalized blur, he'd still remember the kiss was real. And beyond the kiss and beyond all things fragile, there would be that which could never be destroyed or taken away. That thing he'd shared with everyone, even Malone.

These days H.I. thought a lot about Malone. She wasn't the same. Hadn't been since she'd emerged alive from Bell Tower. He'd first realized it while watching her try to lie to the Brits back on the ice. Sure she'd taken charge of communication. But she'd barely been unable to look any of them in the eye while claiming that she'd been the pilot on an unregistered flight. She'd struggled while telling them that due to shock, neither she nor the others remembered the crash. And no, none of them knew the location of the plane. Not any more than any of them knew the source of mysterious radio burst that was long enough to be triangulated and bring the Brits to the rescue. At one point Malone had actually looked to be on the verge of tears. Not fake tears. Real tears. And watching her, H.I. had instantly realized why. Probably for the first time in her life, Malone had found herself conflicted about lying to other human beings. In this case human beings who had helped save her life.

Maybe over time, Malone's story might become the version that would make the most sense to her personally. But even then, she'd have to grapple with something even more powerful. She'd died. No doubt about it. She'd stopped all life function and been pronounced dead by two doctors. How long she'd been dead was unknown. And what she'd experienced while dead, she was refusing to tell. Multiple times H.I. had tried to get it out of her, and multiple times she'd simply changed the subject. Not said she didn't remember. Just changed the subject and looked away. So maybe she was somehow still trying to lie to herself. Maybe even trying to believe the last lie she'd told the Brits, that no one knew the source of the radio signal.

H.I. promised himself that he would always know differently. H.I felt pretty sure about where the signal to the Brits had originated. By the time of the rescue on the ice, the source was far out in space and getting farther by the second. One day it would be back. When he'd told the Brits that part, they'd nodded with the sympathy they'd show a lunatic.

But the truth was indestructible, as it always was in the long run. Humankind had reacted to Bell Tower's arrival with enough suspicion, fear, and hostility to kill it. But killing it had only given it strength, and in return it had shed its healing blood before returning home.

On the ice, Americans had come for them within days. The rest was hazy, everything from the minute the military transport had put down outside DC until the day Doc had sprung H.I from Walter Reed. Looking back, H.I. decided that one day in the isolation unit at Walter Reed had been much like the next. It was a blur of windowless rooms negatively pressurized to protect the rest of the building. There'd been endless needle sticks and blood work, all normal. With all of their needle sticks, he and April and Malone should still look like drug addicts. But the sticks and veins had healed without a trace.

There were other things that still woke him at night. Those were flashbacks of repeated visits to the endoscopy suite where fiber-optic scopes had been shoved into every orifice. Sometimes he'd still experience the claustrophobic sensations left over from all of the of the endless waits he'd suffered inside steel tubes where repeated MRIs had scanned every millimeter of him looking for tumors, anatomic changes, or lymph nodes. All had been read simply as "within normal limits." There had been cultures taken from every place he could imagine and some he couldn't. "No Growth" the reports read. They should have at least read "normal flora", because all humans are colonized by bacteria. But theirs had read "no growth." And none of the test animals injected with his body fluids had shown any sign of disease.

All that had remained and would continue to remain were alien blood cells living in his blood and April's and Malone's. The alien cells could only be seen with electron microscopy. They wouldn't replicate outside of their bodies in lab animals. They wouldn't kill or cause disease. But they could eliminate cancers from tumor bred mice.

Doc's thinking on that subject had been and still was very clear. Doc, like Dr. Kay, had been released early from the isolation unit. The two of them had then become shadows on the other side of pressurized glass or voices on the intercom. Eventually Malone, April, and H.I. had been released. And during that time, Dr. Kay had announced a personal decision of the life altering kind.

Three weeks had passed since H.I.'s return. And now he was pretty much a free man. The first comfort he sought was a night in his own bed. The next morning, he got up early and left Doc's house without a sound. He drove, for a change happy to be in control of something. He knew where he was going, but wasn't happy about what he was going to find there.

It was seven a.m. when he got to the Waterstone house. It was empty. A pile of untouched morning newspapers lay on the front steps. The papers weren't his doing. He'd been replaced the first day he'd missed his route. That was the way the real world worked. He stood in the front yard and looked a long time.

The house was empty and would stay empty. Not that it would do any good, but he ripped the "For Sale" sign out of the frozen ground and hurled it over the back fence. He had one more place to go.

It was seven forty-five am, when he entered Adams Day School. The halls were empty as he expected. He still had makeups for finals. He'd been absent when they'd been given to everyone else. And besides, he'd returned expecting to suffer the expulsion that headmaster Clayfield had promised him. About that he'd been wrong. He was not being expelled. Clayfield had a new autographed photo on his wall and a new friend in congress, someone named Senator Bledso. Bledso had pulled strings on H.I.'s behalf. Still, it didn't matter to H.I. that he was staying in school. His reason for staying was gone.

The first person he encountered was Jefferson Parrish. Jefferson greeted him with a high five and a hug. They didn't have much time to talk. Jefferson was en route to an exam makeup of his own.

"There're all kinds of rumors floatin around here bout you, H.I., Baby."

"Promise you none of them are true."

"How you know till I tell you what they are?"

"Someday, I'll tell you. Right now I'm in a hurry too."

It was nearly 8:00 a.m. when H.I. found the classroom where April was seated alone.

He found her seated in the front row, bent over a text and a notebook, and unaware of his watching her. He stood in the doorway and watched her for a long time. He felt good just looking at her. She was the same April, the same beautiful April. But she also was a different April, an April who was at school early and sitting in the front row. She was wearing glasses. He had never known she needed glasses. The glasses reminded him that Bell Tower had repaired its human passengers, not engineered them into something they weren't. Or had it?

She must have felt his presence in the doorway. She looked up and smiled. The smile was worth a million dollars.

"Hi."

"That's my name."

"No. I meant 'Hi.'"

He locked the door behind him and walked to her desk. He had things to say, things that were tearing him apart. He started by asking her why.

"Because it's for the best."

"Best for who?"

"For Mom and for me!"

"Government work is out. You're in. Is that it?"

"That's it," she answered. "Me and Grandpa and a teaching job at Hopkins. Mom and Grandpa are actually speaking after all of these years."

He heard his voice crack. "So you really are moving away for good?"

"Have to. Commuting's a bitch." Her voice cracked a little too. "Mom drops me here at seven, and that barely gives her time to..."

Her eyes were a little wet. They were deep eyes, liquid and blue and teaming with everything beautiful. Without thinking he held her, and the two of the kissed a lot. Between kisses, he told her that life was very unfair. She answered with her lips against his ear. "I'll be here another two or three weeks. And this summer..." She knew better than to finish. Summer was a long way away.

He looked at April a long time. "Do you feel different?"

"Every day. Do you?"

He nodded. He knew they were both different, always would be. Doc had warned them that the long-term effects of having Bell Tower in their blood were a complete unknown. The levels were declining, but Doc told them they would both still have to undergo periodic tests. April had told him they'd have to find her for that. And she would not make it easy on them, the part about finding her.

"You think it will ever be back?" April asked.

"Bell Tower? Not in our lifetime."

"What about Rykoff? You ever think about Rykoff?"

"He's long gone," he told her. "We won't ever see him again."

* * *

Thousands and thousands of miles south, the Jivanos built their great hut and watched as the forest returned under the face of one moon. The forest buried the evil things left by the cloth-covered people. The new Shaman ordered a celebration.

The women stuck blades of grass through piercings in their jaws and draped red straw over their loins. Some prepared the blood paint for the men, while others prepared a feast of monkeys. The men disappeared into the forests to take the heads of the cloth people who were killed when the Earth took its vengeance. They returned with the heads of the Earth's enemies shrunken to the size of oranges. The new Shaman ordered a dance of the avenging soul, banishing the spirits of the Earth's foes forever.

The Jivanos left the Earth's healed wound and followed their Shaman to a place he'd seen in visions. It was in the place where the sun slept at night. Overlooking that place were mountains so old and wise that their tops were capped in white.

The shrunken heads of the Earth's enemies were left behind. One head was found by an old Indian who was not of the Jivanos. The old Indian draped it from his neck and traveled east to the edge of the great river, to the marketplace of white people where he tried to sell it.

This shrunken head had a shaven scalp and a bearded face. It was adorned in a round ornament of metal that pierced one ear. The old Indian did not know what the ornament was. The white man who bought the head did know.

The white man flipped the ornament with his fingers and called it something the old Indian did not understand. He called it a grenade ring.

* * *

Still thousands of miles further south, the captain of *HMS Endurance* leaned against the reinforced glass of his enclosed bridge and scanned the ice. Through binoculars Captain Stivers could see the plane wreckage but couldn't identify the markings. A large section of the fuselage was intact. Beyond the wreckage the last black wisps of the signal fire faded into the snow-covered rock of an island named only by a number. Stivers looked again for penguins on the frozen rock beach. There were no penguins. There should have been hundreds.

"Let me know when the Lynx is back on deck."

"Aye, Captain."

"All back on turbines. Steady in the cut, zero four five."

The helmsman echoed the orders. Stivers swept the horizon searching for his Lynx helicopter. It was nowhere in sight. There was only the seasonal ice, three feet thick at its northern edge, solid and fixed to the shoreline rather than adrift. As he'd cut his way west of Robertson Island and in toward the signal fire, the hull of the *Endurance* had fought the ice, and the going had been slow. So Stivers had ordered that the Lynx proceed to the wreckage.

"Red Plum, this is Lynx. Do you copy?" The helicopter copilot's garbled radio voice echoed inside the steel and glass bridge. Red Plum was the nickname given *HMS Endurance* in recognition of its bright red hull. Hearing the transmission Stivers looked again. He spotted the copter heading back toward his ship.

"This is Red Plum. We copy you. Over."

"We are on final approach, Red Plum. We have one survivor."

Stivers ordered that the Lynx be given clearance for landing. He ordered that the survivor be taken to sick bay. Stivers scanned the fast ice one last time, then the plane wreckage and the beach. Why were there no penguins? The beach should have been crawling with penguins.

"Captain off the bridge."

The first officer acknowledged, and Stivers dropped aft, negotiating the passageways toward sick bay. Still dressed in his Nomex flight suit, the Lynx pilot met him halfway. They took their time walking.

"You found only one survivor?" Stivers asked.

"That's all, just one. He says he's the pilot."

"Aircraft identification?"

"American C-130. Bloody big Hercules. The markings match."

"But it's on the wrong bloody side of this continent." Stivers shook his head. He saw that his Lynx pilot looked shaken. Stivers thought he knew why. "Were the others bad?"

"The others are bones." The pilot wiped sweat from his brow. "Our survivor says he's been here a month, and his mates are nothing but bones. Now that doesn't make sense. Not in this climate."

"You saying the survivor's a cannibal?"

"I'm not saying anything except he's been alive here for a month and his mates, who should be a neatly frozen as steaks in a frig, are stripped to the bone. I'm telling you they're nothing but bones and still in their flight suits."

"What's the survivor's story?"

"He claims he stayed alive on penguins."

"Did you see any carcasses?"

"None."

"Did you find anything else?"

The helicopter pilot stopped and lowered his voice, even though they were alone in the passageway. "We found weapons at the sight. Automatic weapons."

"Put a marine at the sick bay door. I want one there on all shifts."

"Aye, Captain."

Stivers entered the sick bay alone. He found the ship's pharmacist mate doing paper work. The survivor sat on a cot, his face and body hidden by a heavy blanket. The blanket did not hide the fact that the man was tall and powerful.

"You're onboard Her Majesty's ship, *Endurance.* I'm Captain Stivers."

"My name is Smith." Under the hood, something moved. The captain caught a flash of light hair and a beard.

"Are you American?"

"Yes."

"Are you the pilot?"

"Yes."

"When you're feeling better, I'll have questions."

"I'm feeling better already."

Under the blanket, the man shifted positions. The movement was powerful. It shouldn't have been. After a month on the ice with nothing but meat to eat, the survivor should have been depleted of body fat. He should have been weak. He wasn't. Captain Stivers reflected on what kind of meat the man might have eaten. The thought made him cringe.

"Get your rest, Mr. Smith. I'll have questions later. There will be plenty of time."

"What kind of time?"

"*Endurance* is on station another few months. Then back to Portsmouth."

"Another few months?" The blanket shifted again, and Stivers got a brief glimpse of the survivor's eyes. They were intense and probing. They were violet.

"We'll be steaming home, so to speak, just in time to avoid winter down here," Stivers said. "You're lucky you didn't go down in winter, Mr. Smith. You're lucky to be alive."

The blanket shifted again, and Stivers caught another flash of the eyes. Violet and probing, taking in their surroundings as if to study them the way a predator studies terrain.

"Did you hear me, Mr. Smith?"

"I heard you. But winter wouldn't have mattered." His voice became soft, almost hypnotic. "I'm hard to kill."

The End

Made in United States
Orlando, FL
13 September 2024

51469864R00171